Melusine

BY THE SAME AUTHOR

The Marvelous Story of Claire d'Amour
The Call of the Beast
Priscilla of Alexandria
The Angel of Lust
The Mystery of the Tiger
The Poison of Goa
Lucifer
The Blood of Toulouse
The Albigensian Treasure
Jean de Fodoas
The Brothers of the Virgin Gold

Melusine

by
Maurice Magre

Translated, annotated and introduced by
Brian Stableford

A Black Coat Press Book

Visit our website at www.blackcoatpress.com

ISBN 978-1-61227-703-5. First Printing. January 2018. Published by Black Coat Press, an imprint of Hollywood Comics.com, LLC, P.O. Box 17270, Encino, CA 91416. All rights reserved.

TABLE OF CONTENTS

Introduction

This is the eleventh volume of a twelve-volume set of translations of Maurice Magre's prose fiction. It contains translations of the novel *Mélusine, ou le Secret de la solitude* (1941) and the collections of vignettes "Le Côté d'ombre des âmes" and "Révélation des mondes invisibles" from *La Beauté invisible*, as "The Dark Side of Souls" and "The Revelation of Invisible Worlds."

Volume One, *The Marvelous Story of Claire d'Amour and Other Stories*, contains translations of early short stories, including the collection *Histoire merveilleuse de Claire d'Amour suivie d'autres contes merveilleux* (1903) and six other stories from various sources published between 1901 and 1913.

Volume Two, *The Call of the Beast and Other Stories*, contains translations of his first three works of prose fiction in volume form, *Les Colombes poignardées* (1917), as "Stabbed Doves," *La Tendre camarade* (1918), as "The Tender Comrade" and *L'Appel de la bête* (1920), as "The Call of the Beast."

Volume Three, *Priscilla of Alexandria and Other Stories* contains translations of the original version of the story collection *Vies des courtisanes*, first published in *Oeuvres Libres* 23 (1923), as "Courtesans' Lives" plus the additional story added to the version published in volume form in 1925, and the novel *Priscilla d'Alexandrie* (1925), as "Priscilla of Alexandria."

Volume Four, *The Angel of Lust*, contains translations of the novella, *La Vie amoureuse de Messaline* (1925), as "The Love Life of Messalina," the novel published as *La Luxure de Grenade* (1926), as "The Angel of Lust," and the chapter from *Magiciens et illuminés* (1930) entitled "Christian Rosenkreutz et les Rose-croix," as "Christian Rosenkreutz and the Rosicrucians."

Volume Five, *The Mystery of the Tiger*, contains translations of the novella *Le Roman de Confucius* (1927), as "The Story of Confucius," and the novel *Le Mystère du tigre* (1927), as "The Mystery of the Tiger."

Volume Six, *The Poison of Goa*, contains translations of the novel *Le Poison de Goa* (1928), as "The Poison of Goa," and the prose poems contained in *Le Livre des lotus entr'ouverts* (1926), as "Lotus Blossoms."

Volume Seven, *Lucifer*, contains a translation of the novel originally published under the same title in 1929 and the novella *La Nuit de haschich et de l'opium* (1929), as "The Night of Hashish and Opium."

Volume Eight, *The Blood of Toulouse*, contains translations of the novel *Le Sang de Toulouse* (1931), as "The Blood of Toulouse," and the chapter from *Magiciens et illuminés* entitled "Le Maître inconnu des Albigeois," as "The Secret Master of the Albigensians."

Volume Nine, *The Albigensian Treasure*, contains translations of the novel *Le Trésor des Albigeois* (1938) as "The Albigensian Treasure," and the collection of vignettes "Communication avec la nature" from *La Beauté invisible* (1937), as "Communication with Nature."

Volume Ten, *Jean de Fodoas*, contains translations of the novel *Jean de Fodoas: aventures d'un Français à la cour de l'empereur Akbar* (1939) as "Jean de Fodoas" and the chapter from *Magiciens et illuminés* entitled "Le Mystère des Templiers," as "The Mystery of the Templars."

Volume Twelve, *The Brothers of the Virgin Gold*, contains a translation of the novel *Les Frères de l'or vierge*, first published posthumously in 1949.

Mélusine ou le secret de la solitude has a similar narrative structure to *Le Trésor des Albigeois*, its brief chapters mingling a number of mini-essays and prose-poems with a continuing first-person narrative that, although clearly fictitious and exceedingly rich in the fantastic, is proffered by an unnamed protagonist who is clearly an *alter ego* of the author.

The three-year gap in publication of the two novels—if they can really be considered as novels—probably does reflect a three-year gap in their writing, but if, as seems possible, both took aboard separately-written pieces when they were patched together, the composition of their elements might have overlapped, and also overlapped that of *La Beauté invisible*, whose component vignettes have much in common with the vignettes included in the novels.

In the biography *Maurice Magre: Le Lotus perdu* [Maurice Magre: The Lost Lotus] (1999), Jean-Jacques Bedu, having seen a manuscript entitled "Roseline ou la Tentation du crépuscule" [Roseline; or, The Temptation of the Dusk] bearing the date 6 April 1941, states unequivocally that Magre wrote *Mélusine*, "one of his last masterpieces," after the German occupation of Paris, while he was occupying a room in a rest home in Nice, but he gives no further details regarding the precise contents of the manuscript that he saw. Whenever their various component parts were composed, however, in terms of their narrative strategy, *La Beauté invisible*, *Le Trésor des Albigeois* and *Mélusine* can be seen as a quirky trilogy of sorts, dealing with the same themes and experimenting with a similar literary method—or re-experimenting with it, as Magre had used something similar earlier in his career in *Les Colombes poignardées* and *La Tendre camarade*.

Given that Magre certainly brought the novel to a conclusion on 6 April 1941, and presumably delivered it to the printer then—the publication date is given in the text, printed in Avignon, as 21 November, twenty days before Magre died, on 11 December 1941—it may seem ridiculous to raise the question of whether the book is actually finished, but it might be worth pointing out that at least one plot-thread introduced in the early chapters and subjected to some slight further development is abandoned without any hint of resolution. It is, however, not impossible that Magre's decision to consider the text finished was an abandonment rather than a completion, determined by the belief that he would not have time to bring it to a more rounded conclusion, either because he expected to die before December or because there was other work to which he wanted to give priority.

If work on *Mélusine* was, in fact, cut short, the latter of those alternatives might be the more probable, as there were two larger projects on which he might have been still working, perhaps hoping to finish at least one of them before he died. One was the massive patchwork *Les Frères de l'or vierge*, of which a version was published posthumously in 1949, although its principal narrative thread was clearly incomplete, having been provided with a curt termination incompatible with its early chapters, possibly supplied by an editor, although it is more likely that Magre applied the patch when he decided that he could go no further. The other was his final non-fiction book, *Le Livre des visions divines* [The Book of Divine Visions], similarly published posthumously, in

1943, and probably also less full than the writer would have liked—Bedu judges it inferior to its two predecessors, *Les interventions supernaturelles* [Supernatural Interventions] (1939) and *Le Livre des certitudes admirables* [The Book of Admirable Certainties] (1940).

It is also possible, of course, that Magre was too sick to do any more work after deciding that *Mélusine* was finished, and that both of the posthumously-published projects were already as complete as they would ever be in April 1941. If so, then *Mélusine* might have been his swan song, and its delicate imaginative flourishes the last gasps of his prolific and fecund imagination. In spite of the problems of their internal chronology, the revision of the classic legend of Mélusine of Lusignan contained in the story, and its overlapping with the invented legend of Saint Eleutherius and Roseline's fantasies, is ingenious. The visionary sequences depicting the protagonist's communications with nature are vividly effective, and demonstrate that Magre's poetic gifts had not waned—a conclusion also suggested by the last of his nine major collections of poetry, *Le Parc des Rossignols* [Nightingale Park] (1940).

Seen as an ensemble, *Mélusine* is poignantly elegiac, providing an entirely apt complement to the vignettes collected in "Révélation des mondes invisibles," but it also has a strong component of wry humor, especially in its dealings with the desertion and return of the "sublime friends," which similarly provide a quirky complement to "Le Côté d'ombre des âmes." Like his previous quasi-autobiographical novel, *Lucifer*, published more than a decade earlier and similarly associated with a burst of confessional non-fiction, *Mélusine* is surely reflective, looking back to an earlier phase of the author's personal quest. Indeed, it finds its narrator not

11

only still questing, but still on the threshold of his final attempt to find peace of mind in solitude, which he had first attempted long before, having left Paris in the late 1920s and having lived in various more-or-less isolated locations since then.

According to Bedu, with support from the final chapters of the two posthumous volumes, Magre "found God" in the last months to his life and sought solace in the orthodox Catholic dogmas that he had long rejected as inadequate and injurious. If so, it was presumably in the spirit of a drowning man caching at a straw, and says less about the hopefulness of the gesture itself than the inadequacy of the conviction of having reached a successful conclusion that he had tried to assert in "Révélations des mondes invisibles" and *Le Livre des certitudes admirables*. In that regard, *Mélusine* is perhaps a more honest work than its non-fictional companion-pieces, in its wry acknowledgement that any apparent conclusion to a spiritual quest can only be illusory, because it can only be a forward-looking arrival on the threshold of a new beginning.

In one sense, the narrative terminus at which *Mélusine* finally arrives has more in common with the first of the author's three quasi-autobiographical contemporary novels, *L'Appel de la bête*, than with its more immediate predecessor *Lucifer*. Whereas *Lucifer* picks up from the initial phase of earlier novel the notion that the Magre's earlier erotic obsessions could be seen as a kind of demonic possession, and develops that idea into a graphic horror story, the final chapter of *Mélusine* is more closely related to the final chapter of *L'Appel de la bête*, in which the protagonist appears to have freed himself from that possession and is ready to face life without it, equipped with a new maturity. In its tone and attitude, however, *Mélusine* is strikingly different from both of the earlier novels, whose hauntings are far more intense and oppressive, and it represents a translocation to a contemporary setting and an intriguing further development of the dry laconism of *Le Trésor des Albigeois*.

Far less melodramatic than *Le Trésor des Albigeois*, which mingles its quiet fabular chapters with a plague, a black mass and an excommunication—all supernaturally effective—*Mélusine* is able to concentrate almost entirely on the sense of wonder communicated by its supernatural intrusions rather than any sense of threat. Although Roseline, like Laurence in *Lucifer* and Rose-Thé in *L'Appel de la bête*, can certainly be seen as yet another incarnation of Claire d'Amour, Magre's first incarnation of the essentially-treacherous allure of lust, she is treated with a nostalgic indulgence that takes much of the venom out of her bite; although, like her famous ancestor, she has covert serpentine qualities, that is as much a source of legendary glamor as threat, and her fantasies have an esthetic quality that goes beyond, and is arguably more rewarding than, her sex-appeal.

If *Mélusine* is construed as an allegorical transfiguration of a personal predicament, therefore, in the same self-exploratory vein as "Histoire merveilleuse de Claire d'Amour," *L'Appel de la Bête, Lucifer* and *Le Trésor des Albigeois*, it seems to represent and embody a significant shift in attitude. It is not a conclusion to that literary quest, and could not have constituted a conclusion even if the author had manage to finish it in a more rounded manner than he did, but it certainly represents progress of a sort, and perhaps the only sort that is really possible in that kind of quest, in spite of the greater pretentions and higher ambitions to which "Révélation des mondes invisibles" aspires. Although it is not without a few structural flaws, therefore, Bedu is certainly not wrong to reckon *Mélusine* as one of the author's masterpieces.

Bedu was able to ascertain that Magre did not die alone; his ex-wife, who was still living in the south of France, was with him at the end. Bedu concludes from that circumstance that, whatever had caused the break-up of their marriage twenty years before, Jeanne Rosen still loved him. She must, at least, have felt sorry for him, and wanted to offer him what consolation she could. As Bedu conscientiously observes, however, she might have been wiser already to have been thousands of miles away in her native America. In fact, she stayed in Vichy France until she was rounded up by the Gestapo in 1943, for the crime of having Jewish ancestry, and she was deported, dying not long thereafter in a German concentration camp.

There is, alas, no encouragement in that narrative conclusion for any reader who would like to believe that there really is a solution to the existential problem of *désespoir* that Magre had spelled out in the preface to *La Beauté invisible*, or that one really ought to be glad to suffer from that kind of despair, provided that one can live with it. But Magre's career, and literary achievements, do suggest that writing fantastic fiction can help, in some measure, and perhaps reading it can, too.

The translation of *Mélusine ou le Secret de la solitude* was made from a copy of the 1941 published in Avignon by Édouard Aubanel. The translations of "Le Côté d'ombre des âmes" and "Révélation des mondes invisibles" were made from a copy of the 1937 Fasquelle edition of *La Beauté invisible*.

Brian Stableford

MELUSINE; OR, THE SECRET OF SOLITUDE

THE GREAT BOOK OF GOD

It was written...

When they look back on life, many people say: "It was written!" But written where? No one knows exactly, for men are ignorant. But I have ended up knowing that all things are written in the great book of God.

That is a great prodigious book with letters of all colors and illuminations on every page. The binding is in orichalcum with a golden lock whose key is magical. For God utilizes magic, white magic and black magic, and also a certain magic blue in color, which is occupied neither with good nor evil but is only concerned with the subtle essence with which souls are created.

As for the characters of the text, perhaps they do not correspond to any human language. They are simultaneously akin to Hebrew and Sanskrit, and might well have been Devangari, the language that the beings called Devas once spoke, who were half-human and half-divine.

It is impossible to say on what occasion it was given to me to cast a rapid glance over the great book of God—oh, very rapid, in truth, and only the page concerning me.

Naturally, I did not understand the text, because of my ignorance of divine things; but I have seen little illustrations that are in the margin, sketches and portraits that seem swiftly designed, with a superior negligence. And at the very top there was my mother's face, with the tranquil beauty of her immutable love. I did not linger over gazing at the illustrations of my youth, and the subsequent years of my life. Was I wrong? It is a matter of knowing the measure I which remorse is mingled with memory.

Because of the force of the present, I only looked at the designs that dealt with my journey to the mysterious land. And there was an insignificant little house with a cypress standing beside it, like a friend. In spite of the absence of detail, one could see that the door of the house was only pushed to, and that a light phantom was holding it with a transparent hand. In fact, was it a phantom, or the memory of a woman, thus represented?

A little lower down there was a young woman with a pony-tail, a straw hat and the face of a moon, wonder-struck because it was rising in a blue sky. Then a crow, then a tortoise, and then an hourglass. And I noticed that there was an unfinished silhouette of a traveler with a staff, which might become, with a few strokes more, a windmill or a family gathering by the fireside.

Marvelous uncertainty! Similarly, there were blank lines in the text. Certain modifications were possible, then! Thus, it was possible, by a personal decision, to add a pleasant adventure, or remove a cause of chagrin. One could introduce the word reverie or the word happiness. Yes, assuredly, it was possible to modify the great book of God. But only if one had a profound knowledge of Devangari.

THE LETTING AGENT AND DESTINY

It was written that I would go to the most mysterious place on earth.

How did all that happen? Can anyone tell me why I rented the house, took the train, bought a hat of slightly conical form with a Tyrolean plume on the right side, in order to have the external appearance of a traveler? How can one know the enchantment of causes and effects and know whether there is, at the origin, the suggestion of an invisible protective spirit?

Perhaps I was insane to rent a house without seeing it. Perhaps no protective spirit acted, and the first link in the chain of events was in the determination of the letting agent who rented the house. Perhaps that agent had no determination and was simply in a hurry, that morning, to get rid of me.

"A very small house for one person, in a solitary place where there are no factory chimneys, no Sunday fair, nor an inn with a gramophone, nor a blaring casino—that's difficult to find. Oh, you want a forest all around? That increases the difficulty. And the sea a short distance away? That complicates thing further. You'd prefer a monastery in the vicinity, and bells don't bother you. Damn! That's a matter of a very exceptional location. And yet, I can sort you out. I have to hand the very small house you need. It's exactly suitable. It's a long time since it's been let, which is inexplicable, in view of the charm of the location. And by a curious coincidence, everyone's fighting over it."

The letting agent had got up, had gone to his office door, opened it for a moment and came back to me with the shining eyes and bright smile of someone about to tell an unimportant lie.

"You've heard all those rings of the doorbell that have just succeeded one another. They're clients that have made me offers for the house. Perhaps they're thinking about some overbid on the price, which is very minimal. They're numerous and they're waiting. But I'd like to give you the preference, because one isn't the master of one's sympathy. You have only to sign here, putting *read and approved*."

I knew that I had just accomplished an irrevocable action. It would be an insensate prodigality to rent a house, only to change one's mind thereafter and not live in it. I had engaged and entire year of existence on the spur of the moment—and I experienced an interior thrill at the audacity of running a risk.

"Can you tell me why this house, so desired by a crowd that is murmuring in your antechamber, has remained untenanted for such a long time?"

The letting agent's face became suddenly impenetrable. Then as he put the lease bearing my signature in a file, he said: "Unknown...rumors run around...a solitary house...you'll see..."

THE ARRIVAL IN THE MYSTERIOUS LAND

It is a former domain of pines and mimosas where houses were once born. In the middle is a large château. Not far away there is a railway, which has frayed a path through the pines, a village of people, stony expanses and hills full of silence—and then the rest of the world.

Anyone arriving at sunset receives a warning that comes from an infinite distance. And I knew, as soon as the first evening and the first minute, that there was a great mystery in that place.

In truth, mystery is universally widespread. Is there a place on earth where everything is not incomprehensible? The laws, the powerful divine laws, are only half-immutable. Nothing obeys reason exactly, and the more reasonable people seem to be, the more they deviate from reason.

The little station gives the impression of only being there by chance, and as soon as the train has drawn away with a great smoky sigh, one would think that it shrinks, and disappears among the trees that enclose it. The guard has pushed the barrier. A carriage moves off. A star lights up in the distance.

"You only have to go straight ahead, and then turn left."

Perhaps that mass in the distance is the monastery. How high and dense the trees are! The solitude will be greater than I thought. But night lends itself to the illusions of solitude. It's necessary to go uphill, and then down again. That blue in the distance must be the sea. There is a big house at the end of a driveway. Over there I can see a small one.

"Bonjour, Monsieur; doubtless you're the tenant," said an old man carrying a rake, who emerged from a mimosa.

New tenants must be recognizable by their suitcase, their overcoat and their appearance of having come from far away.

"I'll go fetch the keys."

I considered the house. It belonged to the same architectural family as all the houses to let in that maritime area, but with something particular. If it could walk, it would have limped. But it was motionless, and stood with a slight slant, with an overly large coiffure that resembled an archbishop's miter. And as it was surrounded by bougainvilleas covered in violet flowers, it was reminiscent of an archbishop of small stature who gave the impression of keeping a secret.

I had put down my suitcase and I was waiting in the garden for the old man who had gone in quest of the keys. It was then that I seemed to perceive furtive footsteps inside the locked house, which were slightly sad, if a sound of footsteps can possess sadness.

I advanced toward the silent door of the house in order to make sure of the reality of the sun, so light that it might have been produced by a shadow, and shadows produce very few. I was about to put my ear to the lock when, having looked first, I distinguished the movement of a living creature there. And I recognized an insect with two hooks, the same one that a familial legend, a lesson useful for the fourth year, gives as the normal inhabitant of old locks: the earwig, with which I had often been threatened, at the time when my head was precisely at the level of locks and when I did not have to bend down in order to listen clandestinely.

Since my childhood I had calculated that there must be many more earwigs than locks, and that many families belonging to that genre of insects must find themselves devoid of lodgings. But pity has so many other subjects of exercise! I was in the presence of a favored earwig that had spent the entire winter in a profound lock. Had I been in any danger? Did that insect merit the name that it bore, and did it have the habit of plunging into human ears and depositing the seeds of thousands of little earwigs there?

I did not have time to meditate those problems, nor the new problems posed by the remark I heard. For I heard a remark. It was very quiet, or seemed to be. And perhaps it was not perceived by the organ of hearing but by some mysterious interior faculty enabling insects to communicate with humans—a faculty long lost, if it existed. The remark that the earwig made was: "It's her who is walking. It's necessary not to disturb the spirit of the one who is dead."

THE LANGUAGE OF INSECTS

I took a few steps back, and my first thought was one of wonderment. An astonishing phenomenon had just been produced. An insect had spoken to me and I had understood what it said.

But in that case, I understood the language of insects! That was a prodigious faculty that I had often dreamed of having. It is true that I had been obliged to renounce the ambition. But now I had just received a special confidence, which I had understood very clearly. I lent an ear to the sounds of the nature around me, and it would not have taken much for me to be obliged to start running in order to calm the agitation into which I had suddenly been thrown.

In reviving by means of memory my arrival at the house, it is impossible for me to evaluate the time that that inconceivable comprehension lasted—perhaps only a few seconds. During those few seconds—or those few minutes, I don't know—I had the perception not only of the speech of insects but of all animals.

It was not exactly words of which they made use. They expressed simple and complex sentiments by means of prolonged rhythms. Only sometimes, personal relationships motivated exclamations that had the value of words. I was struck by the extreme coarseness of what can be called a language. A dog, in the distance, was repeating insults addressed to another dog that were equivalent to our most base vocabulary, which were a sort of evocation of filth. A donkey was proclaiming a resigned malediction regarding its miserable life, in terms that were almost repulsive, by virtue of the stupid disgust they expressed.

On the other hand, a bird on a branch was warning a sleeping family about an owl that had taken off but was still distant, and there was a certain amicable grace in what it said. Not far away from me, in an unkempt garden plot, a cricket was repeating untiringly, in a continuous fashion, its joy in learning, the development of its knowledge of the world. I was so surprised that I advanced toward it, which immediately caused it to fall silent. On leaning over, I distinguished little tremors in the grass, which corresponded to sentiments of fear. That fear was the dominant note of all the sounds.

I heard an interrogation that was addressed to me personally, and which came from a bird. Was it the same one that had announced the advent of the owl or another? It had turned toward me and it said, approximately, with extreme rapidity: "Who are you? Where do you come from? Why are you here?"

And then everything ceased. The marvelous perception was interrupted. There was no longer anything but a chirping in the branches. The donkey and the dog had fallen silent. The cricket resumed a monotonous chirping in which it was impossible to distinguish the joy of knowledge.

"Excuse me," said the old man, "but I couldn't find the keys."

And he showed me over the house. The rooms did not have the dead character of long-uninhabited rooms. A certain life was expanded there, which was manifest in the quality of the folds of the curtains, and in the manner in which the mirrors reflected images. A woman must once have presided over the arrangement of that small house.

I was struck by the sight of a large clock in the ground floor room. The old man saw my gaze.

"It's necessary to warn you that it marks time as it pleases. It doesn't go fast or slow, but without anyone being able to explain why, every time it's midnight, it chimes thirteen times."

THE FIRST ENCOUNTER WITH ROSELINE

The first time I encountered Roseline it was in a place that was half street and half road: a street because of the presence of a house, a grocery that was also a café and a tobacconist of sorts; and a road because there were hedges of rosemary and mimosas to the right and the left.

She was supposed to be talking to a semi-venerable lady, to whom a certain scatterbrained quality removed a little of the gravity. The conversation had just stopped abruptly and Roseline was staring obstinately at my hat, in such a way that her gaze, the color of flowing water, glided over my head like a silent blue arrow.

The beauty of young women! One can promise one-self not longer to pay any attention to it, but one is surprised by its appearance, as if by the movement of a star that, interrupting the order of celestial attractions, has started to make zigzags in the sky, giving all the signs of its liberty.

I had renounced it some time ago. When I gazed at myself in a mirror, I could only distinguish the two white patches that my hair made at my temples. Those patches were, moreover, augmenting with surprising rapidity, and a curious phenomenon was localized there. Every time that I met the gaze of a woman in which there was a subtle transmission of sympathy, I immediately felt a slight pressure on my blanched temples, as if the hands of wisdom were reminding me of the reality of time. That pressure was so real that I put my hand involuntarily to my forehead with the confused hope, or perhaps the apprehension, of seizing a mysterious, icy, in-human hand in its merciless solicitude.

Roseline's beauty came, above all, from a faculty of astonishment that radiated from her. It was not only my hat that astonished her but the color and perfume of rosemary, the quality of the morning air, and the light beat of her pulse. One sensed that she could not accustom herself to being alive without being astonished by it. She was holding her arms along her body, as if, suddenly freed from the laws of gravity, she were about to rise up toward the sky by virtue of a spontaneous elevation.

She was perfectly ravishing and tastefully dressed, but, without it being possible to discern why, there was something slightly ridiculous about her. Oh, very slight, which was only manifest in a fleeting fashion. It did not come from the silk of her neckerchief, nor the color of the flowers in her hat, but perhaps from the exaggeration of sentiments, the vehemence of sincerity.

My hat must remind that young woman of something, I thought, during the few seconds I took to arrive level with her.

And I saw her features covered over by a light mask that only the soul is able to fabricate, a mask woven with surprise, simulated reverie and observant inattention.

I had gone past and was continuing my route when I heard a burst of laughter. As I turned round, I saw that Roseline was still looking at my hat, and laughing. Was the form of the hat so amusing, and could it motivate such hilarity?

And as I tried to put a certain severity into my gaze with regard to the impropriety of the laughter, I saw that her eyes had the particular gleam that the sunlight brings to the mist of tears. Could a hat of slightly conical form provoke laughter and tears simultaneously?

And at the same time I heard a remark made in a low voice, a remark as mysterious to me as a legend: "Isn't that the new tenant of the House of the Crow?"

THE CROW

The House of the Crow? So my house was like the house of a crow! Why? And what crow?

Did a bird of that species live in one of the old trees in the little garden, or was it accustomed to perch on the slightly inclined roof of the house? But didn't that happen to all trees and all roofs? No species is more common than that of crows. But perhaps it was a matter of a special bird, remarkable for a strange life, an incarnation of a dead poet and the possessor of a secret that it could not transmit.

I did not like living in a house thus named and I thought that it was necessary to find it a name, if only in order to designate it to myself.

I might call it "the house of good luck," but that is imprudent. It is necessary not to name good luck.

I might call it "the house of wisdom," but is that not too boastful? It is true that I aspire belatedly to wisdom, but it was still very far away.

"The house of reverie," then? Reverie leads to idleness by a gradual slope; it prevents the soul from realizing itself.

I might call it the house of the realization of the soul.

Isn't that a rather abstract name? How difficult it is to designate one's own house to oneself.

Let's think. What am I, in sum? A miserable grain of dust that would like to know, understand and pray in order to travel toward perfection in solitude. I might call the house "the house of the grain of kneeling dust," but I won't tell anyone that name, or fear that it won't be understood. Anyway, for houses as for humans, the true name ought to remain secret.

Mathieu Lapeyre, the man with the rake, the guardian of the keys when there was no tenant, shook his head several times, put down his rake, and ended up agreeing that there was indeed a story about a crow, but he did not know exactly what it was. As for the crow itself, it existed; he had seen it. It was a prodigiously old crow.

"It sometimes comes out of the forest of cork-oaks over there and comes to perch here. It's necessary to know that crows, in growing old, instead of going white, like men, become black, a black more somber than the darkness of the night, a black that causes fear. And that one has bristling and worn plumage, as if it had been burned by the sun and frozen by the cold."

Ancient seasons must have passed over it, curling up its beak and making its eyes redder, and when one saw it, one felt ill at ease, because of the tenebrous color of its plumage, similar to the color of Hell, if Hell exists—which is controversial: the Hell where souls go to grope.

Mathieu Lapeyre saw my interest in my eyes. One likes to charm an interlocutor. He searched for some memory relative to the life of the crow.

"I haven't seen it for a few months. Perhaps it's dead, by dint of living for a long time, and is being eaten by ants and carrion-beetles in the hollow of a cork-oak. Perhaps nothing remains of it but a curled beak, for the beak outlasts the bones. But it might make its lugubrious cry heard this very evening—for it has the custom of screeching lamentably, as if it were calling to something absent, And I can tell you, Monsieur a means of making it come, from which it's better to refrain, because of that sad appeal. It's a bird attracted by a cross. I don't know the reason, but I've observed it myself.

"All the Lapeyres are buried in the cemetery here, next to the cypresses that extend between the Armitelle and the château. One day, my wife said to me: 'The Lapeyre cross has fallen down. It broke as it fell. It's necessary to make a new one and put good paint on it.' I'm a carpenter in my spare time, and I made a tall and handsome cross that I stuck in the garden, awaiting paint and varnish. Did the crow see it from afar? It's necessary to suppose that it was on the lookout. Scarcely was the cross there that the crow was on top of it, speaking in crow.

"I tried to chase it away because of the noise it was making, but in vain. I went after it with a stick, and Noah, the dog, barked. The crow kept coming back and perching on an arm of the cross, as if it owned it. And at night we couldn't sleep because of its cries. I put the varnish on in haste and ran to plant my cross where it ought to be, where the Lapeyres are resting, where my wife is now, and where I'll be in my turn. And the crow didn't come back again.

"It could have taken up residence in the cemetery, where there are a thousand crosses next to one another, but no. It knows full well that the circle of the long white wall next to the cypresses encloses a city of the dead. One might think that a cross here, near the house where you are, or mine, which is next door, reminds it of something. One doesn't know the souls of men, much less those of crows."

THE LUSIGNAN FAMILY

I no longer know on what insignificant occasion I made the acquaintance of the aged lady. Her name was Madame Tournadieu. As I went into her garden, without any hidden agenda, conscious or unconscious, I saw that Roseline was there, and that Madame Tournadieu had just laid out the cards to tell her fortune on a little iron table.

With a joyous volubility and without worrying about any preamble, Roseline started talking.

"I belong to the world of spirits much more than that of humans, the world of aerial spirits. It's in an entirely accidental fashion that I've been placed in the ancient Lusignan family to play the role of a young woman. But I'm only on the earth because I have a mission to fulfill. A certain number of privileged beings have missions, but most of the time they don't know it and they go through life uselessly. Do you know yours?"

The aged lady, who had the responsibility for the subject of the conversation, smiled benevolently and nodded her head. In spite of a slight eccentricity, I had estimated immediately that her essential quality was a great common sense. I showed humility and was afflicted by the vulgar character of my nature. Thus, when I chatted with my friend Porcastre, who had come to resemble the images of Plato that we possess, and whom I called the philosopher, I sometimes didn't understand and was humiliated by my inferiority. I sensed that Roseline was far above me in the spiritual scale of creatures.

I made an evasive gesture and, lowering my eyes, I admitted that, at least thus far, I had no certainty regarding my mission.

Roseline nodded her head. But, as if she had already forgotten the importance of missions, her eyes bright with curiosity, she asked me if I liked snakes. My response would not have been useful, for she added, without waiting for it: "It's necessary to like them. You'll see a large number of them. Perhaps you've already seen some. The whole region is full of them. But there's a marvelous quality of those creatures that gives the illusion of coldness. They pullulate in certain places; they're in all the walls and under all the trees, and humans don't suspect it. In any case, don't come to the château at night without taking good care. I have a sister who is so beautiful that one can't see her for the first time without fainting. What would happen if you fell unconscious on a pathway in the park and the snakes...?"

I had attributed qualities of common sense to Madame Tournadieu imprudently. I saw that her face had a grave expression and that she was considering the hypothesis that had just been put forward as quite plausible.

"Yes," Roseline went to, "my sister is a little like the ancient Medusa whose head Perseus was obliged to cut off. Her power is so frightening that I wonder whether it might not be necessary to do that some day."

She paused and meditated for a few seconds, while Madame Tournadieu continued to approve.

"Every Lusignan has a curious particularity. Thus my father...if you've met him, you'll have noticed it because of his beard...he has two beards. My father has a frightful habit and I argue with him incessantly about that subject. He has a benevolent air about him but he's a very cruel man. He kills his enemies and he nails them to the wall with long steel spikes. If he weren't so rich he'd have been condemned to death a long time ago. I love him, though, because he's my father.

"How can wearing that beard be explained—that beard divided into two parts, one of which is longer than the other? I think he'd prefer it if the two parts were symmetrical, and he suffers from that inequality. But it makes me suffer much more when I kiss him. And I kiss him often because I have a heart overflowing with love.

"And yet we have thousands of butterflies that separate us! Poor butterflies that he martyrizes, I love you for the inexplicable length of your agony! 'You don't understand anything about science,' my father says, laughing. It's necessary to tell you that my father is one of the greatest scientists of our epoch, perhaps the greatest of all. He knows all the species of butterflies and moths that exist, even the American species, even those of the North Pole. But how can the science that knows deadly poisons for humans not have found one for butterflies, which are much tinier?

"And I wonder if the butterflies, after having palpitated for a long time in a glass box, even end up by dying. I believe they make a semblance of it. They resign themselves to having a pin that traverses them and they wait silently for the duration of a collection—a duration that might be immense.

"Once, I set one of them free, the most beautiful of all. 'It's at least a hundred years old and it's Russian,' my father told me. It was covered in gold powder and wore a little crown. It was a mummy of a butterfly. Its eyes were a centimeter long. It flew away with a great sadness. The garden was too young for it.

"When I told my father what I'd done, he chased me around the house shouting that I was a monster, and I believe that he would have nailed me instead of the butterfly if I'd been on the scale of the box and the pin. One is sometimes saved by a difference in dimension."

CONCERNING THE OBJECTIVE
OF THE VOYAGE

Why had I come to that land of solitude and that house that nobody had rented for a long time?

That was a question that I dared not ask myself. Frankness practiced, with a clear gaze, with regard to a stranger, produces an interior voluptuousness, but with oneself it is difficult to realize, because one does not dispose of the magic of speech and the soul is then diminished instead of being glorified. Nevertheless, it is necessary to recognize why one is here rather than somewhere else.

In truth, it is necessary not to expect too much of solitude. To begin with, one cannot find it anywhere. Perhaps there are islands in Oceania...but one then finds the problem of nourishment as absorbing as that of the presence of humans. At that time and at that turning-point in my life, I believed in the virtue of solitude.

For I was at a turning point. I had entered the period when the smile of women who look at you changes its meaning. One distinguishes a hint of respect therein. Unwittingly, and simply by the play of years, one no longer finds oneself on the same equal footing with them. In their eyes, one is an important person, with whom communication will be mingled with a certain ennui. One has been pushed, without being aware of it, into a new condition of life.

I had remained as long as possible without wanting to think about that change. But I had received a warning, like a ringing bell. On going into a Metro carriage once, a well brought-up young man had got up precipitately to offer me his seat. My God! It is little, unimportant events that force one to make great decisions.

As far as I can go back in my memories, I can see therein the resolution to devote myself, at a certain time of my life, to the search for the truth, perhaps to what is called, in Christian language, salvation. I had arrived at that moment and I knew that it entailed the renunciation of the former reasons for living.

Contrary to my expectations, I did not experience any difficulty in renouncing all the pleasures that were not those of the spirit—or rather, almost all the pleasures, because there is the pleasure of the air one breathes, the sunlight that penetrates you, creatures with which one sympathizes, pleasures that never quit you. I was intoxicated by the joy of the new horizons I glimpsed. The spiritual world was abruptly revealed, like the panorama at the top of a mountain. How long I had taken! How insensate I was to have delayed for so long! But it is necessary to take the first step, to commence with renunciation, otherwise the summit of the mountain remains obscure and one remains convinced that there is nothing behind the clouds.

I had accepted joyfully the appearance of egotism that the first step toward wisdom provides—for there is no detachment without egotism. "Wretch! You're a ingrate! You're forgetting your family," one hears quite frequently. It cannot be otherwise. It is necessary to be an ingrate and forget one's family. The amity of the gods does not entail that of humans. There is an inexorable choice between the paths. They are the paths that once presented themselves to Hercules. In our day, Gauguin also found them before him, and he knew that, in order for art to be a divine path, it had to be accompanied by renunciation.

It was a great ambition that impelled me, perhaps the greatest of all, that which only requires, in order to be realized, the gleam of a tranquil eye, combined with the light of thought. Perhaps one is aided by certain books, by the sound of the wind, by the quality of the atmosphere. But perhaps it is necessary to have within oneself the dormant source of a welling beauty. Perhaps it is necessary to be marked by a predestination whose sign is invisible.

What if I were not worthy of that attempt? What if I had chosen the place in which to make it imprudently? For there must be some places that are more favorable than others. I had heard talk of places where the spirit breathes, and even of an inspired hill. There must, therefore, be soulless hills, valleys that the spirit cannot reach. What significance did the presence of a very old crow have? And above all, was it a favorable commencement to encounter, when I had scarcely arrived, a young woman with eyes the color of flowing water?

MELUSINE WITH THE LONG GREEN HAIR

"You haven't yet perceived anything?" Roseline asked me, with a gesture that designated the land around us.

I had just said something banal about the beauty of the region.

"What might I have perceived?"

Roseline burst into clear laughter in which there was an undisguised scorn.

We were walking on a hill that day, between a little pine wood and a field of leafless vines, the stunted trunks of which were reminiscent of as many sorrowful dwarfs.

"I won't tell you anything because it's necessary to divine it for oneself. And then, perhaps you're one of those who are fated never to understand: fortunate innocents who traverse life which a blindfold over the eyes. Anyway, what's the point in knowing? Knowledge of those mysteries came to my father a long time ago and he hasn't yet found the solution. I've never known whether he bought the château in which we live in order to delve deeper into the question, or to console himself for having a daughter who transforms into a snake."

Roseline uttered a profound sigh and lowered her head slightly, like someone who is bearing the weight of a beautiful but ineluctable destiny.

It was only at that moment that the old legend of the Lusignan family returned to my memory. Henri de Lusignan went on a crusade with Saint Louis at the time when he was King of Cyprus.[1] Then he married a young woman of great beauty called Melusine, whom he brought back to his château in Poitou.

"Melusine with the long green hair," sang the poets of those distant times.

"She must have difficulty in understanding the mysteries of our holy religion," said the prior of Lusignan.

That Queen of Cyprus remained somewhat pagan, unable to traverse the great forests of centenarian oaks and chestnuts, where the rain made the underwood rotten with dead leaves and vegetal waters, without having fruits of nostalgia and distraction.

"I'm going to clear the area of trees and our woodcutters will become laborers," said the Seigneur de Lusignan.

On the day before every Sunday, the young wife locked herself in her bedroom, and she had demanded that the Seigneur de Lusignan never attempt to enter it, under the pretext of unleashing an irreparable misfortune. He could not resist the temptation, and one evening he peeped through the keyhole. He saw, to his great dolor and an equally great surprise, that the woman he had married was only a woman in the upper part of her body, and a snake in the rest. He heard a heart-rending scream

---

[1] In the earliest written version of the legend of Melusine—and hence of most of the literary versions based in it—the hero is named Raymondin. The Lusignan family ruled the island of Cyprus from 1192 until 1489; the first of them to be called Henri became king in 1218 while still a baby, assumed control in 1232 and ruled until 1253; he was the only one of that name who could have been associated with Louis IX, alias Saint Louis (1214-1270), who became King of France in 1226 and participated in the seventh crusade, launched in 1248, and the eighth, launched in 1267.

and Melusine with the long green hair, which must also have been wings, flew out of the window and disappeared in the direction of the profound forest, from which she never returned.

In vain the Seigneur de Lusignan went to kneel down at the edge of the forest and begged his wife to come back. In order to have her he would have consented to her keeping her half-animal appearance, even though it was not fitting for a good Christian to have a wife with the form of a serpent. A man in love is willing to make great concessions. Only on certain evenings at Pentecost did he hear a desperate cry emerging from in the depths of the forest, whose accent he recognized. And that was all. Then he grew old, and died. Perhaps the race of serpents cannot be reconciled with that of humans.

Roseline allowed to pass over her face the expression of slightly sad softness that the evocation of memories provokes.

"I've often thought about my ancestor Melusine, and I know that I resemble her."

"Have portraits of her been conserved?"

"No, no portraits—no portraits painted on canvas, at least. But so many mirrors and springs have reflected her image! Even close to the place where we are. She leaned over the sea when she disembarked at Fréjus, the towers of which we can see from here. Fréjus was a great port and she stayed there for several days in the bishop's house. That holy man didn't suspect anything, and advised her to take communion at least once a week, on Sunday. And that didn't please her. But she loved the bishop's garden. It reminded her of her youth—for my ancestor Melusine was born in the sunlit place in the Orient, not far from the Tigris and the Euphrates, where the terrestrial paradise was located. And a marvelous cactus grew in the bishop's garden, with nine leaves full of colors, falling back harmoniously in proportions fixed by the law that regulates cacti."

I marveled that such precise details should be known to Roseline after ten centuries had gone by,[2] but I thought it better not to ask her how she knew them.

"Poitou didn't suit her, because the sun is too pale and neither palm trees nor cacti grow there. And yet, my ancestor Henri had done everything necessary for the abode to delight her. As much to please her as to astonish the inhabitants of Lusignan, he arrived at his château, after years of absence, with an extraordinary cortege. Melusine with the long green hair was to his right, on a white horse, in a robe befitting the Queen of Cyprus, the color of a pool, the color of beech leaves, with a necklace of emeralds and a crown of woven jade. Behind came negroes wearing green armor and huge sabers in the shape of a quarter-moon. They were laughing and showing their teeth. And as the people of Poitou had never seen men with black skin, they were astounded, and pointed at their woolly hair and bizarre tattoos. After the negroes there were fakirs and charlatans with cabalistic objects related to magical things, and hen a camel at the end of a rope, which lowered its head pensively. Then came the followers of the Queen, all princesses of Arabia, Palmyra or other places; then cavaliers in large numbers; then slaves carrying a crocodile, with its mouth open, its jaws sustained by ivory colonnettes in

---

[2] According to the dates logically implied by the version of the story just cited, fewer than eight centuries have gone by, but other details added to the story is subsequent chapters suggest a different chronology.

order that its teeth could be seen. And the oddest thing of all, surely, at the end of the cortege, was a sort of Oriental clown, an acrobat of a certain age, with a long nose and a graying beard..."

"A graying beard?"

"Which stirred over his breast while he played a psalterion..."

"A psalterion? Are you quite sure?"

"Yes…and who performed a comic dance on his own in order to entertain the audience."

And, at the idea of that psalterion player at the end of the cortege, Roseline, forgetting her ancestor Melusine amid the forests of Poitou, emitted a loud burst of laughter—a burst of laugher so long and filled with joy that I thought she was about to start dancing, like the bearded acrobat.

THE OWNER OF THE AGRIPPA

I could see from my threshold a house with a low roof illuminated by a slightly ruddy light, and it gave me a bad impression. I asked Mathieu Lapeyre who lived there and whether his commerce was agreeable.

"It's the house of a bad man," he said, "an assuredly wicked man. And what's more, he's foreign to the region."

Now, a few days later, the wicked man died. Whether he is good or bad, death awaits a man at his hour.

Guillard—that was his name—had a bad reputation in the locale. It was known all the way to Fréjus, and perhaps even beyond, that he had an evil nature.

"He's very careful of his money. He's cross-eyed, which is a sign. His house faces north. And he has an Agrippa in his possession, also known as the Egromus."

That Agrippa is well-known—I mean, known in the region. It is a large book with an embossed cover, whose parchment pages are full of sorceries and singular figures. At least, it is said to be parchment. Perhaps it is vulgar paper, but garnished in the margins with fingerprints with distinct lines. It is said that there is an Agrippa, or an Egromus, which is similar, in every Christian parish, and that the man who owns it is a left-handed Christian.[3]

---

[3] The name of "l'Agrippa" [the Agrippa] is derived from an apocryphal volume appended after his death to the survey of occult science compiled by Cornelius Agrippa von Nettelsheim (1486-1535), which acquired a considerable repu-

In addition to such a possession, the bad man was bad because he conserved, no one knew for what purpose, a small bone in a green bottle, a bone like a minuscule dorsal spine, that of a little-known animal or a human dwarf—all things that are characteristic of evil.

He had been seen through the windows, one evening, reading his book and moistening his finger in order to turn the pages. He had been seen after dinner and in the morning, the candle still burning. But it went out subsequently, as all candles do, and the door did not open. One night passed, and then several, and the house seemed lower and more deeply sunk in the ground, with a certain air of not wanting anyone to go there.

When several days had gone by, an old woman named Catherine and a retired individual named Malassis, who sometimes visited the wicked man, were informed by the postman that the door was still closed and that an unused pot of milk was still in the same place. They discussed the matter, and, as they were very pious people, they went to fetch the curé. Having a presentiment of what had happened, they penetrated into the house.

The man was on his bed with his face rigid, but almost as calm as if he were asleep. Two candles had been consumed, one to his right, the other to his left, as if Guillard had carried out the funeral service for his own death.

And the book was there, in fact, but much smaller than had been believed: a book touched by many fingers.

---

tation as a handbook of black magic. "Egromus" is a trifle enigmatic, but is cited in works by the folklorist Anatole Le Braz as one of several alternative names employed in Brittany for the same grimoire.

Everything was quite ordinary, for death overtakes the living with great simplicity. Everything except one thing. It is well-known that the human body, as it dissolves, destroying itself, returning to putrescence, gives off an insupportable odor. Only great saints, it is reported—although very few have witnessed it—escape the common law and emit a sweet odor that is known as the perfume of sanctity. Now, Guillard, lying on his bed, his hands closed, turned to stone and his face taking on the elongation of death, emitted, with no doubt about it, a delicate odor of roses, an odor such that, when it had been respired, the soul was penetrated with delight.

At first, no one wanted to believe it. But the perfume was increasing. Several people had come to see, for death attracts, and all of them were embalmed.

"There are roses somewhere," someone said.

But no, there were no earthly roses.

"Personally, I don't smell anything," the curé had said, remembering that Guillard had died without confession or extreme unction ad could not pretend to any sanctity. Then, from the corner of his eye, he had seen the Agrippa, also known as the Egromus, the sole example in the parish.

"Perhaps it's a miracle," said someone. "There's a saint at La Mothe who has been preserved, shrunken, under a glass bell-jar, who also exhaled a sweet odor when she died. But that was in the time of legends, and she was a saint when she was alive."

I was only informed later, and the placement in the bier had just taken place. All of that is truly exceptional and very difficult to ascertain.

The members of one group, by the door, were wondering whether the wicked man really had been wicked. But there was a great deal of evidence. His wife, while she was alive, had been a punch-bag. He had thrown stones at children. He killed cats and rabbits, and always did so slowly. If anyone reproached him he said: "I'm a scientist, I study pain scientifically." And then, there was the dorsal spine of the dwarf, which his brother had removed. A wicked man, no doubt about it! It was necessary that the world was upside-down for there to be that delightful perfume of roses.

"There has been a miracle! A great miracle!" said someone near me, two or three times, who was exclaiming in a low voice and did not seem to be entirely serious.

The dead man's brother, frowning, watched the gestures of the visitors, doubtless fearing that someone might take the book, even though he had hidden it somewhere.

"I've come from Auvergne for the burial," he said.

In a corner, no one knew why, a young boy was holding his nose ostentatiously.

I breathed in with all my strength and I sensed the perfume immediately.

"It's extraordinary," said Mathieu Lapeyre, beside me. And he added: "Isn't it?"

And I saw that the extraordinary character of the thing was partly dependent on my judgment.

I breathed in again, and no longer sensed the odor of roses.

"Someone's just opened a window," said a short man, as if he were apologizing for the insufficiency of the miracle. "If only you'd come a little sooner."

Outside, I heard people exclaiming. Nothing is any longer as it was before. The fault is in all those modern machines. A wicked man dies like a saint. One is even deceived by God.

THE DISAPPEARANCE
OF BROTHER ALPHONSE

"I'll take you to visit the Camaldolese monastery," Roseline said to me, "And I'll say a prayer to Our Lady of Pity, for the realization of my mission and yours."

In the harsh, arid mountains that overlook the village of Roquebrune-sur-Argens there is a Camaldolese monastery: not a great monastery like an ant-hill of cells and meditations, but a monastery only grouping a few white monks together around the ancient chapel of Our Lady of Pity.

An automobile carried us along the road to Roquebrune.

"The superior is a joyful man," Roseline told me. "He likes flowers and birds and is able to talk to them. Between us, I think"—Roseline lowered her voice, perhaps in order not to be overheard by the driver—"that he's received certain instructions from Saint Francis."

"Saint Francis?"

"The Saint Francis who lived in Assisi, to whom the angels talked," said Roseline, with a smile full of softness that gave her, for a second, a certain resemblance to one of those angels. "But it's necessary that I warn you. When we climb the mountain to get to the monastery, be careful to walk exactly in the middle of the path. No road goes to the monastery and it's a quarter of an hour's walk on foot. Now, many of the trees one goes past are former humans—irritated humans, perhaps humans who are being punished. I don't know why so many former humans, with their sorrow and their sins, find themselves on the slope of that mountain, but if you pass too close to them they try to seize you with their branches."

When we began to walk under the trees, Roseline repeated those recommendations regarding the former humans.

"I believe they're hardened souls," she said.

And I saw her walk with great prudence, taking care that her dress did not brush the tree-trunks. For my part, I could not distinguish the slightest abnormal movement of the branches.

Roseline uttered a sigh of relief when the path went through an unwooded area.

"I say prayers for them," she said, raising her voice, "but they can't know that. They can't hear under their bark. Oh, what a separation there is between the worlds!"

Suddenly, she stopped.

"Perhaps you don't know the story of Brother Alphonse? It wasn't very long ago. It happened right here. Almost every evening, shortly after sunset, when the monks had had their meal, Brother Alphonse limped down through the pines where we are to the village. He went to collect the scraps that a pious butcher's wife set aside for the convent. That wasn't for the monks, of course, but it's necessary to feed the animals.

"Brother Alphonse was rather old, short, and like a romantic king's jester. Outside of any monastic rule, he wore a beard like a necklace, in the fashion of certain mariners. Why had he adopted that form of beard? For it's necessary to get to the bottom of things. Perhaps because of the inclination and force the hairs on his chin. Perhaps in order to conform to a certain ideal of beauty that is only realized in the form of beards. At any rate, that is the way it was.

"One evening, because of the density of the shadows and certain animals that are hidden and come out at nightfall, he took a lantern for the return journey and held it up in front of him. From Roquebrune it was easy to follow that light, which veered slightly to the right and the left because he had a limp.

"That evening, the butcher's wife, who was sad and was gazing into the distance for that reason, and other people who were joyful, and doing the same thing because of their joy, could all see Brother Alphonse's lantern distinctly as he went through the tall pines. He was also visible from the convent. One monk, a great lover of dogs, who was waiting for the scraps in order to share them out, saw the glow approaching.

"When all of them were interrogated, it was that lantern-glow they talked about; but the monk named Alphonse, the old man hardened to labor, with his necklace beard, his slightly twisted knees and his short arm lifting the lantern, was never seen again, not the following day, or ever, in the sequence of infinite time. He had gone no one knows where, with his bag of scraps.

"In vain, the men of the village, the gendarmes of the commune and the monks of the monastery retraced the route a hundred times. They searched the area, in vain. A monk who resembles a romantic jester does not pass unnoticed. It was the wearing of that beard that made evil tongues and the pagans of the Mairie say that Brother Alphonse was weary of doing nothing but running errands in a convent of monks and that he wanted to drink to life.

"Absolutely nothing was discovered. There was no sandal-print, no revelatory beard-hair hanging like a thread of an old cobweb on some branch of wild laburnum. Absolutely nothing. Evidently, people claimed—

there are always evil tongues—that a limping man resembling Brother Alphonse had been seen in Marseille. But we've arrived at the tree. Look carefully to your left. There, the path seems to bend and, instead of pines, there's a row of old willows. I'd swear that at one time, the one that is closest to us didn't have the same form. All those old willows resemble one another. It's necessary to remember that, in the language of trees, the willow signifies punishment. And doesn't that one give the impression of a thickset monk, slightly inclined to one side, with a sort of necklace of bark, whose legs have lost their separation? It's wiser to go past quickly. Assuredly, the heavens and the earth aren't regulated with the simplicity one might think."

YOU DON'T LOOK YOUR AGE

How did that conversation about ages come about? I can't remember the point of departure. I only remember that I had a desire to deflect it, that I had the sentiment that it was dangerous for me. Why dangerous? Had I anything to hide on the question of my age? Had I not renounced? Has someone who has renounced the concern of having, or having had, or appearing to have any particular age? Ought not someone who has renounced be glad to be at last a hundred years old?

A centenarian, if he has not attained wisdom after having pursued it, at least has the appearance of it, and that is already a great deal.

I believe that we began by talking about the age of plants. I said that one can recognize the age of trees by the fine circular lines that are inside the wood, and Roseline stated to laugh, and said that she had learned that at the age of four.

Slightly vexed, I declared that I had only made that affirmation in order to talk about certain very old large trees in California. When they were examined it was still believed that the age of the earth did not surpass six thousand years, but one of them gave evidence of a past of eight thousand years. Did Roseline know that?

She did not know that—fortunately, for I had invented that tree eight thousand years old, so much did I desire to shine, to appear erudite. And I thought I had surpassed such paltriness!

I have retained a remorse or that, but it was much less painful than what was to follow.

Roseline told me that her father knew the ages of all species of creatures. First of all, the age of butterflies. They had lives of great brevity. That was easily understandable. There must be an exception for the old sad king that she had set free. Oh, she would like to find him again! But had he recovered from his wound?

She had often heard her father express astonishment at certain strange longevities, like that of the crocodile. After studies of that animal, her father had come to believe that crocodiles were only victims of their own ferocity. They ate one another. But he was convinced that certain animals of that species, having attained a superior degree of strength, and having nothing more to fear from their fellows, could not die of old age. There must be crocodiles as old as the earth itself.

"What experience they must have," I said, in a bantering tone.

"Age doesn't give experience—on the contrary. Haven't you noticed that age gives old men, even intelligent ones, a puerility greater than that of children."

And it was thus that the conversation was orientated toward the ages of people we knew: the age of her father; the age of Madame Tournadieu.

"One is as old as one appears," said Roseline, with a bright smile. "For example, you don't look your age."

That was equivalent to asking me what it was, and I told her without any hesitation. But what was the obscure force that impelled me to lie, and rejuvenate myself by five years?[4]

---

[4] Magre was 64 when *Melusine* was published, but the narrator appears to be younger than that, although he is careful not to provide any precise information.

I perceived a hint of surprise on Roseline's part. And at the same moment, I registered the accuracy of the expression "to look half-fig and half-grape." I had never understood that assimilation of a facial expression to two different fruits, but I suddenly understood it. Roseline had an expression half-fig and half-grape on learning my age, an age that wasn't true! She thought that I was older than she had believed. I had lacked audacity. I ought to have rejuvenated myself by ten years.

But why? What did the impression that she might have of my age matter? Was it not perfectly indifferent to me? While I said something or other about ages, an interior conscience reproached me on the subject of lying, not because it is necessary not to lie, but because of the hidden state of the soul that it reveals. What about the resolutions made? What about the absurd past of which I had so gloriously proclaimed the conclusion? Was that self-esteem of lost youth only an obscure reflex or the sign of a vivacious force that as only dormant?

Nothing is more bitter than discontent with oneself, the surprise that one has in catching oneself red-handed in mediocrity. I nearly said to Roseline that I had only wanted to see what she thought, and gave her my true age, but aging myself by ten years.

I was about to do that. But like a drifting boat, the conversation, of which I was not holding the tiller, suddenly took another direction. It seemed to fly off toward subjects a thousand leagues away. It was too late. Roseline looked at me from time to time covertly, perhaps seeking in my intonations or my gestures the manifestations of a fugitive youth.

THE TURTLE

It was in the evening of the day of the conversation about ages that I found a turtle in my garden.

Along the sandy Argens, where paludal rushes grow, numerous secret turtles live, which remain invisible. They are marine in origin and there is no way of knowing why that tribe selected that sand and water one day in order to seek a dwelling there.

But who knows the secret of animal migrations? Where to the locusts go, overwhelmed by the weight of their numbers? Where do the wise birds go that traverse the air on a day fixed by the September moon? What fixes that day? What guides those collective voyages? Which perspicacious bird, which erudite turtle, which studies the moon and the sea, measures the fatigue and hope and gives the signal to its people? No one knows. But the turtles had come to the shore of the Argents, into the midst of the paludal rushes.

Now, along that river, which pours its water into the sea near the city of Fréjus, there was in that fecund spring, without anyone knowing the cause, an abnormal multiplication of that tribe of turtles. Whence came that greater force of the generative faculty? Those turtles reproduce in accordance with a certain rhythm, and suddenly that rhythm was broken. Did that spring transport in its breezes, in its rain or in its sunlight, a particular quality acting on the sexual potency of those little carapace-bearing animals, and on them alone? For nothing abnormal was observed in the birth of dogs or that of crickets, and horses reproduced in a regular proportion—

at least, no remark was made by the owners of stud farms.

Or is it necessary to suppose some oral order given by the mysterious leader that directs migrations, a leader with a more beautiful carapace, a longer beak or a keener eye? Or did the order come from higher up, from the power that regulates species, counts individuals, and has a prodigious great book in the form of a world map from which depart, in accordance with the country, the different sorts of creatures, distributed in proportion to terrestrial production, in order that there should be a harmony between grass and sheep, flowers and bees, zebras and lions?

That, one cannot know, but the turtles in the vicinity of the Argens became, that year, more concupiscent, more procreative of new turtles, more productive of minuscule eggs. And there were so many births, so many little turtles avid for nourishment, that the banks of the Argens could not nourish them, and they spread out through the neighboring terrains. They were seen on the beach at Saint-Aygulf, they passed under the Roman aqueducts of Fréjus, they traveled beneath the white laurels of the Valescure and through the shady hollows of the Armitelle.

And it was thus that one of them came into my garden: the turtle that was there under a branch of rosemary.

It stretched out its neck and scrutinized the profundities of the sky. And suddenly, I established a relationship between it and me. Perhaps it had knowledge of divine things and a despair of not being able to attain them sufficiently was manifest in that elongation of the neck.

Was it not folly to attribute human motives to it? But perhaps it had them, in an animal proportion, quite obscure and quite unconscious.

It was possible that it only aspired to deposit that heavy carapace on the ground and to be a vagabond, light and dancing. But through the ages, its desire for protection, and its terror of the monsters that might devour it, had materialized on its back a house that was simultaneously a fortress. That was how we resembled one another. My appetite for pleasure had ended up producing, at length, a carapace of desires by which I was covered. I would dearly have liked to get rid of it; but one is bound to the past that one has created.

When would the turtle be able to dance without a carapace? When would I have set down the heavy burden of desire?

THE MYSTERY OF SATURDAY

Behind the little fence that encloses my garden, I perceived Roseline, who was making signs to me. She was even waving an umbrella. She evidently had something to say to me. She did not wait until I had opened the gate and shouted to me, joyfully:

"I forgot to tell you that my ancestor Henri was fat. No portrait of him has been conserved, any more than for Melusine, with the consequence that no one knows the proportion of that obesity, but he was fat, since he is mentioned in the genealogies as Henri I, nicknamed the Fat.

Possessed by an idea, Roseline neglected the formality of salutations. With a gesture, she invited me to accompany her on the road, and she continued:

"He was fat, which explains everything. Could a woman like Melusine love a fat man? And note that he had been a prisoner of the Saracens, which had not made him thin. He therefore had a natural paunch, which did not lend itself to attenuation. When one sees engravings or paintings depicting ancient times, one never finds fat men therein. Why? There were some, however. In order to have been dubbed the Fat, my ancestor Henri might perhaps have had an obesity that went as far as deformity. Did Melusine love him? It's a problem of knowing whether one can love a very fat man."

Roseline stopped then, she moved her head up and down, and, looking at me out of the corner of her eye, she murmured, as if it were an observation to herself: "In sum, you have the good fortune to be slim."

Why did that remark fill me with disturbance? Roseline considered it a possibility, then, that I might still inspire amour? I felt an internal wave of satisfaction. And immediately, I said to myself: *What importance has that? It's a general reflection that signifies nothing. But the tone in which she said it! And why attach that tone to me?*

Meanwhile, Roseline continued:

"A woman who changes into a snake once a week has a particular mentality, and ideas of her own about thinness and fatness. I wonder first of all why she consented to come to Poitou. To be Queen of Cyprus is already an enviable status. Henri I, nicknamed the Fat, who came to marry her, had emerged from the hands of the Saracens after having paid a ransom, and must have been very glad to find himself back in his fortified town in his comfortable palace. My father, who has studied these ancient questions, assures me that luxury was then highly developed, and that people in Cyprus enjoyed all the improved means that had been in usage in the Roman Empire. The central heating, for example, was better than ours, for there was a system of hot water pipes passing under the floors; the bathrooms were extraordinary, with a steam bath and mosaics, which was very important for Melusine on Saturday. It was in the bathroom that she locked herself, and on the day of her marriage it had been expressly agreed that her husband would never make any attempt to know what she was doing in there. The misfortune of those who love too much, most of the time, comes from the fact that one of the two does not keep their word."

Roseline paused again and, making an inexplicable comparison between me and Henri I, nicknamed the Fat, she asked me, with the same sideways glance: "I hope that you keep your word?"

And I was troubled again by that remark. She had made it with regard to two individuals lost in the shadows of a distant legend, but all the same...might Roseline not have a hidden agenda?

"My ancestor Henri didn't keep his, and he wanted to know. What great folly! In amour, one should never know. It's necessary to respect certain feminine mysteries. Have you noticed that one is always punished for a desire to know what ought to be hidden? Especially in the exceptional case of a man who has a wife who changes into a snake once a week. Fundamentally, the human heart is always the same. Would you, for example, be the kind of man to look through the keyhole of a bathroom, to listen anxiously to the rustle that the scales of a wet body make over the mosaics?"

I remarked to Roseline that, as she had just said, the case was exceptional, and I could not have reflected upon it.

"I'm going to tell you a family secret. It's a matter of a tradition that is perpetuated among the Lusignans. It's called the mystery of Saturday. Since the epoch of Henri and Melusine there has been, in an irregular manner, a daughter of the Lusignan blood who has received the singular faculty of changing into a snake on Saturday. Sometimes, several generations pass without the phenomenon being manifest. It is thought then that the fabulous epochs are over. Then it's perceived that they are not. A child is born who has a few scales on her skin in the first few months, which disappear. That's the fatal sign.

"What must happen can be avoided by condemning the young descendent of Melusine to virginity. My an-

cestors, who were all pious people, locked the poor creature away in a convent from which she never emerged
again. Prayers, the monastic life and faith in God prevented the transformation of the woman into a beast.
And still it was necessary that the cell in the convent in
which the young woman lived did not overlook a forest.
It appears that, in that case, all sorts of hissings and
slitherings in the grass were heard by night outside the
window of the cell, as if all the snakes in the forest were
assembled there. And that gave a character of dubious
worth, a trifle diabolical, to the pure virgin who did not
know what the cause of those strange assemblies was.

"But that was only possible in olden days. Once
can't lock up a young woman in a convent by force. And
try to explain the reason to sensible men nourished on
science! I'll tell you something else. The descendant of
Melusine is always born with a passionate temperament,
a sort of internal paganism, a flame that she can't master,
and which burns her."

As she spoke those words, Roseline bent down and
picked a poppy that was growing beside the path and
appeared to be extending its petals to her. She crumpled
it in her hand.

"Look at the color of this flower, still wild, that the
cuttings and artifices of gardeners haven't been able to
alter. Its color isn't the color of blood. It's a unique rd,
that of passion. I know that by night, snakes eat the
stems of poppies. It can't be said that the poppy has an
odor, but something special is emitted from that bloody
corolla, which contains peace and ardor at the same time.
It's necessary to have its juice on the lips to understand
that mixture."

Roseline held out the poppy to me. Perhaps thinking that I didn't take it quickly enough, with an abrupt

gesture, she crushed it upon my mouth, and for a few seconds I respired an insipid odor, I felt the greasy humidity of the juice of flowers, in which an aftertaste of a feminine hand remained, a hand that prolonged its contact a little too long, intentionally.

THE POND OF THE SOUL

What happened to me presented itself to me like an image, like the décor of a comparison.

I saw a pond, with fresh water of an extraordinary purity, clear luminous water susceptible of reflecting ambient beauties. And the landscape that surrounded the pool was made of delicate trees and well-ordered flowers under a sky full of nuances.

I cannot explain how, but in the water of the pond was my good intention, my desire to be intelligent, more sensible, humbler and purer in heart. Or rather, the water was itself that good intention, mine, and, at the same time, the good intention of a pond that is ready to reflect the surrounding landscape like a well-behaved mirror that renders the forms that pierce it, embellishing them slightly, thanks to the mysterious power of water and the prestige of that which is seen inversely.

The pond offered itself to the flowers, the trees and the sky, to the thousand colors of the air and to their rainbow marriage in the depths of its tranquil crystal.

And then, suddenly, something happened to its purity, as if its innate faculty of reflection had been damaged. No stone had fallen, provoking that circular geometry and radiating ripples. Aquatic inhabitants of the mud had not engaged in combat, striking one another with batrachian tails. No, the interior quality of the water had diminished its potentiality of light. A deformative power had been born, which was only manifest by virtue of unexpected curves, magnifications and oscillations of things reflected. The sky in the pool became gray, the trees became ridiculously thin or accumulated together.

The globe of the sun had irregularities and a slight blackening.

The good intention of my soul as not changed into evil intention, but it had been neutralized, it was no longer anything but a vague desire, on which appeared, here and here, certain stains of regret.

How can I describe what I saw, how can I measure the perception of myself by means of the image of a pond become a mirror of nature?

Slender rushes, slightly inclined over the water's edge, which were pure ideas turned toward the spirit of the sky, lost their rectitude, twisted and inclined in the direction of the earth. Blind tadpoles, emerging from the unconsciousness of the mud, traced circles, and caused an obscure mist to rise. A water-lily, the ideal of the soul, became black. The essence of the mirror, the ineffable virtue of reflecting the image of nature, was extinguished like a lamp whose oil has suddenly become an incombustible substance.

Then I raised my head above the pond. But instead of the ineffable blue of the celestial infinity, I saw a woman's face, the substance of blood and flesh—and that face was not reflected by anything.

MY FRIEND PORCASTRE

My friend Albert Porcastre came to see me. He was staying in a small inn situated on the road, some distance from my house.

"So I won't trouble your solitude," he said to me, with a smile.

He was a professor of philosophy and had scant esteem for my own intellectual faculties.

"Tell yourself that you don't know anything," he often said to me.

I understood immediately, as soon as our first conversation, that he was slightly irritated by my attempt at retreat and detachment from the world. In any case, although he often talked about the ideal, I believed that he could not imagine the possibility of human perfection.

"Men are dogs who only seek their nourishment on the dung-heap. And it's necessary not to try to get them out of it."

There were two men in him: the one who loved vulgarity, vulgar language, obscene jokes and bar-girls, with a sincere amour; and the other, who was summoned ardently toward things of the spirit and always had Plato's *Timaeus* in his pocket or the *Meditations* of Marcus Aurelius.

His physique reflected his double nature. He had a heavy build, broad shoulders, and fleshy lips, abnormally red to the point that one could believe that he had drunk wine a few seconds before, but a forehead in the form of a lyre and a blue gleam in his eyes, always fixed a little higher than the heads of his interlocutors, attesting to his love of thought.

Although attached to the pursuit of women of inferior quality, he had no concern for costume. He did not wear braces, and that obliged him to the repetition of the same gesture. He put both hands in his pockets in order to hitch up his trousers. And that gesture ordinarily coincided with a bitter remark that he took pleasure in uttering frequently. He laughed afterwards, and one understood then how one can qualify as gross a laughter that is, in itself, devoid of dimension. He had the tranquil certainty of having within him a power of seduction. "I do not know how that can be," he had said to me once, "but I have a fluid that attracts all women."

And, in the secrecy of his heart, I am sure that he rejoiced in being vulgar, for the fluid had a certain connection with his vulgarity. In the meantime, he was full of good will.

"You're very nicely lodged here," he said, considering my house while we were walking in the garden, "but how bored you must be!"

"Not at all!"

"To remain face-to-face with oneself, not to be bored in solitude, it's necessary to have attained a certain spiritual development."

"You think that I haven't attained it?"

"You know that I always tell the truth. I don't believe so."

"That's quite possible. But I can assure you that I'm not bored."

He started to laugh—a laughter far more delicate than usual, for that was a characteristic of his two-sided nature; he had several varieties of laughter at his disposal. In this case, the delicacy of his laughter added force to what he was expressing.

"Boredom," he said, "is like happiness. At the moment, one does not know that one is bored, any more than one knows that one is happy. You don't know that you're bored. Then again, there's something else. For someone who believes in survival and the afterlife, I find this house a little troubling."

"Why?"

"I've told you before that you have no intuition, you who believe in intuitions. I, who don't believe in them, have them."

"So?"

"Your little house, which seems entirely inoffensive at first glance, gives me the impression of a house of phantoms."

"Explain yourself."

"We've only traversed the rooms; I found that everything was very genteel, very well-arranged, but there's a certain something…something that one can't render in speech. Strictly speaking, it might be called the sentiment of a presence."

I was stupefied. I remembered the extraordinary phenomenon produced on the evening of my arrival—so extraordinary that I had thought, on reflection, that I had been the victim of an aberration. My God! Was there not question of a dead woman with furtive footsteps? But was it reasonable to pay any heed to such an implausible communication?

"That, in any case, is of scant importance," Porcastre went on. "You'll be so bored that you'll prefer to talk to a phantom than not talk to anyone. Unless..."

His face took on an expression of base hilarity that was typical of him.

"Unless you return to what you call your former errors. Yes, that's what will happen. And I've just encountered the creature that will bring you back to them. Moreover, she isn't bad."

"What do you mean?"

"She's the first person I saw on arriving here. I immediately thought of you. I'd scarcely deposited my suitcase in my room. She passed along the road with a slightly vulgar dance, which was reminiscent of a procuress. I asked the proprietor of the hotel who she was and he replied: 'That's Monsieur de Lusignan's daughter."

"I do know her, in fact. We've taken several walks together."

"Of course! I guessed. There are moments when I could believe that I'm a sorcerer."

My friend started to laugh, but that laughter had taken on the amplitude of men who have just told or heard an obscene joke.

"Why are you laughing? There isn't anything funny about it. I haven't made a vow not to talk to anyone. It's a matter of a very intelligent young woman, slightly eccentric, simultaneously very modern and reminiscent by her education of the young women of an earlier era."

Pocastre fell into a wicker armchair that was at the foot of the only pine tree in my garden and made the gesture of holding his sides to mark how comical my words seemed to him.

"There's a canine quality in men that never perishes. What's the point of trying to deceive yourself? I'm sure you've found the remedy against ennui."

I shrugged my shoulders.

"I've entered without regret into the last part of life. I have a goal. It's not to launch myself into stories. Anyway, the question doesn't arise. I know full well that nowadays all young women…but this one is an exception."

"It's a pity that I can't stay longer. I would have asked you to introduce me, and I would have made a bet with you. In fact, perhaps I have the time."

Porcastre had told me that he was only going to spend three days with me.

"If the canine quality of men is powerful, that of women is even more so. Yes, in sum, I have the time. Introduce me, and you'll see."

THE POSTMAN

But no, I'm not bored. I'm only waiting for news. That's perfectly legitimate.

Is that the postman's footsteps resonating at the end of the road? It's too early. What impatience! Here I am, leaning on the fence in the attitude of someone waiting. I am waiting. In any case, I'm not impatient. But what am I waiting for? What might the postman bring me? Among my friends, some don't have my address and the others have nothing to say to me. No, I'm not expecting anything from anyone.

Is that straw hat really his? Doesn't he wear a kepi? He's stopping at every villa. So, everybody gets letters. What characterizes the postman is that he never hurries. Is it possible to accept a glass of wine at such an early hour? If I put Bordeaux at his disposal, would he bring me more letters? Perhaps. There are such inexplicable correspondences between things. I ought perhaps to get some Bordeaux.

Now the sun's getting hotter. There's no point in staying here, since no one can have written to me. Isn't that a great benefit, in any case? One waits for letters and they only ever bring bad news. And then, afterwards it's necessary to reply. For a single amicable letter there are twenty that demand tedious explanations. The fortunate man is one who never sees the face of the postman. Let's go back in quickly before he gets here.

But I can hear a bicycle. I'd forgotten that the postman has a bicycle. In an enormous leather bag he's carrying a gigantic correspondence. I can glimpse packages of attractive books. It's impossible that, given the number, some of them aren't for me.

He's going to stop, for sure. How preoccupied he seems! One would think that he's a profound thinker. He touches his kepi as he passes by. He's passing by. It's a mistake. He has a light mind, in spite of appearances. And then, all those glasses of wine! He'll come back.

But no. He continues his route. What if I run after him and catch him up?

I can see him now in the distance giving to others with full hands. Here's someone in a driveway coming to meet him. He's handing out newspapers and brochures. I'm the only one this morning, absolutely alone, not to have any mail.

Oh, ingrate hearts! I would never have believed...

Come on! On the contrary, I'm glad to be forgotten by everyone. I'm delighted. No letters! No news! So much the better! So much the better! Oh, the joy of solitude!

A CONVERSATION WITH
MONSIEUR DE LUSIGNAN

I have made the acquaintance of Monsieur de Lusignan.

"I'm very content," he told me, "that for once, by chance, my daughter is taking pleasure in the company of an older man. She has such a liking for bad company. And that's not saying enough. She has a liking for hooligans. She gets it from her mother. It's an unimaginable thing. For her mother, it was a badge of honor to have been in prison. But for all that, she was a delightful woman.

"Oh, women! I've begun to wonder, in growing older, why the creator made two different sexes. I know what you're going to tell me: two sexes are necessary for reproduction. But not at all! That's an error. Primitive cells reproduce and even multiply in a surprising fashion by simple separation. If God had made a little more effort, he would have been able to enable humans to live without the frightful drama of sexuality. But perhaps God did it deliberately. Division is necessary in order for one to have the merit of union. It's necessary that there should be women to bring us back to evil by hiding under pure faces and angelic forms."

In order to take advantage of the mildness of dusk, Monsieur de Lusignan had received me in his park, which was vast, and tended by careless gardeners. Grass was growing in the pathways; the trees were full of birds.

Monsieur de Lusignan was holding his double-pointed beard in his hand and sometimes tugging the shorter part. He was much taller than me, which augmented his authority.

Suddenly, he stopped, and looked at me intently.

"You're doubtless in this region for the same reason as me? What is there not to learn? But we're not the only ones, unfortunately. The region has attracted the good, and also the wicked. It appears that a man died recently who had in his possession the Agrippa, also known as the Egromus. I've questioned people to the right and the left on his subject. No one was able to tell me why that man had come to establish himself in the area. It certainly wasn't for the same reason as us."

I was about to reply to tell him that I didn't know the reason to which he was making allusion, but he stopped me.

"No, you're certainly of my opinion; there are things that it's better not to talk about."

While walking he looked to the right and the left into the branches of the trees.

"Give me a sign, but without appearing to do so, if you see the sphinx Atropos with the death's-head.[5] There's one in the park at present. I've only glimpsed it. It's a black moth with a death's-head on its wings. I ask you to make me a sign without appearing to do so because the sensibility of moths is incredible, and has never been studied intelligently. Have you noticed that, by dint of directing the research of the mind toward a goal

---

[5] The reference is clearly to the death-head hawk moth *Acherontia atropos*, a member of the family *Sphingidae* [sphinx moths]. The image of the death's-head is, however, on the thorax of the actual species, not on the brown wings.

that one believes to be utilitarian, one arrives at neglecting everything that is truly interesting?

"Thus, the sensibility of moths is completely unknown. It has never even been remarked that the substance of their bodies belongs to another kind of matter than our terrestrial matter. And yet, it's easy to take account of the fact that the tissue with which the bodies of moths are made is neither animal nor vegetable. It's a substance that comes from the spirit world. Lepidoptera are an exception, they constitute a divine experiment.

"Evil does not exist among Lepidoptera. One does not see them striking one another or killing one another. They are not submissive to the needs of nourishment. And they are very sensible to the amour that they bear. Those who have attempted to domesticate them have received tender marks of affection. Alas, I cannot deliver myself to such trials. I have killed too many of them in my lifetime. I only learned belated the divine origin of butterflies. Oh, ignorance! I only liked their beauty. I traversed the body with a pin in order to enjoy it more. Each individual butterfly or moth would not recognize me as a killer of its fellows. But the soul of the species knows it.

"The sphinx Atropos would turn away from me if it succeeded in recognizing me. Unless it brings me a message. For moths are often messengers. The popular soul knows that, since it considers the presence of a death's-head moth as the announcement of an imminent death. And that's logical. If there are gods above us—I say gods, plural, which is to say, intermediaries between God and us—when they want to warn us about something, they make use of these singular little beings, who do not know evil and are made of divine matter.

"But there it is; it's necessary to know that sacred language, the divine language and the secret of the identification of ideas with the images of nature. My daughter tells me that you have certain knowledge. Do you know any of the symbols that the gods employ?"

I was obliged to confess my ignorance of those symbols. Monsieur de Lusignan looked at me with surprise, and a little sadness. I had caused him a disappointment.

"Evidently, it's very difficult. Veer few men know. Are you also ignorant of the veritable language of flowers?"

"Alas!"

"I speak of the veritable language because the one that is found in little popular books is, in general, erroneous. Flowers are also made with an extraterrestrial matter. They also serve, in certain cases, as vehicles of divine thought, especially the flowers of plants that posses a power, a natural virtue, like the poppy, rosemary or hemlock. But the gods have conceptions so different from ours that it is very difficult to grasp their language, even when they make serious efforts to make themselves understood. In sum, the greatest cause of our woes comes from the rigorous barrier that separates the worlds."

Monsieur de Lusignan spoke to me for a long time about subjects that all had a certain character of the marvelous. I sometimes looked at him covertly and I realized by his gestures, his way of walking or tugging his beard and the fashion in which he searched the sky for the sphinx Atropos, that he was a man living entirely outside reality. I thought I might risk a question without fear.

"Do you think that it is very difficult to understand the language of animals?"

"Very easy!" he exclaimed. "Infinitely easier than understanding the language of men, with words and rules of syntax! I ought to say that personally, I have never arrived at the perception of any animal speech—but that's my fault, for lack of love! For it's only an interior reaction to one's love for living creatures. If you're capable of that impulsion of love for an animal species, you understand the expression of its confused thoughts naturally. Evidently, that impulsion of love is rare among so-called civilized men. One finds that certain solitary individuals, living in the bosom of nature, have ended up identifying themselves fraternally with the animals that are close by. And yet, they almost always have a desire to eat their brethren, in the same way that I, who loved butterflies and moths, could not resist the desire to traverse their bodies with a pin. As the poet says, each man kills the thing he loves. A sad law! But the man who is strong, who is filled with love, has only to listen, and he will understand.

Monsieur de Lusignan stopped and looked at the ground in a melancholy fashion.

"He will, in any case, only understand poverties. It has sometimes been given to me to listen to the conversations of great professors of philosophy or medicine, and great writers, men of genius, or reputed as such. They only talk about mediocrities of the lowest order, if it is not about the dinner they have just had and the dishes they love. So, what can you expect from what the magpies are saying in the trees, or the frogs on the edge of the pond?"

UNCERTAINTY

And what if I'm mistaken? Is solitude really a road to becoming better? It isn't a matter, in any case, of absolute solitude, but that which a man can support who hasn't broken his attachments to the world, who remains bound to it by friendships, by books, by a sympathy for certain landscapes, and by his former liking for playing a role.

There is no guarantee that solitude will not develop that which is bad in us. Everything depends on the road one discovers in oneself. Not all roads lead to God.

Then again, solitude is subordinate to the frame in which it is exercised. There are favorable places and there are contrary ones.

The strong man breaks all his ties, does not see faces around him, does not know that there are trees, fields and stars. I am not that strong man. I make an attempt at solitude and I expect aid from the beauty of the country that surrounds me. But how tempting beauty is, and how closely linked to sensuality! Beauty does not push you forward toward the pure realm. It stops you in a sensual exaltation, in a paganism that has no other objective than joy. There must be a fashion of opening one's soul to beauty in such a way as to be enriched thereby.

I've hired, at random, a house with a garden, in order to read there and meditate there, in the hope of becoming a little more intelligent and progressing in the knowledge of the marvelous world that is around us and which we do not see. I've sat down in the shade of a tall pine tree; I've gazed at the plants and insects; I've talked to a neighbor, made the acquaintance of an old lady, a young woman, and her father. I know that, in one direction, there is the sea, and in the other, dense woods. All of that is very ordinary.

And yet, I sense a great mystery around me. Perhaps that mystery exists everywhere, and is only making itself felt in me because I'm more attentive. But perhaps there is something here that isn't elsewhere, the influence of which is acting upon me.

Who is it that I ought I to ask to enlighten me? Men are so ignorant and so blind. The majority confuse superiority with ironic doubt. And if one appeals to invisible beings, how slow the response is! All the more so as one has contracted the habit of indentifying an appeal with the syllables of the name of the entity to which one is appealing. And then, how can one appeal to those who no more have a name than a form?

THE APPEARANCE OF THE CROW

I was in my bedroom; it was hot, the window was open, and I was on the point of going to bed. I had switched off the lamp because of mosquitoes and I was looking at the garden, faintly illuminated by a moon that was about to disappear over the horizon.

Suddenly, I heard the caw of a crow. It was coming from the tall pine in the middle of the garden.

"The crow!" I exclaimed. "There it is! It's come back."

And almost immediately, the marvelous phenomenon was reproduced. I understood the language of animals again! The caw of the crow was no longer a cry devoid of meaning. It was a brief sentence which could be translated as: "He's not there!"

And I understood another remark, slightly longer, which was a dolorous exclamation: "How sad I am to be alone!"

The crow only had strictly limited sentiments, for it recommenced: "He's not there!" and after a pause it went on: "How sad I am to be alone!"

So the crow was looking for someone, observing his absence and affirming its sadness in solitude. It experienced the need to proclaim that in the night, and I heard it, for a few minutes, expressing those simple things in the shadow of the pine. Then there was a flutter of wings and it flew away.

"Blood! Blood!" sang a mosquito in my ear. It had to be prey to a blind desire, for it expressed it untiringly.

I went out into the garden precipitately in order to hear other voices, the expression of more animal sentiments. But the night was particularly silent. I had been reading under my lamp and it was late. Many animals were asleep. Doubtless many had no need to express what they were experiencing vocally.

Suddenly, very close to me, at my feet, a cricket intoned its song. It was not paying any heed to me. It must have been the same one that I had heard on the night of my arrival, an exceptional cricket, a luminary among crickets, whose sharpened senses permitted it to know that it was not running any danger by virtue of my presence. Doubtless it had exercised its observation since I had been walking around the flower-beds amid which its existence unfurled. What it said surpassed infinitely what one might have supposed to be the sentiments of an animal species.

"The night is protective! Nature is rich and marvelous! Everything has been created for crickets! How the trees are glorified by providing the leaves in which we find both nourishment and knowledge. For the veins of leaves form characters of a divine language, in which the secrets of the world are traced. Those characters are innumerable and it is necessary to learn them incessantly in order to know the meaning of the indefinite enigmas that surround us. But crickets possess patience and the delight of spiritual labor. We have arrived at knowing how there are periods of light and darkness, how roots plunge while dividing themselves into the earth, and have the extraordinary power of taking water and transmitting it to the branches, and how various creatures are, some of them inoffensive and others armed with sharp darts. We have arrived at knowing how transformative death is beneficial, and yet it is necessary to attempt with all one's might to delay it. All is well, everything is ordered, the earth is soft—as is appropriate in order for us to hollow out profound dwellings therein to shelter from wasps—the rain falls when necessary, and the sun fills us with joy."

My comprehension was abruptly interrupted, as it had been the first time. The song of the cricket became once again that monotonous noise to which I was accustomed.

What could be the cause of such a phenomenon? Did the advent of the crow have something to do with it? When I had gone back up to my bedroom, I meditated for a long time, leaning on the window sill. But no plausible explanation occurred to me.

Hazard would to put me on the path, a little later.

A VISIT TO SAINT ROSELINE

I had not seen Roseline for several days when she came to find me in order to go with her to the village of La Mothe. There, in an old chapel, in a glass reliquary, the body of the saint whose name she bears is conserved.[6]

We had talked about Saint Roseline, in regard to the death of a certain Guillard and the abnormal conservation of his body after death, a conservation all the more strange because it had been accompanied by a sweet perfume of roses.

"We'll go to see Saint Roseline at La Mothe," Roseline had said to me. I had wanted to fix the day, but she had decided to fix it herself. She had added, with a clear gaze: "My father has a little farm at La Mothe. I'll take advantage of it to see the farmers and bring back butter and eggs."

All that was normal. As we were about to climb into the automobile, for La Mothe was about half an hour away, Roseline said to me, negligently: "Oh, if by

---

[6] The body of Saint Roseline (1263-1329) was deposited in the chapel in question following its exhumation five years after her death, when it was allegedly found intact and well-preserved. The reliquary apparently only contained her eyes until the mid nineteenth century, but remains that were embalmed in 1894 were then placed in a glass case and still remain on display today, accompanied by a mural mosaic by Marc Chagall. Roseline's legend includes "the miracle of the roses," when food that she was removing from the family reserves to give to the poor during a famine was supposedly transformed into a bouquet of roses.

chance you see my father, it's not worth the trouble of telling him that we've been to La Mothe. There are little secrets in the family that it would take too long to explain."

My God! All that, strictly speaking, was normal.

We set forth. The weather was fine. Roseline was particularly cheerful and in a mood for confidences.

"You haven't had a Russian mother?" she asked me, point blank.

"In truth," I replied, surprised, "my mother was born in Toulouse."

But the precision was unnecessary. Without paying any heed, Roseline went on: "You can't know what it is to have a Russian mother. To begin with, one loves her much more. And then, there are the stories of a Russian childhood, a maternal childhood that went by long ago, and which one can never forget. The people have names so complicated that one can't retain them; it's a matter of indeterminate steppes, phantom forests and fortresses, perhaps Siberian, perhaps Caucasian. Cavaliers go by with fur bonnets that come down to the chin and they have lances so long that they're lost in the clouds. There are Cossack hunters who crack their whips and show sparkling teeth like rows of icicles when they laugh. Others have bearskins on their backs, on which they've left the head intact in order to put it on their own head, so that they seem to have two heads, one human and one ursine. There are journeys by sleigh under fir trees, with packs of wolves howling behind, whose red eyes can be seen shining like living embers. There are icons in the chapels in translucent gold, into which drunken princes go with their violet boots and crimson gloves, falling to the flagstones weeping and demanding vodka while proclaiming prayers."

Roseline stopped and raised her hand as if to seize a piece of Russian silk fluttering in the air.

"A Russian mother! I must have been thirteen when she died. But what advice she gave me! All my knowledge of the world comes from her. Oh, she didn't have ideas like everyone. 'My daughter, there's no true love,' she often said to me. 'I'm speaking in the interests of your happiness. It's necessary not to occupy yourself with prejudices. When you're twenty, remember what I've told you. Love whom you please and don't occupy yourself with anything else. For there's an immense conspiracy in society to prevent young women from seizing the miserable portion of happiness that nature accords to them. Oh, a very miserable portion! And in spite of that, parents, friends, and the whole world are in league to take it away from them.'

"And once, shortly before she died, my mother took me in her arms and she murmured to me, as if it were a secret: 'Never marry a scientist, especially a scientist who loves butterflies!'

"For it's an anomaly in the Lusignan family to love creatures other than snakes. The love of snakes is transmitted like a tradition. Note that my father maintains an entire collection of them in the depths of the park, in a locked place to which he might take you some day, if he thinks you're worthy. And they're mostly venomous snakes. He has them sent from distant countries and sometimes spends hours watching them sleep. I'm sure he'll end up getting himself bitten."

Roseline remained pensive momentarily, but not for long. Then the fear of bites vanished.

"What can one do when one has a mother who has advised you to love and a father who engages you every day never to love?"

That contradiction could not have weighed excessively on Roseline's soul, however, for she took a small mirror out of her handbag and hastily put on lipstick. We had arrived at the entrance to a park, in which the chapel was situated.

"What time is it?" Roseline asked, with a hint of anxiety. "Is it three o'clock?"

I relied that it was quarter to three.

"Oh! Good!" She seemed reassured.

"There's no urgency."

"No, evidently not."

One does not take cognizance of certain observations at the moment when one makes them. It was only in the evening, when I had returned to the House of the Crow, that it occurred to me that Roseline, during our visit to the saint, had been absent, hurried and as if detached from what she saw. To be sure, it was not the first time that she had contemplated the extraordinary case of the incorruptibility of Saint Roseline. She was only showing it to the stranger that I was. But there was something strangely hasty in her attitude and in her manner of assuring me that, except for the glass reliquary, nothing in the chapel merited retaining the attention.

Saint Roseline, who had died six centuries before in the convent of which she was the prioress, had left, as a testimony to her perfect life, a purified form that death had not altered. The bodies of saints, in those distant times, were consigned to numerous displacements. Churches and monasteries made one another pious gifts of miraculous remains. The still-intact body of Saint Roseline had been transported hither and yon. During the wars of religion it had been so well-hidden, in order to preserve it from the impious, that it had never been found again.

It was a blind man who, in the course of a fervent prayer in the chapel, where her place was empty, suddenly saw with the mind's eye the secret place where Saint Roseline reposed. She was restored to the place where it was given to me to contemplate her. But in the meantime, she as visited by Louis XIV. The powerful king was accompanied by his physician, named Vallot.[7] That man must have been animated by the spirit of skepticism. The supernatural gleam of the eyes, after a lapse of three centuries, made him fear some trickery. Sheltering behind the authority of science, he made a slight incision in one of the eyes, and the divine light of the gaze vanished forever, for miracles are not repeated in accordance with human caprice. Behind the lowered eyelids, however, enough of the delicate substance of the eye was discernible to admire how our fragile flesh can receive eternity by virtue of the passage of a pure soul.

"It's utterly extraordinary," said Roseline, distractedly. "Wait for me in the park. How tedious these farmers are!"

And she drew away with a particularly light and rapid step.

I made a tour of the cloister several times, and then walked along the pathways under the old trees. Mimosas alternated with laurels and eucalypti derived of their bark, reminiscent of young men clad in white abruptly sprung forth from mantles that still lay at their feet.

---

[7] Antoine Vallot (c1594-1671) was Louis XIV's physician from 1652 until his death. He and the king visited Saint Roseline's reliquary in 1660.

The reasonable time for a conversation with a farmer went by. What could the questions of butter and eggs be about which Monsieur de Lusignan ought not to know? I remembered that it was appropriate to give a tip to the concierge and as I perceived him near the gate I went to him. We exchanged a few words of great banality. I prolonged them, without really listening, in order to pass the time. However, I heard him complain about the birds that ate his fruit. He set traps, which were futile. He did not like crows.

"There are crows here?"

"Considerable numbers that come from those woods above Arcs."

And, after several hostile remarks about the race of crows I heard him say: "Oh, I couldn't live with a crow, like Saint Eleutherius."

This time, my attention awoke. So Saint Eleutherius had lived with a crow? But when and where? What was this Saint Eleutherius? I asked him for details about the life of that saint, but he did not possess any.[8] There are celestial saints whose names are cited with veneration without anything being known of the causes motivating that veneration. Perhaps Saint Eleutherius was our contemporary and the guardian of the chapel of La Mothe had heard mention of him from people who had lived in his intimacy and had noticed the presence of a crow in his vicinity.

Nothing of the sort—that even made the guardian laugh. Could there be saints in our day? I supposed that

---

[8] The Catholic Church recognizes several saints named Eleutherius [Eleuthère in French], but none associated with the region in which the present story is set; the one featured in the story is a pure invention.

he must have lived in the times of Jesus Christ. There was only Monsieur Spéluque, the great scholar of Fréjus, who would know when Saint Eleutherius had lived, if he had even existed—for so many stories are told.

Meanwhile, time continued to pass. I saw, a little further away, on the road, the driver of the vehicle that had brought us, marching back and forth with a vivacity that testified to the length of the wait.

Young women have no sense of duration, I said to myself, to excuse Roseline.

In the end, I was obliged to suppose that something unforeseeable had happened.

I looked at the surrounding country, and I suddenly saw Roseline emerge from a little house that opened on to a little path some distance away.

That house had no connection with a farm, or with any place where farmers might reside. It resembled one of those detached houses that pullulate in the suburbs of cities and are often fitted out for the use of strangers in the vicinity of spa towns. Newly-painted shutters gave it a sort of coquetry. I distinguished a minuscule garden with the bright colors of a few flowers.

By for the sake of discretion, I did not linger over the examination of the house. My rapid glance saw Roseline make a sign of farewell with her hand, and it seemed to me, in a flash—nothing is more deceptive than visions that only last for a second—that I distinguished a silhouette on the threshold...

No, I cannot say that I distinguished a silhouette: such a fugitive impression has, so to speak, no existence, and ought not to be retained. When my gaze posed on the house again, the door was closed and Roseline was advancing toward me, smiling.

"As long as I haven't made you wait too long," she said, simply. "You have to excuse me. I'm so talkative."

No unforeseeable event had occurred. And, in order to justify that loquacity, Roseline started talking about all sorts of subjects with a joyful volubility.

Yes, something unforeseeable did happen: a bitter sentiment that made me relive scenes of my youth, which resuscitated forgotten faces and lost hours. I was confounded by astonishment to be gripped by so much force by that sentiment, which I had thought dead. And it only grew within me. I had a desire to interrogate her, to know, and I only succeeded in maintaining silence by means of an effort.

"*Au revoir*. See you soon. Perhaps tomorrow. That excursion was charming. Another time, I'll show you the banks of the Argens. And I must go back to La Mothe one of these days."

But no, I had not seen that silhouette on the threshold. The world is full of illusions, of false images. Roseline had not given reasons because there were none to give. Some things are so simple that one does not think of explaining them.

THE PRESENCE OF BOOKS

The silent beauty of books...

They had taken a long time to arrive in their boxes, but in the end, they had arrived, thanks to the everyday miracle that is the organization of railways. I had lined them up on brand new shelves, which, thanks to a marvelous harmony, had a secret understanding of things, having been brought by the carpenter, their author, the day before the arrival of the boxes.

The paint was slightly sticky, but not enough to cause the books to adhere.

I arranged the books lovingly. A large surface of wall had been covered with bound books, and another with paperbacks. I had formed groups in accordance with the color of the binding, taking pleasure in admiring the fine effect of reds and garnets united on the same shelves. The books with intact paper covers had been gathered together. A few pariahs with miserably torn covers had been exiled to the lowest shelf, the one at which one does not direct the gaze.

When, after a considerable time, that had been concluded, I had begun again, because it was more harmonious to arrange the books in accordance with their dimensions, the large with the large and the small with the small, making an exception for the pariahs, which retained their inferior position.

Only then did my error appear to me. Were the books a décor, part of the furniture? Had I a mind sufficiently vulgar to subordinate the order of the books, those receptacles of thought, to decorative questions of color or format? I had, in truth, just been conducting myself like an upholsterer, an organizer of interiors for the use of rich bourgeois. Everything had to be begun again.

I recommenced with ardor. One sole law ought to preside over the organization of books, a law that takes account of the authors who have written them. How can the value of a book be recognized, if not by its author? And what is it if not ingratitude not to take account uniquely of the true creators of books?

I worked with pleasure, praising in passing the abundant writers for their abundance and the sober writers for their faculty of condensation. Memoirs ought to be with memoirs, philosophy with philosophy. To take an example, Maine de Biran's journal ought to be detached from the rest of his works and seated next to Goethe's memoirs. But stop there! Was it not necessary also to take account of the date when the books had been written? How difficult the classification of a library was! However, I set to work to obey the reason and justice that ought to preside over the ordering of books.

And it was only when the last volume was standing in the place that I thought legitimate, at the moment when I was about to utter a sigh of relief, that enlightenment finally dawned.

A library only has a reason for existence by virtue of the services it renders. Books were divided into two categories. How had that not appeared to me sooner? There were those that I had read and were there in order to be reread, taken up from time to time, or even merely to be consulted, and there were those that I had not read, which were intellectual promises for me, future pleasures of discovery, the riches of days to come. Two different sections! Then there would be no futile searches, no forgotten book. And even the pariahs ought to participate in that division, emerging from their exile.

That exile had, in any case, been an aberration. Should the exterior envelope matter if it encloses a spiritual beauty? The pariahs ought to be in the place of honor! Even if not the slightest particle of their paper binding remained, if they had lost all covering and were as naked as beggars!

O perplexity! Books are in place in accordance with the convenience of their possessor. Convenience! Should practical considerations outweigh everything else? Is there not something garish about putting *The Imitation of Christ* next to the *Tao* of Lao-Tsu? Would it not be more logical to unite, on one side, the writers of the Orient, and on the other, those of the Occident? Everything has to be done again.

Night has fallen. I'm exhausted. The gilt of bindings is shining, the tears in paper covers attest to the frequent reading of attentive men, and, on looking more closely, one can distinguish the imprints of certain thumbs that provide an indelible sign of that attention. The books can be placed in any order; the essential thing is that they are there, with their colors, their thickness and their numerous pages.

Fecund presence of books! Perhaps it is unnecessary to read them, and their presence alone is sufficient. In any case, they are there. Intelligence is present in the form of characters reproduced on paper. Each book contains its portion of enlightenment within its pages, and it is sufficient to pick it up in order to be illuminated.

Not always, obviously. There are obscure enlightenments, incomprehensible authors. But just because a lamp does not function very well, for reasons of the wick or the mechanism, one is not tempted to reproach its light.

I believe that a peasant who cannot read and who was imprisoned for all his life in a library, although he could not summarize precisely Plato's *Symposium* or Spinoza's *Ethics*, would nevertheless end up being the possessor of a broad and imprecise philosophical knowledge that had filtered to him without his being aware of it.

It is, however, preferable to read books. It is even necessary to reread them. There are some that have the marvelous property of always being new. There are others that only put on fancy dress. But even those have a power of evocation. A spark of thought can be sufficient to ignite a great fire. And it is necessary not to be discouraged if there are mysterious texts. One ought to consider oneself in confrontation with them as an explorer who is traversing a dense forest with difficulty, because he knows that he will find bizarre plants and curiously-formed animals there.

I once knew a lady whose said to me that she read twenty pages of the *Enneads* of Plotinus every evening, in order to stay awake! "It's so interesting!" she added. Fortunate lady! I have just arranged the three volumes of the *Enneads* in the section of books not yet read. They are three thick volumes. Their turn will come. But when I consider them, I admire the richness of the human mind that has enabled certain great geniuses, only accessible to an elite, to fashion human minds merely by the radiation of their work, built on the high summits of thought, like a splendid château, the towers of which men admire without daring to attempt to reach them.

May books be glorified! They are good, familiar and consoling. And yet, what secret hatreds they inspire in the ignorant, who are content with their ignorance, or in those that do not have the courage to penetrate into them! I wonder whether certain stains and rips might not have been made by the wicked, who experience the need to insult intelligence.

The presence of books is admirable! It gives security to a person who is anxious, calm to one who is agitated, and transports to the heights one who wants to rise up. Books border the road of wisdom, they are the instruments of perfection.

THE ADVICE OF A PROTECTIVE SPIRIT

The literate Romans of old attached a great importance to a phrase in a book opened at random and the page on which the finger posed on closing the eyes. It was necessary, at the same time, to invoke a protective spirit, if you knew one. It was a means of permitting destiny to give you a slight indication of its intentions. And even if one admits that destiny does not have direct and conscious communication with particular individuals, I am personally rather tempted to believe that a protective spirit can, in certain cases, make use of that means to give you a warning or a piece of advice. I can even say that I'm convinced of it.

Protective spirits can only have very slight effects on our lives, but their influence is exerted on impulses and they are quite capable or impelling us to choose one book rather than another and stopping our finger on a page. It is also necessary that we favor their effort by pausing the movement of our thoughts, and that we have summoned them beforehand by persistently requesting their aid.

I had never made any appeal to any power. I was impelled most of all by a liking for handling a book, for touching it. I picked up the first that came to hand, opened it and designated a sentence.

I read: *Insensate is the man who, favored by the human condition, a state so difficult to obtain, does not profit therefrom to find God.*

Surely that was a warning given by some wise protector. That wise protector had first wanted to qualify me. I was an insensate. I was not profiting from the human condition. I was not doing anything to find God. It was not sufficient to rent a house in the midst of trees and to arrange books of philosophy in accordance with different methods. To be sure, that was a sign of good intentions, but no more. Was it seeking God to go for walks with an extravagant young woman? Was it not, on the contrary, distancing myself therefrom? Was it not jealousy that I had experienced on seeing Roseline come out of a little house with newly-painted windows that did not resemble a farm? Was temptation not within me?

The sage protector was right. I was an insensate.

And one phrase, in particular, was terrible. The human condition is difficult to obtain. One does not become human at will. Thus, in the afterlife, one experiences unknown difficulties in placing oneself in a human seed and appearing in the terrestrial sunlight in the form of a child. That was unimaginable. No one could have experience of it. And yet that author, an Oriental philosopher, affirmed it with certainty. He was supported by ancient traditions, and there was something in me that impelled me to believe his affirmations. I had received a favor in penetrating into this human form, in benefiting from its complex organs. I ought to profit from that favor in order to find God.

Like all men, I had only thought about enjoying life, in extracting the maximum possible pleasure from my senses. That was an error. The sage knew it. He knew, without saying how he had learned it, that the human form is only obtained rarely, after a great deal of effort, and that it is necessary to hasten to take advantage of it because afterwards, millions of years might go by without one being able to recommence. It was necessary to make haste, and I was not making haste. I was looking at books, I was enjoying the beauty of light, and that of faces, but I was neglecting the goal that I had set myself, of becoming better, more intelligent, and more perfect, getting closer to God.

I went out into the garden and I set about circling the old pine several times. Perhaps one ought to circle a tree if one wants to receive a piece of advice. The tree interprets that fashion of circling around it as a question, and it replies, if it is amicable.

My thoughts immediately took another direction. The first thing to do was to understand. There was something to understand. I was enveloped by a particular atmosphere. Why did an old crow come to my garden? Why had I been able to understand the language of animals? Why had that Guillard, a bad man, emitted after his death a perfume of roses, when that seems to be a privilege exclusively reserved to saints? Things around me were going against what is normal. Was I not at risk of experiencing in my own being an analogous reversal?

Was it the response of the pine? A name presented itself to my mind: Monsieur Spéluque, the great scholar of Fréjus. I would go to see that great scholar, and perhaps he would enlighten me.

MONSIEUR SPÉLUQUE

It is very agreeable to hear a man tell you that he knows nothing, especially if he is a great scholar, which causes you to suppose that he is very learned.

"I don't know anything." Such were Monsieur Spéluque's first words. But I was not sure that he was a great scholar, and perhaps he was expressing the simple truth.

I had deliberated over the matter of how to present myself to him. Ought I to have a humble and modest attitude? Should I introduce myself as a writer from Paris, or as an erudite person? No, my habitual method was the right one. One always has something to learn from someone, even someone ignorant. It is always necessary to present oneself as a student avid for instruction, as a naïve pupil prompt to admire.

Monsieur Spéluque's house was one of the last in Fréjus, on the road to Cannes, and he had doubtless chosen it because of a fragment of a Roman aqueduct that served his garden as a boundary wall. I noticed a little metal plaque on the entrance door, on which a rather rudimentary bas-relief represented a god, Pan, playing the flute.

Monsieur Spéluque opened the door himself. He was not wearing spectacles, or a frock-coat. He had arched eyebrows after the fashion of Mephistopheles, and his cranium was completely bald. He was poorly shaven, but he had shaved. He was reminiscent of an ancient faun who had become, in aging, a primitive Greek sage. He warranted that title, moreover, for, from the very outset, he said things like: *I have a pagan soul, I ought to have been born in Athens*, and *I am a contemporary of Socrates*.

I saw that he had a great many books and I mentioned mine by way of a recommendation, but he seemed to wave them away with his hand. He looked at me curiously. On point seemed to interest him. Why had I come to install myself some distance from Fréjus?

I dared not tell him that it was only at the insistence of a letting agent. I replied that friends had praised the area to me.

"Really?" he said. "I would have thought that perhaps you had come for the same reason as me."

Monsieur de Lusignan had said something similar to me. I was still wondering what that reason might be, but he deflected the direction of the conversation.

"Yes, I know the lives of the saints who have come to this region. Many saints have come here—come expressly, you understand, or attracted by an interior necessity. Evidently, they came for the same reason as us."

There must have been a visible stupidity on my face because, having scrutinized me with his gaze, he shrugged his shoulders, like someone who has made a mistake.

"Saint Eleutherius, yes…a curious individual. Was he a veritable saint? That seems dubious to me. In these distant times, people were prompt to attribute the title of saint to people who had only accomplished acts external to sanctity. Was he a veritable saint? I'll tell you his story. You can judge for yourself."

Monsieur Spéluque made me a sign to follow him into his garden. A eucalyptus provided shade there. He designated a wicker armchair to me. He sat down on a block of ruddy stone.

"This seat is a trifle hard, but these stones are a vestige of the ancient aqueduct built by the Romans to aliment Fréjus. I thus have an imperfect contact, but a contact, with the men of old who possessed strength and wisdom in equal doses, and the remoteness of whose times I regret."

"Eleutherius was a monk at the abbey of Lérins.

"You know how honorable that abbey, founded by Saint Honoratus, was. In any case, when one thinks about it, the cause of everything that followed, the cause of our presence here—mine, at any rate—was the foundation of the Abbey of Lérins by Saint Honoratus.[9] The manner in which events are connected, reproducing the episodes of the same eternal struggle between good and evil, is a great and marvelous mystery.

"Before Eleutherius it's necessary to talk about Saint Honoratus and snakes. Snakes had pullulated on the two isles of Lérins. They were the masters there when Saint Honoratus chose one of the islands as a place of retreat. He had previously lived in a grotto situated on the side of Cap Roux, not far from the place where you live. But the renown of his sanctity was so great that all

---

[9] The largest of the Lérins islands off the coast of the Riviera near Cannes is the Île Saint-Honoratus, so-called because of the abbey founded in the year 410 or thereabouts by Saint Honoratus [Honorat in French.] An old fortified abbey still stands, but the present day monastic community inhabits a much more palatial complex of buildings nearby. According to the contemporary writer Sulpicius Severus, the island was swarming with snakes until Honoratus arrived, but they were expelled. The patron saint of Ireland, Saint Patrick, who probably arrived there from Lérins Abbey, was credited with a similar success.

sorts of ascetics came to install themselves around him. In order to recover solitude he went to Lérins, the abode of snakes.

"He exterminated all the reptiles on the island with his crosier, engaging in a struggle that is not yet concluded. He was victorious, temporarily, and when the island was purged of snakes and Saint Honoratus was able to devote himself to prayer, uniquely lulled by the sound of the waves, all the ascetics and all the monks that had followed in his tracks threw themselves into boats and settled on the island, which was soon resounding with hymns and actions of grace.

"Then Saint Honoratus resigned himself. 'Perhaps one can attain God while only being a good organizer of a monastery,' he said to himself. And he founded the abbey, toward which all the literate monks of his epoch flooded. For there is in those islands a source of spiritual radiation. The abbey became its receptacle, and in a natural fashion, the most precious manuscripts of the epoch flowed there and formed, in the course of the centuries that followed, an incomparable library. Lighthouses were placed on the shores to guide ships, but that library was a beacon that illuminated a vast region of the earth.

"Here commences the story of Eleutherius, about five centuries after the death of Honoratus.[10]

---

[10] The chronology of the story is confused; the massacre of monks described in next chapter occurred in 732, not "five centuries after the death of Honoratus"—but neither can the latter date be fitted with the era attributed to the career of Melusine in an earlier chapter.

THE STORY OF ELEUTHERIUS

"Eleutherius, as I told you, was a simple monk of Lérins, of ordinary origin. He left for the crusade with the Seigneur d'Antibes, and it was on his return that he decided to devote himself to God. He doubtless went to Lérins rather than elsewhere because of the library. Eleutherius was literate.

"The abbey of Lérins then had as its abbot a saintly man named Porcarius.[11] That saintly man was a visionary. He saw numerous and clear images of the past and the future. However, those of the future were less numerous and less clear. Thus, in those distant times, the ascetic life led by certain men gave them revelations and gifts of prophecy that are rare n our day.

"Now Abbot Porcarius was informed by a particularly precise vision that on the tenth day after the vision the pagan Saracens would disembark on Lérins, pillage the abbey, burn the library and exterminate the monks and the saintly abbot. Thus warned, Porcarius could have fled, or asked for help from the Seigneur d'Antibes. That appears logical to our modern intelligence, but he did not judge the matter thus, doubtless because of the character of his vision. He was not warned of a misfortune in order to avoid it, but he saw what the future had to be in accordance with the order of destiny.

---

[11] Abbot Porcarius eventually became Saint Porcarius. The story of his premonitory vision is part of his legend, but other versions of the legend suggest that he sent a considerably larger number of monks to safety as a result.

"God, for hidden reasons, wanted all the monks of the abbey to be exterminated and the library to be burned. It was necessary to submit to it. That submission had to be the only solution to adopt for whoever was not a rebel, for Porcarius assembled the monks, who numbered five hundred—five hundred and five, says the monastic historian in his rigorous exactitude—and he made them party to his vision without attenuating its horrible character, and they were all of the same opinion as him. They were all determined to obey God and await death—all except one. And that unique exception was Eleutherius.

"Eleutherius declared himself a partisan of collective flight, but he was not heeded. A few adolescents and overly handsome young monks, who might have been spared and sent to Africa to suffer treatments more terrible than death, of which it is better not to think, were sent away. A few precious relics were confided to them, which must not be allowed to fall into the hands of infidels, and they waited.

"Eleutherius did not leave. He was a weak soul. He dared not brave the reprobation of the five hundred and five monks avid for martyrdom. Who knows? Perhaps he had doubts about the reality of the vision.

"Nine days went by. On the morning of the ninth day, an angel appeared to Porcarius and warned him that one a few hours separated him from death."

At this point, I could not retain a cry of admiration, and I interrupted Monsieur Spéluque's story.

"How close the relationship was between that abbot and the invisible world!"

"It's true," said Monsieur Spéluque, in a melancholy fashion. "Certain barriers that separate us from the world beyond did not exist in those fortunate times. It was a little later that human materialism attained its maximum. And it still at its maximum! Perhaps it is even aggravating."

But he set aside that redoubtable thought and went on: "That evening, at sunset, the monk charged with watching the sea blew the trumpet. He had perceived sails of Saracen form on the horizon.

"Then Eleutherius could not hold back. He drew with him a certain Columbus, who admired him—for he must have had visible qualities of seduction—and by favor of the night he quit the monastery.

"The two monks went to hide in a grotto in the cliff, which was partly invaded by water at high tide. There, Eleutherius confessed to his companion the secret reason, of which he was scarcely conscious himself, for which he was so attached to life. In the Orient, he had seen a woman of such striking beauty that he could not reconcile himself to dying without having seen her again. It was a platonic amour, which did not entail any desire for possession, since he had renounced the world on entering Lérins, but he retained the hope of rediscovering the sweet exaltation that he had known once.

"Everything happened in conformity with the vision that Abbot Porcarius had had. The Saracens disembarked in large numbers, invaded the island, and entered the abbey easily, for they were led by a Christian traitor, Grimaldi, a perverse younger son of the great family of the kings of Monaco. All the monks, Porcarius the first of them, were put to death. Many were tortured in an atrocious manner whose usage has fortunately been lost. That was with the objective of making them confess the location of the abbey's treasure. The ingenuous monks indicated the library, and the tortures were redoubled. The Saracens burned the ancient manuscripts of Lérins, without knowing that they were burning the treasure for which they were searching so avidly.

"In their grotto, Eleutherius and Columbus could only see a portion of blue sky. They knew what was happening, however, for in that portion of sky they saw the souls of five hundred and five monks passing, abruptly extracted from their bodies—which leads us to suppose that both of them, in spite of their attachment to life, had acquired, either by personal effort or by means of the practices of meditation in usage at the time, a great clairvoyance of the spiritual world. Fortunate times, when visionaries were so widespread!

"In the evening, Eleutherius and Columbus slipped into the rocks. The church, the monastery and its dependencies illuminated the island and the sea as they burned. They saw the last Saracens embark, and recognized with horror the traitor Grimaldi, carrying a solid gold cross on his shoulder.

"A great despair took possession of the souls of the two monks, and also the regret of not having been part of the joyful troop of their companions, gaining all together the mysterious regions beyond death. For both of them, they subsequently reported, had remarked, in spite of the distance, an expression of intense delight on the faces of the airborne souls that were drawing away. Perhaps the profane memory of the woman glimpsed in the Orient gave Eleutherius the courage to jump into a forgotten boat and confide himself, with Columbus, to the sea.

"For reasons of a divine order, a tempest blew up and agitated the sea furiously for many days. Eleutherius and Columbus awaited death lying in the boat, but the waves died down one morning and a dazzling sun appeared. The two monks raised their heads and saw that the currents had deposited their boat on a luminous shore dominated by a city with beautiful houses. In the weakness caused by hunger and thirst, they thought that they had died without perceiving it and that it was a matter of some celestial city, where they were going to find Porcarius as well as other familiar saints.

"But Columbus, a son of fisher folk, recognized Fréjus, his natal city, its beach and its harbor, where he had met his father's boat, laden with fish, every evening in his childhood. Then the bells rang and there was a quality in the sounds emitted by the bronze that could not be forgotten.

"The story of the destruction of the abbey of Lérins had flown from mouth to mouth and all Christian hearts had been rent by it. The inhabitants of Fréjus gave a triumphal welcome to the last survivors of the martyrs of Lérins.

"Now, the Bishop of Fréjus had recently died. In those ancient times bishops were still appointed by meetings of pious notables and eminent ecclesiastics. The seat of Fréjus was vacant and risked remaining so, the notables and the ecclesiastics not being able to reach agreement in the course of meetings, the last of which had been scandalous because of the violence of the candidates.

"Eleutherius had charmed all the inhabitants of Fréjus by his noble attitude, his eloquence and the story of his supraterrestrial vision of the passage of souls from one world to the other. When someone proposed proclaiming him Bishop of Fréjus, the agreement was immediate. Even the monks of the monastery of Roquebrune accepted it. They formed a little community of pure and ascetic men, which was hostile to the ostentation of the century and the relaxation of mores. They had promised to come armed on the day of the meeting in order to prevent the election of the rich Abbot of Montrieux, who was rumored to have bought votes. 'The sea has deposited a saint on the shore in order that he should be Bishop,' was the popular word that ran from Marseille to Nice.

"The bishop's palace was a magnificent Roman dwelling that overlooked the sea. There were large cool rooms, painted mosaics, and an open gallery overlooking the harbor, each marble column of which was made of the statue of a saint. Images of the ancient gods had been replaced by pious individuals. Artistic bishops had always demanded works of great beauty. Now, those works were rare. A few pagan figures remained here and there, even including an Aphrodite with two doves on her shoulder and a hibiscus branch in her hand.

"The first day when Eleutherius gazed at the sea from the gallery of the bishop's palace, he saw a large ship in the distance with strange flags, which was heading for the harbor. The Comte de Provence had sent an ambassador to Fréjus and many seigneurs had come with great pomp. They had been alerted to the arrival of the King of Cyprus, the Seigneur de Lusignan, who had just shown his château in Poitou to his wife Melusine.

"Eleutherius, wearing his Episcopal miter for the first time, went to bless the sovereign on his arrival. In the wife of the King of Cyprus he recognized the woman whose beauty had transported him with enthusiasm somewhere in the Orient, among men with a bronze tint and sabers curved like lunar crescents.

"He went back to the bishop's palace prey to a great disturbance and reverted to an earlier self. He realized that he was possessed by pride. He, the simple monk of Lérins, had become a powerful bishop. Immense wealth was at his disposal. He consorted with kings. Who could tell? Perhaps the Aphrodite with the hibiscus branch was awakening dormant passions within him.

"He took off his Episcopal garments. He put on his old monk's habit and he only kept the crosier, from which he removed the gilt and the precious stones, and which became a simple staff again. He waited for the night to be profound and for Fréjus to fall asleep. Then he left the palace, slipped into the rocks along the shore, for the city gates were closed, and he reached open country.

ELEUTHERIUS AND THE CROW

"Eleutherius walked all night through the dense forests of ash trees that extended along the coast. He reached the rocks of Cap Roux. He climbed the steep slopes and, when the sun appeared, he fell exhausted, in Baume, the same place where Saint Honoratus had once lived, which was still quite similar to what it was when saints came to seek shelter there.

"He lived there in prayer and mortification, drinking from a spring that ran between the stones, only quitting the shelter of the grotto to go in search of the wild fruits necessary to his nourishment. Assuredly, he must have been content with very little.

"One day, when he had just woken up with the rising sun, he heard pious hymns in the distance. He leaned over from the height of a ridge and saw, here and there, the tonsured heads of monks in brown robes; one of them was lighting a little fire, another planting a cross. They had picked up his trail.

"His flight had increased his reputation for sanctity. All the monks who had a taste for the eremitic life, and thought of elevating themselves in the hierarchy of beings by mortifying themselves, had come to install themselves near him, a little lower down on the slopes of Cap Roux, in order to mark, by a spatial distance, the distance that separated them from such a great saint.

"Note this well. The same thing had happened to Saint Honorat in the same place, a few centuries earlier. Events have a tendency to be reproduced in a near-identical fashion, if they have been thought forcefully by those who have produced them. That law explains many things.

"Eleutherius judged himself severely. He did not sense any sanctity in his soul tormented by passions. He was not worthy of the respect of those well-intentioned ascetics. He waited for night. He descended silently among the sleeping hermits and plunged into the thickest part of the forest.

"He lived for years without anyone knowing the place of his retreat. Legend fixes him, perhaps arbitrarily, in the vicinity of the place where you tell me that you have rented a small house. The same legend reports that he lived in a commerce so narrow with the wild animals of the forest that he ended up understanding their language and even talking to them. He responded to the howling of wolves and the hooting of owls, and he cawed with the crows.

"He acquired a strange power over animals. A peasant's donkey made a long journey to find him. Flocks of birds perched in the trees surrounding his hut and took up residence there. At night, if he woke up, he saw the gleam of amicable eyes in all directions, mingled with innumerable glow-worms. His power extended over insects. But it was the attachment of a crow that remained popular in the stories that speak of him, and which have been transmitted through the centuries. That crow loved him to the point that he always had it on his shoulder, and spoke to it as to a confidant.

"Those birds can be placed n the first rank of animal creatures from the viewpoint of intelligence and even wisdom. You know that Dupont de Nemours, who studied them for several years, has composed a dictionary—not very thick, however—of the words they employ.[12] The amity of a crow must be inestimable for a hermit.

"Eleutherius grew old in the forest. When he had attained an advanced age, he became convinced that his human mission was to rebuild the ruins of the abbey of Lérins. He departed one day with his familiar crow. He went to Saint Honorat's island, where snakes had begun to pullulate again. He exterminated them with his crosier, aided by the crow, which threw itself upon the smaller ones. For a native hatred has always existed between the species of crows and that of snakes.

The news of that return spread rapidly. Monks came running from all directions. A monastery was built, as well as a fortress, to defend it against the incursions of pirates.

"Eleutherius, heaped with honors and burdened by years, regretted his solitude. In spite of the universal affirmation that he was a great saint, he often wept for himself, claiming that he was the dwelling of a great sinner. It was in the secrecy of his soul that the battle was delivered between purity and impurity, and no one can know anything about it. He departed, with his crow on his shoulder, for the hut in the forest where his animal friends were. While walking, he held the crook of his crosier inwards, to symbolize the fact that his spiritual effort would henceforth be directed inside himself."

Monsieur Spéluque paused. Then, as he saw that I was still attentive, he resumed:

---

[12] The naturalist Pierre Samuel du Pont de Nemours (1739-1817) included a supposed dictionary of the language of crows in his *Quelques memoires sur différens sujets, la plupart d'histoire naturelle* (1807).

"That's all. His legend says no more. No one knows whether he or the crow died first. No relic of Saint Eleutherius remains anywhere."

The afternoon was reaching its end, and it was time for me to withdraw. I got up.

"It's one of those stories of saints, of which there are so many," said Monsieur Spéluque, by way of conclusion.

"Let's suppose," I replied, while we were walking through the garden, "that the legend reposes on a basis of truth. Let's suppose that Eleutherius lived with a crow and that he died before that crow. How long might the crow have lived, after the death of its master?"

Monsieur Spéluque looked at me, surprised by the unexpectedness of my question.

"Perhaps for a very long time. I believe that crows form an exception in nature and can attain an extraordinary longevity. But no one is sure of that. People go to a great deal of trouble to make complicated machines in order to destroy one another, but have not yet studied the simplest things of nature."

"Might Eleutherius' crow have been able to survive until our own day?"

"My God, anything's possible."

We were on the road and I had just shaken Monsieur Spéluque's hand. As I was about to draw away, an idea occurred to me and, at hazard, I said: "Well, I can admit it to you. I'm here for the same reason as you."

Monsieur Spéluque's face brightened. "That doesn't surprise me. I can even say that I was sure of it. I saw that at the first glance. Come back and see me, and we'll try to clarify the mystery."

THE MESSAGE OF THE AMARYLLIS

So there was a mystery—but what? I asked myself that question the following morning as I was pacing back and forth, on a small scale, in the microscopic garden that surrounded my house.

I had examined all the plants that grew in that fragment of ground, rejoicing in the proximity and the amicable influence of a certain number of tress grouped respectfully around the central pine. I had noted the ones that were the receptacle of a vegetal personality and were susceptible of conversing, when there was no wind, with the religious soul of the old pine. For trees only have exchanges in immobility and silence, and they fall silent, by contrast, and only exhale vulgar plaints when their branches are agitated and we think we hear them speaking.

There were young innocents that were not yet animated by the descent of any soul, which were only thinking about games, which are for them the passages of birds from one branch to another. On one side of the wooden fence there was an egotistical acacia, and on the other a cork-oak radiant with bounty and the pleasure of giving. They were facing one another, affirming the diversity of arboreal natures. A rosemary hedge, with the mysterious depth of its meditation on the beyond, almost separated the garden into two. There were two or three bizarre yuccas, an aloe avid for a quarrel, and a white laurel that launched its joy of life in all directions.

Nothing had escaped me in that narrow parcel of land, over which I exercised a sort of right of possession, and from which I received, by way of imperceptible breaths, delicate little blessings, such as only vegetables are able to give you, by means of their imponderable sympathy. And I had noticed a narrow strip that was completely sterile.

That marred a corner of the garden slightly. Why had the soil produced nothing in that place? Perhaps it had been forgotten in a distant time when someone interested in the garden had raked and planted. Perhaps the cause was in the quality of the soil, for weeds seemed to be making a painful effort to grow there.

Now, in going past the disinherited strip, I saw that there was a large amaryllis flower in the middle.

I considered it with admiration. An amaryllis is formed by several marvelously roseate lilies arranged in a circular spray at the end of a woody stem. Books say that the amaryllis comes from Mexico, which is important to know, Mexico being full of maleficent plants. That amaryllis had seven calices, very regularly blossoming, and the woody stem sustaining it, doubtless owing its thickness to its Mexican nature, was straight and came up to my knee.

"Mathieu Lapeyre!" I shouted.

By raising my voice, I could be heard by Mathieu Lapeyre, whose house, hidden by shrubbery, was not far away. In the morning, he devoted himself to small domestic tasks outside his door.

I had no doubt that Mathieu Lapeyre, by way of a joke, had stuck the amaryllis stem in the sterile strip.

He appeared almost immediately at the fence and I asked him the provenance of such a beautiful amaryllis. At the same time I tugged the stem, which I supposed to be simply embedded. But it resisted strongly. I pulled harder and understood that in order to oppose that resistance it must have profound roots, ramified in radicals, with the complication and tenacity that plants employ in order to hold firmly to the ground and aspire water and juices.

But how had those roots and radicals been able to plunge down so rapidly? Mathieu Lapeyre's face reflected a slightly stupid astonishment that left no doubt as to its sincerity, for sincerity is always accompanied by a slight expression of stupidity. He had not paid any attention to that strip. So? The amaryllis must have spring forth there like the plants that fakirs cause to emerge from the earth by extending their hand. But I had not seen any fakir coming into the garden.

There was something mysterious in that conjuring trick of a terrestrial order, that sleight-of-hand of nature. And a thought immediately occurred to me. Was that not an indication, an advertisement of some superior power? But what was the mechanism of the prodigy? Nothing comes of nothing, and a superior power requires elements in order to produce a prodigy. An amaryllis bulb must repose beneath that slightly sandy strip. That bulb was doubtless destined to die miserably like so many other seeds. The marvelous element had intervened by giving it an extraordinarily rapid growth. The amaryllis had grown in one night—for nature has a certain margin to permit potencies that are unknown to us to accomplish extraordinary things without violating her laws entirely.

In a single night! So, if I had come down into the garden at midnight with a lamp and I had sat down beside the strip, I would have been able to see the movements of the flower, see with my eyes the most secret mystery of the earth, the hatching of a flower! No gardener-poet has been able to flatter himself with having perceived that. No one has heard the delicate sound of subtle silk tearing that the narrow bud of a flower makes in blooming. Perhaps the crickets are charged with singing in order that the rustle of divine fabric in question goes unperceived. There is a modesty of nature with regard to humans.

But what had the power that had manifested itself in the amaryllis wanted to tell me? Would it not have been simpler to express itself in direct speech? Perhaps human language was difficult to materialize for a power that does not have human organs, while it could dispose of a creative breath permitting it to give life to an amaryllis seed.

Monsieur de Lusignan had told me that butterflies and moths were utilized for divine messages because of the matter of which they are made. Flowers were also made of divine mater, without analogy with anything that there is in the world. By virtue of its complexity, that amaryllis must have an extended meaning. What was the message of the amaryllis?

I consulted the language of flowers, which informed me that the amaryllis signified pride. I interrogated simple souls. A vegetable-seller going from house to house, announcing her coming by a cry similar to that of a mariner in distress, replied to me in a surly tone that the amaryllis always announced a misfortune in the house. The vegetable-seller was a taciturn individual of ill augury.

My optimistic housekeeper winked in a malign fashion to tell me that a marriage was in prospect.

My God, who to believe? How to discover the secrets of divine symbolism? And perhaps there was an urgent reply for me to give! How difficult relationships with the invisible powers are!

THE GREEK AMPHORAE

Humans are subject to aberrations and they are even deceived sometimes by false visions. Had I not imagined, for example, that I had seen the silhouette of an elegant young man on the threshold of that little house where Roseline was supposed to be conferring with farmers?

Well, that was an aberration, a play of my imagination. Imagination has always played tricks on me. And I have the certainty of that error. With a great deal of skill, when I saw Roseline again, I steered the conversation toward those farmers of La Mothe, the custodians of butter and fresh eggs. Roseline has furnished me with various very precise details regarding the family in question. There are several children, a son who is doing his military service and two daughters, one of whom is very intelligent and the other slightly innocent. Such are the eccentricities of heredity. Thus, in the Lusignan family, there are two sisters, one of whom is beautiful—that was the elder—and the other ugly, who is her, Roseline.

Naturally, I protest. Roseline laughs and agrees that, strictly speaking, one could accord her the beauty of the devil. Of the devil, that's right. And there are all sorts of differences between the two sisters. There is even an incredible opposition. Her older sister never goes out, whereas she is on the move all the time, obliged to go here or there. One reads and the other does not. One wants the doors to be closed and the other wants them open. One likes red and the other blue. One only likes young men and the other has a predilection for men of a certain age.

I ask negligently which of the two has that rather rare predilection.

It is her, Roseline. Firstly, that predilection is not rare. Secondly, young men have no conversation, they are conceited and know nothing. She cannot remain five minutes with a young man because she gets bored immediately. They can only talk about cars or aviation. To get back to the farmers of La Mothe...

For Roseline returns to the farmers without the slightest hesitation, which she would not do if she has not gone to visit them the other day or if they did not exist.

Internally, I reproach myself sharply for having a suspicious soul. No, Roseline does not lie; she never lies. She is one of those women of whom one can say that they wear their heart on their sleeve. She has certainly told me, once or twice, that she has the faculty of changing into a snake on certain days, albeit not very often, but that must be considered as a fantasy rather than a lie. And then, does one ever know?

We say such things while we go on foot, along minor roads, to the beach of Agay. That excursion has been decided by Roseline.

"You'll make yourself ill by force of reading. And then, there's something very curious to see. You know that Agay was once a great Roman port. Now, one stormy night, a galley was shipwrecked opposite the port on the sandbanks outside the bay. The galley—no one knows how many oarsmen it had—was transporting a cargo of beautiful painted earthenware amphorae full of Greek wine, which has two images on their sides. On one side was the god Dionysus, who changes the grapes of the vine into wine by means of the sunlight, and on the other the goddess Athene, who changes the wine of grapes into joyful spirit by means of the art of transmutations. If one goes over the sea in a boat one can glimpse the galley in the depths, with its benches, its oars and is broken masts.

I ask Roseline whether she has seen the galley herself.

"Of course, and everyone can see it if they go out to sea when the water is calm, and everyone, with a little luck, can buy a amphora with the images of the gods from a fisherman, because from time to time the capricious sea extracts one from the sand and rolls it as far as the shore. My father bought one, and observed that I resemble in an extraordinary fashion the goddess Athene sculpted on one side of the amphora. Yesterday there was a very violent tempest. It's certain that the tempest has thrown up a few amphorae, or fragments of amphorae, along the beach at Agay, which we're going to pick up.

And we hasten our steps, for fear of being forestalled by some lover of amphorae.

It is the time when the mimosas and the while laurels are flourishing along the banks of the Armitelle. It is the time when the air is very pure and one can see from a long way off the contours of the branches of trees on the hills.

And when, at a bend in the road, we perceive the bay of Agay, all blue in the gold of the afternoon, Roseline, exultant with joy, points at the sky and the sea and says:

"You're going to follow the circular line of the sand, attentively examining the extreme edge beaten by minuscule waves. You see that family boarding-house. It's a very small boarding-house where my friend Blanche d'Elbée is staying, in order to do painting there.

I've mentioned her to you, I believe. Blanche d'Elbée is an artist who seeks solitude. She's a little neurasthenic, and any foreign presence, apart from mine, is intolerable to her. Apart from mine—and that's quite exact. I'll go and say bonjour to her for a few minutes. Oh, only a few minutes! She can't bear any more, poor Blanche! Keep a careful lookout for the amphorae! After two thousand years under the sea they no longer look like amphorae at all; they're completely coved in seaweed and it's necessary to look attentively in order to discover them."

And Roseline drew away with such a light step that one might have thought that she was going to fly all the way to the little family boarding-house.

No, no, it wasn't a matter of falling back into the baseness of certain suspicions, degrading for the person who experiences them. I applied myself with great conscientiousness to the search for sculpted amphorae under the robes of seaweed and wrack. But no face of Athene or Dionysus appeared among the seashells and parasitic arthropods. In made a circuit of the beach several times, in vain.

A duration of time that I refused to evaluate went by. Come on, neurasthenic as she was, Blanch d'Elbée was amusing herself conversing with a friend.

In the end I saw Roseline coming out of the boarding-house. Blanche d'Elbée was not accompanying her, but she was followed by a young man. I saw them coming toward me over the sand, exchanging joyful words. The joy seemed to be coming from Roseline in particular.

The young man, who was tall and strong with a square jaw, gave an impression of somber humor, for romantic causes. He was bare-headed, as befits a modern young man, who cannot wear a hat without dishonor, and he had a red silk handkerchief wrapped around his wrist. A large lock of black hair barred his forehead, and he sometimes swept it back with a rapid gesture. That movement allowed the sight of a gold bracelet on the wrist where no handkerchief was wrapped. He had thick red lips and a profile sufficiently regular for it to be called a Greek profile.

"My friend, the Comte de Grimaldi, of the Grimaldi family. You know..."

I did not know anything, but I shook the young man's hand.

Roseline had just encountered him be chance in Blanche d'Elbée's house. What a coincidence! He was an old friend. He had also done paining in Paris, and Roseline had known him on the Lemaître course. The Lemaître course! Those were good times, weren't they, Pierre?

Pierre nodded his head.

"All three of us are going back on foot," said Roseline, in a confidential tone. "The Comte de Grimaldi's auto is being repaired."

"Yes, exactly..."

"In fact, did you find any amphorae?" Roseline asked me, distractedly, as we left the beach.

It did not cause her any disappointment to learn that I had not found any. She had scarcely expected it.

While walking, I wondered where I had seen the Comte de Grimaldi before. I have a vague sensation of having seen not long before the contour of his shoulders and his equally square jaw.

He did not say much, except about one subject that seemed to be a dominant preoccupation for him. That subject was the antiquity of the Grimaldi family.

Roseline must know that, for, doubtless with the aim of making him shine, she said, à propos of nothing: "You know that the Grimaldi family is very ancient."

The young man smiled like someone about to launch forth in a plan mounted on a white horse.

"The most ancient of the Grimaldis," he said, "was a certain Grimoald, who was the mayor of the palace under King Childebert II. He was the ancestor of the kings of Monaco. But there is a tradition in our family that takes the Grimaldis back even further. We don't talk about it, because it's a matter of an exaggerated antiquity."

"Why not?" asked Roseline, whom extraordinary things did not astonish.

"The isles of Lérins were once called Lero, the name of a god, a legendary hero, who was a Hercules of the Ligurian race.[13] That Lero was the ancestor of the Grimaldis."

"Is there any historical basis to that genealogy?" I asked.

"A little," Pierre de Grimaldi replied. "There are no archival documents, but there are moral data, which, without being rigorous certainties, nevertheless have some value."

Then, as we were out to reach the large clump of flowering mimosas that formed the edge of the Armitelle, I remembered abruptly, by a curious whim of

---

[13] Lero, an obscure Celtic god, was invoked along with his female counterpart Lerina as the spirit of the isles of Lérins. The connection with the Grimaldi family, whose generally-recognized historical origin is much later than the reign of Childebert II (575-595), and also later than the date credited here to the life of Eleutherius, is entirely fictitious.

my memory, the place where I had seen the silhouette of Léro's descendant before. It was on the threshold of the little house with the newly-painted shutters where Roseline had stopped at La Mothe a few days earlier.

That memory struck me like a poisoned arrow, whose poison makes itself felt immediately.

But the memory excels in deceiving itself, I told myself, immediately. It transposes scenes, it makes fugitive creations. One cannot add serious faith to it.

And as Roseline had stopped to cut mimosa branches, I picked a few flowers myself that were growing between the stones. Grimaldi did the same, but negligently, without haste, and he only kept one flower. I noticed that it was an amaryllis.

THE NIGHT OF THE CROW

It was a moonlit spring night. I know not what distant bell had chimed a nocturnal one o'clock. I was leaning on my window sill and admiring the delicacy with which the designs of leaves were outlined against the transparent blue of the sky. I perceived the profound meditation of the old pine, and how deeply it felt the dolor of the world, that of things and that of living creatures. Certain aged trees, by virtue of an excess of sensibility, no longer know happiness. They have too great a power of identification with what surrounds them. They experience suffering, but cannot bring any remedy to it because of the chain of roots. They have to be content with participating in it with the continual prayer of their raised branches.

Alongside the pine, the cork-oak was following its own meditation. But its faculty of giving a part of itself permitted it to suffer that much less. For pity is worn away by work accomplished. A young birch was white with respect for the meditation of those great venerable brothers. And a little further away, on the other side of the fence, a cypress, without paying any heed to anyone, was launching an almost visible dark blue prayer, like a jet, straight into the bright azure sky.

I observed that the night was perfectly silent and that even the owls, in the distance, had fallen silent. But as soon as I had made that observation, the silence ceased abruptly. I heard the branches of the old pine palpitate, and then those of the cork-oak. A bird had passed from one tree to the other. But it did not have in flying the precaution, the affectation of silence, that birds have that fly in the middle of the night. That bird was flying somewhat at hazard, bumping into branches, going hither and yon, and it seemed to me that there was something disorderly in the manner of its flight. I leaned out to see and I encountered the ruddy gleam of an eye, and saw tousled plumage. It was the crow.

At the same time, I heard it utter several cries. I had never desired so much to understand their meaning; but the admirable gift was not in me that evening and the thought that I had of obtaining it must have rendered its coming impossible. Everything that comes from the gods is contradictory and fleeting. Nevertheless, I took account of the fact that there was an annunciation, that there was a solemn appeal therein, with which was mingled the idea of death and perhaps the heartbreak of an adieu.

The old crow with the tattered plumage flew to the right and the left in the trees of the garden, colliding with braches, as if its eyesight had deteriorated, and I saw it reach the rim of the well, pitifully, where it took two or three limping steps. There, it uttered a few more cries, but lower, leaning its beak and its plucked neck toward the ground, as if it wanted to give some information to the invisible world that inhabits the vegetation of the soil.

It seemed to me that I understood that information. The old crow was announcing that it was going to die. It had come to that place, where it had lived, and where there were certain bonds and certain amities, to say that it had flown through its last moonlit night. That is what I believed that I sensed confusedly. But one remains incredulous about one's intuitions.

However, there was something abnormal about the garden. Branches were stirring in the trees, and there were a few almost imperceptible chirps of birds, as if, in fact, there were an item of information being transmitted. An animal shifted in the clump of rosemary. I saw a turtle pass under the wooden fence.

The crow, with one last cry, took off and went past my window. No, it did not address itself to me. At least, I didn't think so. All of that was in my imagination. And yet a force impelled me. Who knows? I went downstairs precipitately, I arrived in the garden, I ran into the road, not without noticing that the little calls of the birds in the trees had redoubled and that, here and there, in the bushes, there was the rustle of small creatures in motion.

I looked in all directions and I saw that the crow had not gone very far. It was on a branch of a eucalyptus, at the intersection of two roads. Again it uttered a little sad cry and it flew away: a miserable, uncertain flight, zigzagging slightly, which permitted it to reach another tree, some distance away, but not far enough for me to be unable to distinguish its silhouette with ruffled plumage outlined in the moonlight.

Was the crow waiting for me? Did it want a human witness, and was what I was sensing internally true? Or was I only the victim of my imagination, and it was only pausing in one tree after another because of its fatigue and old age? I could not give myself a sure response, but curiosity drove me forward. I followed the crow, sometimes running in the fear of losing it, cursing the detours that I was obliged to make when I encountered one of those iron wire boundaries with which property-owners have the habit of marking their possessions. I jumped over hedges, went alongside pine woods, and whenever I thought I had lost the crow, its increasingly lamentable croaking resonated in my ears and told me the direction that I had to follow.

I cannot evaluate the time that the march lasted. It must have been longer than I thought while I was accomplishing it. For I was kept in suspense by the idea that I was going to witness one of those scenes to which humans are not usually invited and no not exist for them any more than if they had occurred on another plane of existence to which human reason does not have access.

As I went, my eyes fixed on the low branches of the trees, I wondered whether there was not something abnormal in the fields and the woods. I regretted not having a greater experience of the countryside at two o'clock in the morning. Was the sky always cut like that by the passage of birds? I thought that birds slept, like humans, until sunrise. And what were those movements in the bushes? I knew full well that there was an entire nocturnal life, that hedgehogs only sought their nourishment by night, and that it was only thanks to darkness that foxes slid into henhouses, but I was witness to an unusual activity.

I saw a donkey traversing a field at a deliberate pace. Donkeys do not wander around on their own in the middle of the night. A peacock that I knew well was running in the same direction as the donkey. Often, while out walking, I had stopped to watch it displaying its tail through the gate of the park of an English lady to whom it belonged. Why had that peacock escaped? Other animals that I could not make out were slipping through the wild laburnums, going through the larches that grew under the pines. And they were all heading in the same direction, as if they were being guided by the plaintive crow, whose silhouette could be seen lurching awkwardly in the moonlight.

Suddenly, I made out the shiny undulation of a stream. It was gliding among the paludal rushes, the color of mat silver, and, under the lunar rays, projected gleaming crystal spangles. It broadened and shrank in places, and I recognized, by the sandy banks that its course left behind, that I had reached the edge of the Argens.

The place toward which I was heading, and which the crow had reached, was a large circular meadow covered with peach trees in flower, which the Argens divided in two with the passage of its gleam. A large wood of old trees came down a hillside and bounded the meadow in the direction from which I arrived, while on the other side, small clumps of cypresses stood to attention impressively. It seemed to me that one of the groups framed a stone oratory in ruins, the niche of which was empty, surmounted by a little dome whose cross had disappeared.

A special enchantment resident in the color of the water, the lightness of the peach-blossom and the mystery of the full moon gave the entire landscape a supernatural atmosphere and created a beauty that made one think of the beauty that one ought to contemplate in the other world. I was profoundly penetrated by it, while assuring myself that I was not witnessing anything abnormal, that nature always had that same beauty, under the full moon and in the middle of the night. And I reproached myself for not having made a similar contemplation instead of sleeping heavily in my closed bedroom, preferring dense slumber and its liking for oblivion to the subtle and fluid intoxication that the ensemble of the moon, the night, water and trees provide, by virtue the combination of their relationships and exchanges.

But I rapidly took account of the fact that I had reached the theater of an unexpected and perhaps unique scene.

The sandy Argens, the meadow of peach-trees and the woods of pines and cork-oaks had been chosen for a mysterious animal assembly. Scarcely had I stopped, agape with emotion, when a great flock of birds coming from the north, settled in the trees, but in a silence so great that their wings seemed to be velvet. Another flock, almost triangular in form, striped the sky and came to settle further away, in the trees that bounded the meadow on the other side of the river. I recognized, by the shape of a belated bird, that they were swallows.

At the same time, I had the perception of an extraordinary, varied, moving and meditative life that surrounded me on all sides. I had a wooly sensation in my hand. A large long-haired dog had stopped alongside me. It had been running, and was holding back its panting. A little further away, the donkey that I had already seen was marching uncertainly, as if it were hesitating to advance. Sheep were trampling the grass behind me. It seemed to me that I saw the pointed muzzle, the oval eyes and the tawny fur of a fox. A family of wild pigs, which seemed to have come a long way, descended the wooded slope and stopped suddenly.

Meanwhile, the lunar blue of the sky was striped by the incessant passage of birds. They were coming from all directions. They were letting themselves fall like black rain on to the trees and the bushes. I noticed that they were avoiding the vast wood of pines and oaks that closed one side of the meadow, as if it were a reserved location. There, all the trees were already garnished with motionless birds, similar to one another. They were the crows, the younger brethren and descendants of the old ancestor. There must have been thousands of them. As I looked attentively at the foliage under the night sky, I saw the somber red gleam of their eyes, lighting up and dying away.

Sometimes, a bleat was heard, or a grunt, or the sketch of a cock-crow, abruptly interrupted. And that extraordinary presence extended to the society of the smallest animals. The leaps of frogs were outlined against the waters of the Argens like geometric figures. Swarms of dragonflies vibrated their wings in the reeds. A buzz indicated the passage of a cockchafer. Wild plants shifted at my feet, trodden by hedgehogs, and as I leaned over to see them, I distinguished large quantities of scarabs, like scattered precious stones, and a long file of processionary caterpillars. Glow-worms were keeping their lamps lit, rendered pale green by the moonlight, and some were flying, tracing luminous curves. A white cat slid silently to my side. Along the Argens, doubtless escaped from some park and carried by the current, two swans were advancing majestically. I did not notice the presence of any snake.

I do not know what fateful hour sounded: an hour that did not enter into the human conception of time. Voices suddenly woke all over the place and transmitted an announcement incomprehensible for me. But they were voices quieter than usual, sounds proffered with precaution, very low sounds, which seemed to contain a hint of respect. That began with a few croaks of crows, followed by a demi-bark of the dog, grunts, sighs and even the sketch of a donkey's bray, immediately stifled. A large owl, whose silhouette could be seen outlined at the top of a poplar, terminated it with its call, the sorrowful note of which seemed to summarize a song of adieu that had not been sung.

I wondered where the old crow was. A flutter of wings indicated its presence to me. It was in the stone niche of the ruined oratory, in a circle of cypresses, and I saw that the oratory occupied an almost central position in the extent of the mysterious gathering. There were a few seconds of absolute, total, overwhelming silence, only cut by the wing-beats of the bird in its niche. Then I had the sentiment of being enveloped by an immense animal pity, something greater than human pity, and the dolor of being separated from those one loves: a resigned, bleak, desperate pity unameliorated by any hope. I felt it floating around me in the silence and the pale moonlight.

The crow launched itself outside the stone niche. I thought that it was going to fall in the meadow, for it was flying with difficulty, bumping into the high branches of the peach trees, the light flowers of which took flight around it. It climbed again with that aureole of petals and, by means of a great effort, it succeeded in flying over the water of the river. It held itself motionless in the air for the duration of a second, such as humans are accustomed to measure it. Then it uttered one last croak, a cry that went much further than the desolation that any living organs can express by name: a cry containing, in itself alone, all the wretched life of beasts, since their formation at the origin of the world, with feathers, fur or scales; a cry in which there were thousands of millennia of effort on their part toward the unknown light of intelligence; a cry so heart-rending that it seemed to me that my breast was physically wrung by it—and that cry, which was prolonged in the silence, was abruptly stopped by the interruption of divine death. It alone knew in what measure the expression of dolor ought to be prolonged. The crow's wings seemed to be mineralized, and it fell like a bird of stone into the clear waters of the Argens.

No noise followed it. There was no plaint, by way of a funerary adieu for the departure of that ancestral animal. And the silence was so great that I dared not budge myself, and I held my breath for fear of troubling I know not what solemn meditation. I waited for a time that I cannot evaluate. And suddenly, like the signal of an angel announcing the passage from one world to the other, or a resurrection in light after centuries of tenebrous slumber, a nightingale made audible a song so clear that it was impossible not to think of a flaming sword agitating in the sky.

The mysterious ceremony was over.

Had I witnessed the death of a guide of the realm of beasts incarnate in one of the species in which the intellect is susceptible to the greatest development? Among the creatures subservient to humankind, were there privileged individuals corresponding to what saints are among us? I shall never know.

The silence was scarcely troubled. There were noises in the parted foliage. A hoof resonated on a stone nearby. A thousand little plunges told me that the river-dwelling frogs of the Argens were returning to their element, and I saw a thousand little bright splashes among the reeds. In the distance, the swans drew away. The owl took flight from its poplar.

I took the road of return.

I took a long time. I got lost. The moon was very low in the sky, and a slight blanching announcing the morning competed with its light.

Finally, I succeeded in recognizing the familiar aspect of a road, and a certain gnarled tree that I often passed on my walks. I nearly tripped over a small creature that was walking in the opposite direction to me. I recognized the turtle that had been domiciled in my garden. It was going as rapidly as it is possible for a turtle to go. I would have liked to tell it that it was too late. But how could I do that?

THE QUEEN OF CLUBS

Madame Tournadieu is a sympathetic person. Person is the exact term. There are people of whom one is obliged to say: *That is a person.* Madame Tournadieu is a person. In her presence, one immediately has the idea that sympathy, once observed, must be limited.

Why? Why is it necessary to limit one's sympathy? Is it not contrary to the law that a sage man ought to impose on himself? To cause to radiate from oneself an increasingly great sympathy for all beings, even all persons?

That poses a very important problem, which it is essential to resolve. Ought one to love more and more, in the measure of the possible, or, on the contrary, detach oneself and break the bonds of sympathy that life creates with the hazard of its encounters? The quotidian conduct of the sage man depends on the solution to that problem.

But with Madame Tornadieu, the problem is resolved. Limitation is necessary. She presses the hand with too much force and holds on to it a few seconds too long. She looks at you for too long and with eyes too moist, even though she is not prey to any emotion. She sometimes lets remarks drop like: "I have a reserved nature, but with a passionate temperament." And her oblique gaze gives the impression of adding: *Note that well: you're dealing with a passionate nature.*

Madame Tournadieu has a small house that is only separated from the road by a rather low stone balustrade. Because of that, she has every facility to call out to people passing by. She stations herself behind it, and an array of cards is laid out on a little iron table. She plays

patience, or tells her own fortune, without fear of impor-
tuning destiny or obliging it to contradict her. One never
sees a book on that table. She is part of the category of
people who do not read. That category includes an immense number of people. Perhaps she is even part of the
rather numerous subdivision of those who fear books
and simulate respect with regard to them in order to disguise the fear they inspire in them.

That afternoon, Madame Tournadieu called to me,
brandishing her pack of cards, as I was just hastening my
step in order to go past her house.

"Stop for a few minutes, and I'll tell your fortune,"
she shouted to me joyfully.

She appeared to me to be slightly fatter than usual.
The midday heat caused the reds that colored her cheeks
too abundantly to fuse.

"It's Friday," she added. "You're in luck—you'll
benefit from a day of inspiration."

And I had to sit down in front of the iron table.

"For there are good and bad days. It's truly an inspiration, like that of poets. Yes, it's a kind of muse that
visits you. Today, Friday, the muse has come."

Madame Tournadieu told me that, that very morning, at sunrise or thereabouts, she had told her own fortune. She was personified among the cards by Queen
Argine, the queen of clubs. She was that queen, without
a doubt. That, she sensed profoundly. She was Argine,
as surely was Roseline was the queen of diamonds, the
Rachel that the tradition of card-readers represented as
an evil woman. That didn't mean in an absolute fashion
that Roseline had an evil nature. Personally, Madame
Tournadieu didn't think so. Perhaps one could say that
she was slightly devoid of conscience. Yes, one could
say that, but completely evil was an exaggeration. So,

the cards had spoken. And certain things had been announced relative to the heart. My God! Yes, her own heart.

For she had an ardent heart, which hid treasures of affection—treasures unknown to everyone for a long time, since the death of poor Tornadieu. And the cards had announced to her that she would soon encounter a twin soul—yes, there was a union in prospect for her.

But it wasn't appropriate to talk about such things. It was so personal! It was necessary to keep silent about those personal announcements!

Madame Tournadieu possessed the great art of laughing at her own remarks. She interrupted herself to laugh, as if what she said was not serious. That laughter removed value from certain things that had too much and added it to others that did not have enough. Then too, that laughter permitted her to draw breath, for she was rather short of breath. At the same time, with a rapid gesture like that of a prestidigitator, she pulled up either a girdle or a corset, which had slipped while she was talking and inconvenienced her if it slipped down too far.

"Cut," she said to me.

Then she made me choose and align the cards. One always listens to what is said to you about your future, even if it presents itself under the aspect of the greatest banality.

"You'll make a journey. You'll receive a letter. One, two, three, four... Look, there's an evil woman in your array. I don't invent anything. One, two, three, four. You must mistrust her. The postman again."

Madame Tournadieu was prey to a prophetic muse. She uttered a sigh of relief, as if she were emerging from the anxiety in which she had just been enveloped. The evil woman was combated by another. I saw that her finger, the nail of which was painted bright pink, was posed on the queen of clubs.

She looked at me with shining eyes and resumed laughing. Her girdle had skipped down.

"And there's a union. That's definite. One, two, three, four. And it's even imminent. It's a fortunate union. The queen of clubs. Happiness is before you."

"Don't the cards always announce imminent unions?"

"Don't believe that. The cards don't always speak. Thus, for example... For myself, I draw the cards almost every day in order to know the petty events that are going to happen. And moreover, they always tell me. Well, for many years—many years, I say, long years—there has been no union in my cards. They announced solitude. And now, since this morning, Friday, at sunrise, everything has changed. Isn't that curious? The same thing is announced to us on the same day."

"Yes, there are coincidences..."

"Coincidences is the exactly the right word. There are things that are coincident. Beings encounter one another by coincidence."

I had risen to my feet, and I thanked Madame Tournadieu for having used the faculties of her inspiration on my behalf. Nevertheless, I couldn't help telling her that there was very little chance that the predictions of the cards would be realized.

"At my age, you see..."

Madame Tournadieu almost leapt up.

"But that's the beautiful age! The age of amour! What is the most beautiful month of the year? The month of August, the month of fire, the month when one burns..."

Saying those words, Madame Tournadieu actually seemed to catch fire. She burned on the stone of her terrace, under the spirals of the wisteria intersecting above her head, alongside a spurting laurel.

When I quit her, her thumb was placed on the queen of diamonds, the evil woman vanquished, whom she was crushing against the iron table.

ENCOUNTER WITH A MASTER

Now, with the reaction of hindsight, I have a sharp regret at not having called out to that passer-by with the noble visage...

There is a host of small actions that one would accomplish if one had an accurate sentiment of their importance. But one always thinks that one has time. One does not know that given circumstances will not present themselves again in the same fashion, and that there is a order of admirable things that only come to you once with their infinite possibilities, and which go away never to reappear.

The sadness of opportunities that are offered and never reproduced again! One is timid, one feels ill-disposed, one prefers to put it if until tomorrow. But tomorrow never comes. And because of that opportunity lost, there is a different organization of life, another enchainment of causes and effects, which lead you into gray regions instead of the light that you might have been able to attain.

One fine afternoon, I saw a man going by under the pines and I knew, without any doubt, that I ought to run toward him, extend my hand to him, and talk to him. But I knew it too late. The necessity of knowing that passer-by was at first just a confused sensation to which I refused to pay any attention. Is it customary to speak to someone that one does not know, that one passes on a road? One might be poorly received, or received with an offensive coldness. What tone should one give to the first words? A correct politeness is not engaging. Many people mistrust the amicable joviality, the false cheerfulness that permits talking to everyone. One tells oneself that it is better to adjourn to a subsequent encounter.

When the necessity of knowing that unknown man became clear to me with a certain force, he was already far away, too far for me to be able to run after him.

Only then did I see again the gaze that he had cast over me in passing: a clear, profound gaze, which saw a long way, and in which I had discerned sympathy at the same time as curiosity. But then, I said to myself, if there was curiosity and sympathy, why did he not speak to me himself?

From the top to the bottom of the scale, the law is the same and it is immutable. It is necessary to take the first step. It is incumbent on the man who wants to climb to make the effort to reach the next step on the ladder. The master does not come to you. It is necessary to go to him.

But there was nothing to make me think that the passer-by in question was a master. He was dressed like anyone else. There is no master costume, and, if there were, one could be certain that the man who put it on would really be what he is pretending to be by means of his costume. He was neither handsome nor ugly. A certain pallor attested to cerebral labor. The oval of the face and the crease of the lips were the sign of a nobility of character, a rectitude that cannot be deceptive. Perhaps the hair was a little longer than normal. But in the flash of the eyes and their movement, there was living intelligence in the pure state, unalloyed intelligence.

How many times I had thought about encountering a master! Fortunate are those who have one, and what a pity that religions cannot produce even a fictitious image of one, because of their limitations and their rules, to which the spirit cannot accommodate itself.

Every time that it has occurred to me to expose my desire to encounter a master to people of some education, I have always seen the same expression of disappointed surprise on their faces. The master was in front of me, but I was unable to distinguish him. My blindness prevented me from distinguishing the transcendent merit of my interlocutor. For everyone believes himself to be a master. It requires a great artistry of conduct in life, and no small quantity of wisdom, to remain a pupil, the only title that it is ever necessary to claim if one has any hope of elevation.

So, I did not accost the unknown man; I did not run after him; and when I asked various people the following day who a pedestrian might have been, dressed like anyone else, with slightly long hair and an intelligent gaze, I was indicated by turns the grocer of Bouloris, who had studied in Paris, the schoolteacher, and various individuals from the surrounding area who had no connection with the man I had encountered.

If I had not been the victim of my imagination, why had nature whispered to me the secret knowledge that the passer-by in question had things to teach me, would be a master for me—and why had she whispered hose things a few minutes too late? Are souls the playthings of an invisible director of souls who whispers useful or false intuitions at random? Must I cross the path of wisdom and let it draw away through the pines, as one crosses the path of amour in one's youth, under the appearance of a delightful woman who smiles and draws away? But life is full of delightful women who pass by. One thinks that one will never see them again, and one perceives a little later that they retrace their steps easily. How many times in life does one encounter a master?

THE GNOMIDE

Roseline says singular things and sometimes lets herself go, telling curious stories. She speaks then as if involuntarily. It seems that she is prey to a force that obliges her to recount.

That morning, she caused the bell suspended from the wooden gate of my garden to resound authoritatively.

"I've come," she told me, volubly, "to know what you think about caves. You know the caves of this region, don't you?"

I was caught somewhat on the hop. I asked her what caves she meant.

"You don't know the caves? But the region is full of caves! Everything is explained by the caves."

The caves! I asked her whether she meant, for example, the hole in which Gaspard de Besse had hidden a treasure, alongside the chapel of Saint Pilon.[14]

"It's not a matter of Gaspard de Besse!" exclaimed Roseline, scornfully. "I'm taking about the caves that descend into the depths of the earth, and of which one can only see the narrow opening. There are some in the gorges of Verdon, along the Artuby, and all over the place in the region of Comps. Have you read a book en-

---

[14] Gaspard Bouis, alias Gaspard de Besse (1757-1781) was a notorious Provençal brigand whose preference for robbing strangers won him much local support and legendary status. The rumor that he had buried some of his loot near Cuges-les-Pins attracted treasure hunters for many years.

titled *Unknown France*?[15] A certain Martel has described them and given such a sensation of mystery that when I read the book, when I was about fifteen, I swore to visit the caves and explore them one day. Time passed and I didn't think about it again. One has so many other things to do in life than occupy oneself with caves. But I've been obliged to occupy myself with them. I'll tell you everything. You'll see.

"It was last year, on the evening of Pentecost. Take note that something always happens on the evening of Pentecost. Why? I don't know, but if one is attentive one perceives that something happens. You've seen the window of my room that overlooks the park. It's at the height of a low first floor. Just opposite there's a flower bed of geraniums, bordered by a clump of mimosas and laurels, which is extremely thick in spring. Well, on the evening of Pentecost I was on the little balcony of my room at about ten o'clock. It was particularly warm and there was no moon. I heard my name pronounced in a low voice several times, but it was modulated as if it were sung, by someone with a slight accent. That accent stressed the first syllable, which made it *Rou* instead of Ro: 'Rouseline! Rouseline!'

"My surprise was extreme. I thought it was a joke on the part of my sister, although it wasn't her genre. Then I heard a noise in the clump of laurels. Someone parted its branches and I saw a human form. Human, certainly, but not entirely, for the form seemed to be crawling. It was against the ground and lifting its upper

---

[15] The speleologist Édouard-Alfred Martel published the two-volume *La France ignorée* in 1928-30, summarizing information published in many other works over the previous forty years.

body with its arms. But that upper body was strangely elongated and gave the impression of being nothing but a head. For several minutes I heard the modulation of my name: 'Rouseline, Rouseline...'

"That modulation was followed by a phrase, also sung: 'Come and find us in the subterranean waters...'

"Then it was replaced by another: 'We'll give you a crown of emeralds...'

"The accent was so curious, the form so abnormal that I had a sentiment of fear. I tried to see the face, but there was only the light of the stars and an oblique light coming from a window in the drawing room, the shutters of which weren't closed. I knew that my father and my sister were there, chatting, and for a moment I was tempted to call them. But it seemed to me that in doing so I'd be accomplishing a sort of treason and I remained still.

"Then I heard: 'With the blue and black lotuses that flower in the darkness...

"Then untiringly, the form resumed: 'Rouseline...'

"It was oppressive. There was a silence. The branches creaked and I heard a speech that was equivalent to an invitation to a rendezvous: 'Come to find us near the Duoi wood, near the Avellan wood where the river is born; the cave is deep; we'll wait for you there and we'll tell you to way to the lake...'

"I've been able to remember those words because they were repeated many times, in the same monotonous tone. There was a long slithering sound and everything fell silent. I didn't dare move. I closed my shutters and my window with great care. And yet, take note that in doing so I was struggling against myself. Yes, there was a force within me that incited me to go downstairs precipitately and respond to the appeal that had been made to me. There was even more. I experienced a sentiment of fraternity for that scarcely-human unknown.

"The next morning I went to examine the clump of laurels. Visible traces of footprints remained. The geraniums were crushed. But there were no human footprints. No one had placed human feet on the soil of the flower bed. One would rather have thought that a form had been dragged. But what form?

"Reflecting on the words I had heard, I told myself that the words had invited me to go somewhere with the promise of an emerald crown, woven with blue and black lotuses. I had never seen such lotuses and I thought that, since there had been mention of caves, it was a matter of lotuses flowering in subterranean regions, perhaps above the waters of the lake to which someone was going to show me the way.

"The rendezvous given to me was not so uncertain. There's an old gardener in our park who is always interesting, and when I was talking to him about flowers and plants, never failed to talk to me about the region of his birth, and the village of Comps. He had often mentioned the Avellan wood, where a little stream called the Bruyère has its source.

"I questioned him on the subject, which was dear to him. It's a matter of an area not far from here. Although the roads are poor, it only takes an hour by car to get there. And what an area! The aspect of the rocks is terrifying, the forest trees are twisted and grimacing and the streams flow through impenetrable gorges. One might think that the creator of landscapes had wanted to make a contrast by placing side by side an abode of mimosas, olive groves and roses and the evil access to a world of subterranean things."

"But haven't told me the nature, in your opinion, of the creature that came to call to you by name, under your window."

"I think it's a gnomide."

"A gnomide? In truth, I'd have the same opinion."

I knew that we were in the domain of fiction and I didn't think that Roseline was talking seriously. Nevertheless, she replied to me: "It's certain. Gnomes are small and ugly, but gnomides are beautiful, and moreover, unlike their husbands, they live on the water, on underground rivers and lakes. That one had emerged from one of the caves around Comps."

"Have you seen it again since?"

"In spite of the fear that I experienced, I couldn't resist going to the rendezvous. I took a car, which I left in Comps and it wasn't very difficult for me to find, between the Duoi wood and the Avellan wood, the deserted region where the stream known as the Bruyère has its source. I spent nearly a whole afternoon looking for it. I only found it toward evening. The cave opens in the side of a ravine and at one time, doubtless following the disappearance of some imprudent visitor, a grille had been placed there, which sealed the narrow cavern, in which there is a chasm. The grille must have been there a long time. The lock is entirely rusted and no longer works. One only has to pull it to open it. That's what I did. But then I stopped, because I was afraid. I confess that I was very fearful. It seemed to me that I could hear the voice that I had heard on the evening of Pentecost singing, far underground: 'And we'll tell you the way to the lake...'

"I had the sensation that the voice was drawing nearer and I didn't listen to it any more. I put the grille back as before and I started running as fast as I could through low and very old box-trees, whose trunks scratched my feet. For that's a curious particularity of caves: box-trees always grow around their orifice.

"I found the driver of the car, who had been waiting for me for several hours in a little farm where there's a family of shepherds, and I went home as quickly as possible.

"Afterwards, I questioned my father. He believes that there are gnomides who live underground, but as no one ever sees them, it's as if they didn't exist. He also said that if ever one were to be seen, it would be in the vicinity of Canjuers and Comps, because, according to geologists, under the part of the earth that one can see, which is uninhabited and sterile, there is an entire world of corridors, channels and waters that are invisible to us. And in that world, which no light reaches, there are doubtless subterranean creatures, trees without leaves and tenebrous lotuses."

Roseline was speaking with great seriousness, and I was obliged to set aside any idea of a game. She remained silent for a long time, and then said, pensively: "Perhaps I missed an opportunity, last year, at Pentecost, to learn the way to the lake. Will that opportunity ever return?"

THE ENTRANCE TO THE CAVE

I went to see Monsieur Spéluque again. He received me in his study, in the midst of his books, as one receives someone with whom one has a secret in common.

At first I broached the subject timidly.

"The caves! The wild region of Comps! But all that is of passionate interest!" exclaimed Monsieur Spéluque.

When I told him the story of Roseline and the gnomide, somewhat in the manner in which one tells a fairy tale, Monsieur Spéluque paced back and forth for a while, prey to a keen agitation. He finally paused.

"That could only happen to a daughter of the Lusignans. A gnomide wouldn't come to offer an emerald crown and black lotuses to just anyone. But is the gnomide the fruit of a dream or a reality?"

"What! You could believe...?"

"I believe nothing, but everything is possible. The most extraordinary things happen, the furthest outside any known reality, but they only happen to certain individuals, and not to others. And what is rigorously true for some is folly for the others. If you don't believe in gnomides and creatures of another world, celestial or subterranean, you will never see them. If you believe in them, your faith can constitute, albeit in very exceptional cases, a sort of appeal, a favorable milieu susceptible of making creatures come, and then, it's necessary to take account of the Lusignan legend. Every legend has a basis in reality.

And Monsieur Spéluque began holding forth about Melusine and the legendary history of the Lusignans.

"But in sum," he concluded, "although we have no serpentine heredity in our family, perhaps we might learn something by going to the cave, whose precise location we know. An old grille in the side of a ravine, not far from the source of the Bruyère, constitutes precise information. Let's not waste any time and go there tomorrow."

As a scholar, Monsieur Spéluque was far from any material preoccupation. He charged me with hiring the car and coming to pick him up at Fréjus after breakfast.

I found him the next day at his door. He had kept the long black coat that he normally wore, but he had bright sports trousers, boots and a mountaineer's staff.

"Perhaps there'll be rocks to climb," he told me.

To my great surprise, he had a case under his arm containing a musical instrument. He deposited it in the vehicle very carefully.

"It's my flute. I haven't told you that in my spare time I play the flute."

"But..."

"Music can have an important role as an entry into communication."

I could not disguise a hint of surprise. "In sum," I said, "you believe in the existence of gnomides?"

He raised his faunesque eyebrows and stared at me with his sparkling eyes.

"You're astonished that an old Pythagorean like me, a son of the philosophers of Alexandria—for that's what I am—attaches so much importance to the testimony of a young scatterbrain who, according to what you've told me, continually confounds her dreams with reality. But have you not noticed that, for everything that surpasses ordinary life, we only have data by way of the scatter-brained, people hardly sensate, who are reputed to be unworthy of faith in the eyes of everyone. The knowledge of what is hidden only filters as far as the mind of the sage via the testimony of folly. There is a whole category of people who, without knowing it, are the intermediaries of an invisible world. Now, it's a matter in the case in hand of a descendant of the Lusignans. Think how exceptional it is to have in one's ancestry a woman who changed into a snake once a week."

"It's a matter of an infinitely distant legend!"

"It's precisely because it's distant that it has chances of reposing on a basis of verity. I place the definitive materialization of the human species at a fairly recent date—around the fifteenth century. The form was not definitive beforehand. I believe that until that epoch, in wild forests, uninhabited mountains and deserted shores, the last representatives of the creatures—fauns, satyrs, sirens—that ignorant humans called gods because they had the feet of beasts or the tails of fish. They were only different species, trials made by the creator, who finally decided on the human form, after long hesitation. Perhaps humans gave proof of slightly less animality than their rivals, and it was in their brains, although very primitive, that it was decided that intelligence would be developed forcefully on earth.

"I believe that there are now no longer any creatures different from humans—none on the surface, that is. But that a few living groups might have taken refuge in the earth's interior, in immense subterranean corridors, on the banks of rivers, of which we only see a small part flowing, nothing is more plausible! I could even add that it's logical, and even certain. Where would humans go if the surface of the earth became uninhabitable for them? They would take refuge inside it. Vigorous beings would have adapted their organs in a few generations.

"We don't know whether there might be a light appropriate to the great terrestrial depths, produced by gases or some other means due to the ingenuity of nature. There ought to be one. Perhaps there is also an entire vegetation there, of unimaginable trees and flowers, of a beauty equal to or greater than that produced by the sun in the sky, for perhaps, instead of the subterranean fire that science has ended up doubting, there is a radiant central sun."

This discourse and others brought us to Comps, where the driver collected a few indications regarding the route to follow. It was necessary to reach the village of La Roque-Esclapon, and then set off on foot in search of the Duoi wood, the Avellan wood and the ravine where the grille was.

The rocks, the wild heather and the stunted pines presented an aspect of redoubtable uniformity. Fortunately, we found a guide. He was a very young man. He belonged to the category of those who allow to show on their fifteen-year-old face the one they will have at fifty. That lack of juvenility did not prevent him from knowing the grille.

"It's dangerous," he told us, laconically.

Monsieur Spéluque was increasingly agitated. He walked rapidly, jumping over tree trunks and stones, clutching his flute against his body.

He only stopped to tell me that he had never regretted not knowing Medieval French so much.

"What use would such knowledge be?"

"I situate in the Middle Ages, at the time of the great cultivations undertaken by the monasteries, the retreat underground of the non-human inhabitants of the wild places. The monks systematically deforested the land, not only to plant crops, but with the aim of an exorcism, to expel the sylvan, arboreal or fluvial beings, which they stupidly identified with demons. Those beings were separated from us in the Middle Ages and must still make use of the language that was current at the time. They were not very speculative, and that language was limited in its use for them. They knew enough, however, to have been converted to Christianity if the Church had shown a little fraternity in their regard. But alas, the wisdom of Christ never thought of saving either the animals or the creatures that are not human."

"However, the slightly rhythmic words heard by Mademoiselle de Lusignan were, so far as I understood, in an entirely modern French."

"Well, there is a intelligent elite and an uncultivated crowd everywhere. In the same way that there is a small number of people among us who know many languages, and the majority who only know one, perhaps there are a few individuals among the subterranean creatures who have been able to keep up to date and retain a knowledge of languages, by slipping behind a window in the evening, or listening from the bottom of a well to women drawing water. But it is possible to communicate by other means than language, which is, in sum, a rather primitive and purely human usage."

Monsieur Spéluque caressed the case containing his flute with satisfaction.

The grille was well hidden at the bottom of a ravine and it had an appearance simultaneously mysterious and unnecessary. It sealed a crevice in the rock that resembled any crevice. Very old box-trees grew all around it.

"Box-trees always grow around caves," said Monsieur Spéluque, "And even inside them, since the people of the region descend with ropes in order to extract, sometimes from a great depth, ancient trunks with which balls are made for the game of boules. Box is content far from the sun and one can suppose that the long, sad avenues that extend underground, on the banks of silent rivers, in a light that comes from who knows where, are bordered by box-trees as old as the planet."

We took two or three steps into the entrance of a low cavern.

"It's dangerous!" shouted the adolescent with the aged face. "There's a hole."

Monsieur Spéluque had taken a lantern from his pocket and he aimed the beam at a gaping orifice that opened before us. It was a broad orifice, one side of which was sheer, while the other had vegetation and asperities to which one could cling if one were audacious enough to attempt the descent. I saw in the gloom of the cavern that Monsieur Spéluque was smiling. He opened the case of his flute and brandished the instrument in his hand.

"Fortunately, I have the best means of appeal."

And, placing himself as close as possible to the edge of the chasm, he started to play. He played with passion, leaning forward, sometimes delivering himself to movements so disordered that I dreaded seeing him disappear into the gaping opening, to which he was dangerously close. The tails of his coat were agitating behind him like wings, and I grabbed him forcefully several times, so near did I think he was to disappearing. He could have plunged in his musical appeal and not even perceived it.

When he stopped, I saw that his face was illuminated.

"It's a piece of my own composition," he told me. "One might have thought that I had foreseen...I'll surely obtain a response—or else the chasm is uninhabited and they aren't there. Hold me; I'm going to listen."

He let himself fall face down and crawled until his head and a part of his torso were perched over the void. I had seized his feet. I heard him murmuring words that I could not distinguish.

He stayed in that position for a long time. I thought that it couldn't go on forever, and I tugged him gently by his feet.

He got up, as if regretfully.

"They responded. They're feminine voices. They have singing voices. But they came from very far away."

At that moment the young guide, who had left us, and who seemed to consider the cavern as a malefic place into which it was better not to penetrate, reappeared near the grille. The afternoon was reaching its end, and it was necessary to get out of the rocks and box-trees before dark.

Before going, I wanted to sure myself of Monsieur Spéluque's extraordinary affirmation. He did not show any astonishment. He seemed to consider that only the distance prevented a narrower communication with the gnomides. And he was slightly disappointed.

"In your turn, hold me," I said to him.

I did as he had done, and leaned forward.

What came to me as a prodigious silence rising from the abyssal depths that I saw extending beneath me in a funnel of darkness. I saw it, but at the same time I reflected that I could only have the perception of that depth because I could see somewhere, very distantly, a vague, uncertain glow.

"Can you hear them?" Monsieur Spéluque asked, behind me.

No, I did not hear any song, nothing but silence. But I reflected again that I could only measure the intensity of what I took for an absolute silence because it was troubled by something. That seemed to be coming from another plane of existence; it had nothing of the human voice, nothing that could be produced by human or extra-human organs, and yet there was a voice; it was the speech of living water.

In the distance, at the bottom of that funnel similar to an infinite spiral, there was flowing water: terrestrial water; light water. In spite of the distance, I perceived the softly blue-tinted glow of its essence, and I heard the sound it made on an invisible shore, the song of the water. And that murmur, and that ineffable distant light, were more mysterious than all the songs or apparitions of gnomides or subterranean gods.

For a few seconds I was in communication with the impenetrable life of the secret part of our planet, with a beauty that it is not given to humans to contemplate; I could hear the heartbeat of the earth.

"I heard," I said, afterwards, to my companion.

And while the car carried us away, Monsieur Spéluque repeated several times: "What a mystery it has been given to us to approach!"

I said: "That's true!" But it was not a matter of the same mystery.

THE DIMENSION OF THE MYSTERY

Once we had arrived at the door of his house in Fréjus, Monsieur Spéluque said in a tone that brooked no reply: "Send the car back."

He did not care about the time it would take me to go home on foot. Those contingencies did not touch him. He took me by the arm, and having set down his flute and his staff, he made me take a few steps with him in the central path of his little garden.

"Perhaps you're wondering why an old Pythagorean like me, a Greek sage full of reason and knowledge, adds faith to fairy tales."

"I haven't asked any question."

"You're wrong. I would have replied to you. I'll reply to you without you asking me anything. I've been able to discover a little of my past. I've succeeded in going back as far as my most distant origins, origins that are lost in the night of time. You know that there are tribes in Africa that abstain from killing a certain animal species and render it the worship that one renders to the ancestors. For some it's the buffalo, for others the crocodile. Those simple men know, by virtue of an immemorial tradition, that they were issued from that ancestral animal. And a certain filiation remains in spite of the centuries. Well, personally, I'm a descendant of the beings that are known as fauns or satyrs, half-human and half-goat, inhabitants of the woods, who have a liking for music.

"There remains to me, from them, the conformation of my feet, which had me rejected by the draft board, the form of my eyebrows, and two excrescences that I have on my temples and that have gradually attenuated. Mentally, I've inherited the liking for music, and above all the love of sciences. In the same way that aerial creatures only think of dancing and spiritual reveries, beings close to the earth have a passion for the exact sciences. It's to that relationship with the inhabitants of the subterranean world that you owe having heard the song that replied to my appeal."

"What I heard," I said, "was a distant sound of water that came from an immense depth. Don't you believe that?"

Monsieur Spéluque started to laugh with satisfaction.

"It's always the same. It isn't given to everyone to hear. For one it's the sound of water, for others the delightful song of semi-human creatures. A marvelous phenomenon always present itself under two aspects, one of which is natural and the other supernatural. The apparent order of the world is at that price."

I was slightly confused to be placed in the category of vulgar people who see nothing of things but their ordinary appearance.

"You should have heard the song," said Monsieur Spéluque, forcefully. "And I'll tell you why you didn't hear it. You live in the location where, in my judgment, Saint Eleutherius built his hermitage. Now, a powerful soul turned in upon itself, impregnates the things among which it lives, for an indeterminate duration. The soul of Eleutherius is still floating in your garden. Now, as a Christian, Eleutherius must have had a horror of all the beings of semi-human form that he encountered. In his time, there must still have been many of them in the dense forests of the shore. According to Christian error, however he mistook them for demons. He repelled them with all his power. He refused to hear them.

"It's the refusal in question that is acting upon you without your knowing it: Eleutherius' refusal to hear the nymphs, the gnomes or the satyrs. Whereas he conducted himself differently with the animals, the question of whose nature had been regulated by theology, and with which the devil had nothing to do. Certainly, he loved them and he talked to them, since he has left a reputation as a saint. If you were to tell me that you understand, in a certain measure, the language of beasts, that wouldn't astonish me. That would be all to the praise of Eleutherius and his powerful force of projection. And that is produced here, but not elsewhere. That's the true mystery. Have you not come with the aim of studying it?"

Monsieur Spéluque was speaking excitedly. Sometimes, he gave me a little tap with his index finger. He stopped, and then he started walking again, drawing me along.

"Yes, here and not elsewhere! But within what limits does *here* mean? Are you asking yourself that? For the dimension of the mystery has a great importance. The sacred place of Delphi might have been no larger than the placement of the Pythoness's tripod, and there are accursed places that embrace the extent of an entire mountain. Where ought we to place the limits of the influence that occupies us?"

I did not understand what Monsieur Spéluque was saying at all. It had to do with the motive that had impelled him to install himself in Fréjus. The same motive—at least, he believed so—had brought me to the region. But what was the motive? I did not know. I would have liked to understand and to penetrate that enigma. My embarrassment was visible. Fortunately, he only saw his own thoughts. He lowered his voce.

"In my opinion, it extends, approximately, from the rock of Roquebrune to the highest point of Saint-Pilon."

"Approximately."

"Ah! That's also your opinion. But it's late. We'll talk about it again."

Monsieur Spéluque had a taste for interrupting conversations abruptly. While taking we had arrived near the portal and the obscure road. He shook my hand.

"Yes, we'll talk again. Come back soon."

THE DEPARTURE OF
THE SUBLIME FRIENDS

I should have gone back to see Monsieur Spéluque again the next day, but I did not. I did not even think about him anymore. It was the next day that the strange phenomenon was manifest in me of the past resuscitated.

It began, in an unforeseeable fashion, with the abandonment of certain companions of my life of whose presence I was unaware. And I only knew that they had been around me at the moment when they quit me.

How had they been present without my knowing it, or almost? How had I not been able to take account of such admirable presences? We have witnesses close to us, advisers and protectors of which we have no suspicion. They are there in the form that they had while alive, but that form has become subtle and immaterial, to the point of not being visible. And sometimes, in exceptional circumstances, it materializes for a few seconds and we have a rapid vision of beings who were sitting in our armchairs, leaning toward us while we are writing, exchanging signs with one another on our subject.

What! I ought to have cried. *You were there and I didn't know it?*

And I should have intoned a hymn of praise, glorifying myself for having had such visitors. But I did nothing. I remained stupidly mute, occupied by a prodigiously futile thought which had suddenly taken on a primordial importance.

The first that I saw go out was the one whose work I had read most recently. It was the day before in the evening, when I came home, and I had even murmured, as I chose his book from my shelves, the impious remark: "What shall I read in order to go to sleep?"

And I had chosen *The Ornament of Spiritual Weddings* by Ruysbroeck, rightly nicknamed "the admirable," a book translated perfectly by Maeterlinck.[16] I am obliged to confess that the book in question had played the role I expected of it that evening. For it contains the description of divine ecstasies susceptible, by their great beauty, of causing a passage from the waking state to that of sleep, especially if one has been running around the rocks of Canjuers all afternoon.

It was the admirable Ruysbroeck who appeared to me first, to disappear immediately. I don't know where he was, or even whether he was there. I saw his slightly square Flemish head, his features sculpted by meditation, his eyes sparkling, like the eyes of those who have seen God. There was no discontentment in his face at my inattention while awake. I even thought I distinguished a total indifference. He did not see me, or, rather, he no longer saw me, for I had the sentiment that he had seen me before. He was near the door and he went out.

He was followed almost immediately by a small man with a jaundiced face, deprived of all race and entirely clad in black, like a rabbi of a very distant epoch. I recognized him by virtue of a handful of telescope lenses

---

[16] The Flemish mystic John van Ruysbroeck (c1294-1381) was an ascetic lavish in his praise for meditation and solitude, whose hermitage attracted so many followers that it became a monastery, after the pattern of Honoratus. I have back-translated the florid title of Maeterlinck's French version of his most famous book into English rather than substituting the most common English version, *The Spiritual Espousals*.

that he was holding in one hand and which were shining like his thoughts. It was Spinoza. He followed Ruysbroeck.

As if that philosopher had given a signal, I saw various sublime men who were heading for the door. They gave the impression of emerging from the somber mass of the books. For the entire section of the library that contained the works of philosophers and sages was in the corner at the back of the room, and that corner, because of the branches of the old pine that extended in front of the windows, was plunged in semi-obscurity.

I recognized the author of the *Imitation*, whose name has not reached us, as his modesty was so great that he hid his face beneath a carefully lowered hood.[17] He maintained it with a hand with long translucent fingers, whose mobility betrayed the copyist of archaic texts and illuminations that he had been. Behind him stood a group of Greek philosophers. They impressed me by virtue of the grandeur of their foreheads and their noses. I saw Plotinus, slightly stooped, perhaps for having carried within him for a long time the fifty-four books of the *Enneads*. I noticed that Proclus was extremely elegant, in a robe of immaculate linen that had a broad green-gold border. He took great care not to bump a large sapphire that he had on his left hand, which permitted him to communicate with the worlds of the gods.

---

[17] The devotional text *De Imitatione Christi* [The Imitation of Christ] (c1420) was published anonymously, but modern sources attribute it to the Dutch cleric Thomas van Kempen, known in English and French as Thomas à Kempis—an identification that the narrator apparently accepts, as he calls attention to van Kempen's assiduous labor as a copyist.

Behind them passed the Hindus, whom I revered among all. I saw on their breasts the mark of the interior fire that had burned them. Perhaps they were debating the differences of yogis, but their words had no sound. Milarepa was almost naked and I understood on seeing his unusual thinness and the skeleton designed beneath his skin how young women had mistaken him one evening for a dead man emerging from the cemetery.[18]

There were also Jacob Boehme, Claude de Saint-Martin, Emerson and other authors of books whose promise of wisdom had been my comfort. I did not recognize them all, since they became less precise, seemingly fading away. Their faces did not allow any expression of discontentment or criticism to show. No, they emerged from their books and they went away. They were not interested in someone who did not show them more love.

As for me, I watched them draw away without doing anything to retain them. I ought to have shouted out, fallen to my knees with open arms, attempting to retain them by means of tears and supplication, those great masters who had done me the signal honor of keeping me company. How many times I had called them sublime friends, how many times I had been filled with gratitude for their books, from which I hoped to extract my own elevation. And now I was watching them depart with indifference.

One thought occupied me. I have said that it was prodigiously futile. Can the quality of thoughts be evalu-

---

[18] Milarepa (c1050-c1135) was the most famous of Tibet's yogis and poets, who claimed to have committed evil deeds in his youth, of which he repented bitterly in old age, when he became an ascetic.

ated? At that moment, that thought appeared to me to be the only important thing in life. That thought was related to the solution of the following problem:

The day before, while we were walking, Roseline had taken in her hand a wild flower, some flower or other, a flower whose personality had not been active enough to found a special class with a special name. At least, that is what I thought. She had considered it and she had said: "It has seven petals, as I have seven desires."

That remark had seemed very profound to me and I wondered with a sharp curiosity what those seven desires were. Why were there seven of them? And were those desires orientated, like the petals of the rustic flower, in a semi-horizontal manner? Were those seven desires lightly turned toward the sun or did they tend in the direction of the earth?

Oh, what did the departure of the sublime friends matter to me? It was as if something within me were suddenly consumed. I had become like the man I had been, uniquely preoccupied with problems of sentimental stupidity.

THE POWER OF THE PAST

There is in the human soul a curious passage from intelligence to stupidity. It even seems to be the theater of a constant combat between those two powers. But stupidity has infinitely more strength; it is everywhere, it overflows in all directions, and when one thinks that one has spread a little light over a part of oneself, it frequently happens that stupidity, like a great dark wave, extends again over what one thought one had stolen from it.

That was what happened to me. And, in returning by means of memory to that moment in my life, I am alarmed to think of the rapidity with which one loses what one has taken so long to acquire.

For it is first necessary to remark how much time it takes to progress in an imperceptible fashion. The spirit seems to consist of a subtle matter and all those who talk about it are in accord on that subject. That is an affirmation so frequent that one cannot argue with it. And yet the most vulgar matter is transformed more easily than the spirit. An iron bar, in spite of its apart immutability, ends up volatilizing if it is subjected to a sufficiently high temperature. There is no high temperature that renders an ordinary mind apt for philosophical comprehension.

No matter how convinced a soul might be of the necessity of becoming more perfect and developing virtues, if it is miserly, it remained miserly; if it is prey to lustful imaginations, it continues to find the same temptations in them, due to the force and exactitude of the images. If it fights with all the strength of it will the birth of those evocative images, it will only see them decrease with a despairing slowness. And if it arrives in the end, by means of an express order of the will, in preventing their appearance, the images will not be dead; they will still be there, lurking, like an obliging cinema, ready to emerge in the darkness and unfurl the splendor of possible sensualities, when the will buckles in the evening as one is on the point of falling to sleep but has not yet fallen,

Progress demands immense efforts. Self-modification is only achieved by means of unusual patience. And in a moment, in the time that a woman's glance lasts, a vast edifice, patiently constructed, can be destroyed.

I had not arrived at great results. I had only attained the moment of transition in which one recognizes the vanity of one's past life, in which one sees a new road and in which one is ready to launch forth along it. I had confessed to myself—which is to say that I had exposed the details of my life and the consequences of my errors before a judge who is all the more severe because he has only recently been elevated to the rank of judge and is making an experiment of judgment. I had drawn up the tableau of wasted time, and it was an immense picture. All my life, with all its hours, was inscribed there. I had an entire life to recapture!

The marvelous times of youth, with its facilities, the possession of memory, the joyful delight in learning, I had squandered in the search for the sterile pleasure that women procure. And the epithet sterile is insufficient. Because, not only is that pleasure not productive, but it is destructive. It destroys all the wealth one possesses in the spiritual order.

I am not talking about physical pleasure alone, which is the least dangerous. One pays, in immediate disgust and in lassitude, the debt that any material attachment contracts for you. One liberates oneself from it almost immediately because it demands its settlement in the hours that follow. I am talking about the intellectual pleasure by which one believes one is magnifying oneself in a liaison with a woman, even, and especially, if that liaison has the noble duration of a lifetime. It is more deadly then, because one gives it a mystical and familial range.

It brings, indisputably, quotidian wellbeing, the warm light of the hearth and the absence of sentimental cares; but in setting aside torment, it also sets aside research. It brings the mysterious mediocrity with which the tranquil man is penetrated, with which the heart and the body are equally satisfied. Society favors and glorifies the man who obeys in a docile fashion the rule of unique amour, on which the cathedral of the family reposes, with its pious columns, the bed that serves as the altar and tabernacle of memories. That cathedral has its beauty for men, of meals at set hours, regular prayers and median good sentiments. Society has made it the central monument of the city, because society does not favor the appearance of perfection in humans, and even fears it.

Perfection has to be discovered in isolation, in the darkness of oneself. And the man who wants to discover it, or only to get closer to it—for it is infinitely distant and hidden behind forests of ignorance—must pitilessly reject the being that is known as the affectionate companion, the twin soul, the soul of one's soul, and seek the joyless solitude, the bleak isolation in which the speech of the gods can be heard.

I had only arrived at the point of understanding that necessity. It is a first stage on the road. One sees ahead ennui, bleak evenings, insomnia and awakenings without the hope of a known face. But rapidly, new hopes, with faces that one has never seen, begin to appear. They are hopes that do not ask anything of anyone, which have no need of human aid, like certain flowers in certain gardens that are born without having been sown, by virtue of an inexplicable understanding between the sun and the soil. Those hopes contain a promise so beautiful that once one has glimpsed them, one wants to go a long way on the road on which one knows that one ought to encounter them.

That was where I was. I knew what I could extract from solitude. I knew that books are like instruments of magic, more powerful than the classic circle or steel point. Like a magician, I had disposed them around me. When the light of the rising sum passing through the branches of the old pine colored them, I was conscious of their power. Via them, I had entered into communication. Their reading had given birth to a supernatural light in my soul. I was enlightened—or rather, I would be, for time is required and the repetition of magical ceremonies.

It is not sufficient for a verity to be well understood; it is necessary to live it. The greatest secrets are immediately understood, but forgotten as rapidly. It is necessary to identify with the spirit of those who inform us of them. That is the mysterious operation that must be accomplished in solitude, and the first condition must be the forgetfulness of the past.

That was where I was. And not only had I not forgotten the past, but it suddenly revived within me as if I had done nothing to abolish it. I found myself once again in the condition that I had been in twenty years before. I had the same anxiety and the same desire, the same stupid craving for sentimental words. The exclusive love of a certain quality of stupidity possessed me again. In vain, I had been ashamed of what I had been. In vain I had repeated, while laughing, certain speeches once pronounced, as symbols of the state of mediocrity and aberration in which I had found myself. I was ready to pronounce those same words today, with the profound accent of sincerity.

Nothing had changed, except Roseline's name, a few details of her features and hair-color, the shape of her dress and the tone of her voice.

TWILIGHT OVER THE LITTLE BEACH

One evening, I fell asleep...

Why have I fallen asleep above a little beach, on a slope where clover had grown and which as strewn with pine-needles? I had no reason to feel drowsy and I never go to sleep in the open air. Sitting on the bare ground, I feel the weight of the landscape upon me too forcefully; I am crushed by the celestial metal of the azure, oppressed by the immensity. Then again, comfortable as the place on the ground that I have chosen is, and where I am sitting, there is always some terrestrial asperity, some sharp stone that enters into my flesh. And if it happens that I lie down completely in order to be face to face with the sky, in the confused hope of glimpsing, thanks to that divine confrontation, an immense and benevolent face whose eyes are fixed upon me, I always have the dread that some audacious insect, some creature armed with a minuscule but very sharp dart might penetrate my nose or my ear in order to stick that dart there, out of ignorance or malice.

So, I never fall asleep in the midst of the beauty of nature. But this evening, by virtue of an exception that nothing can explain, I fall asleep.

Everyone has experienced the softness of that moment of a warm and slightly humid evening at the end of May when the sun is about to disappear. If there is a breeze, it drops. The poplars are more attentive than usual to establishing the measure of vegetal time, which is the role assigned to them. The clover straightens up and extends its trefoil leaves, as if to affirm that a fourth would be useless to them and would not bring good luck to anyone. Clover is very satisfied as it is, and asks nothing more. There is no vibration on the telegraph poles. The first marriage of the evening frogs is announced by a croak.

I had gone past the terrace where Madame Tournadieu was weaving her threads of cloth; I had exchanged a few banal words with her and I had said: "I'm going to the little beach."

I had fixed that rather distant point in order that she would not get up with a mutinous exclamation and propose to accompany me. Fortunately, she quickly ran out of breath.

I am noting that brief dialogue because it constitutes a link in the chain of events. I never went as far as the place known as the little beach at the hour when the poplars are occupied with time and the clover straightens up. For me to do so, it required that Roseline knew of my presence via Madame Tournadieu. If I had gone past without saying anything, perhaps there would have been another sequence of events.

The little beach is a strip of sand surrounded by pines of a nature so maritime that some of them advance audaciously into the sea, to the extent that the same tree and lodge a nightingale on a branch and a crab between its roots. Great acanthus leaves cover he slopes that descend all the way to the sea. They are mingled with yellow and green cacti, and arborescent euphorbias respectfully surround an agave that is getting ready to launch its high flower toward the sun. To the right there is a very ancient fig tree that renounced producing figs a long time ago in order to devote itself to meditation, and to the left a group of several eucalypti with their bark cut into strips and a perfume that they mix, like skillful chemists, with the perfume of seaweed and wrack.

An ancient romanticism obliges humans to lean on something and assume the appearance of someone dreaming when the landscape, impregnated with the melancholy of the evening, realizes a beauty that is personal. For a landscape has its autonomy in nature. The little beach, with its fig tree and its eucalypti, formed a whole, animated by a particular reverie with which it was difficult to achieve a rapport. Every time I went past the little beach alone—solitude is indispensable to the comprehension of nature—I had the vision of an arrival in boats, under triangular sails, of African individuals, and I saw thin-legged slaves with red rings throwing carpets over a long, narrow plank, in order to permit several delicate and veiled women to disembark without getting their feet wet.

I was accustomed to the vision of that disembarkation. I leaned on one of the eucalypti. But the chemist was just in the process of giving the maximum potency to the perfume that it manufactures tirelessly, and that inconvenienced me. I took three or four steps into the midst of the acanthi and I sat down.

A nightingale started to sing, as if it approved of my action. It was a pure coincidence, for I am convinced that it was not concerned with what a human might be doing next to the little beach. I noted that the moon was quite high in the sky. A few thoughts of a rather insignificant character passed nonchalantly through my mind, like travelers who do not know where they are going. I had placed my head on my elbow, and sleep took possession of me.

I was woken up by a burst of laughter: Roseline's burst of laughter. She was laughing at finding me asleep. It even procured her an exaggerated hilarity, for the phenomenon of sleep is frequent and familiar. In spite of its frequency, I experienced a certain confusion at being found asleep. As soon as I had felt the tip of Roseline's umbrella, with which she had touched my shoulder, I told myself that an abrupt sleep, at the end of an afternoon, might be considered as a symptom of old age. I stammered, while Roseline continued laughing, but I had sufficient presence of mind to invite her to sit down.

She made a semblance of hesitation, and a semblance of calculating whether or not she had the time, and sat down. And I had the sentiment that she had premeditated everything. How? Why? I don't know. One always thinks that women, submissive to events, are drawn by the combination of circumstances. Nothing of the sort. They make the same decisions as men; the only difference is in the manner in which they realize them. They make a semblance of submission, while they are directing by devious means.

The presence of the moon and the exact measure of its light, the activity of the arboreal chemist and the sweetness of its perfume, intoxicating if one is alone, but bewitching if there are two, the benevolence of the fig tree, the propitious character of the hour and the bewilderment of the awakening, had all been calculated and arranged by Roseline a long time ago. How long? Perhaps five minutes, since the moment when Madame Tornadieu had told her that I was at the little beach, perhaps much longer, since an anterior life dating from the Middle Ages or some more distant epoch.

But in the bosom of the event, who cares about the cause of the event? I knew that it sometimes happens in life that things one has desired are realized as one has desired, even with an unexpected savor that adds to the charm of the realization. It is very rare, but it happens. I had desired, in the depths of my unconscious, to be sitting on clover amid acanthus leaves, by the light of a nascent moon, next to Roseline.

Neither the clover, nor the acanthus leaves, nor the eucalypti, nor the fig tree had been configured in the matrix of my distant desire. I had left nature the faculty of furnishing the accessories and the décor of the setting herself. Nature could have forgotten the moon and I would not have complained, but she had not forgotten anything; she had even thought about a large gray cape that Roseline was carrying. And that cape played a role.

Once Roseline was sitting down beside me, we remained mute, rather embarrassed, she because she sensed that she was sitting a little too close and that it would have been ridiculous to move away, I because I had been surprised while asleep and was searching for an excuse for that slumber. Then too, one is always confused when events are realized too well.

"There's a hint of freshness, all the same," said Roseline, in order to say something, making the gesture of wrapping herself in her cape and hence of isolating herself.

At that moment, there was a general attention around us, the curiosity of which I perceived clearly. I had thought the nightingale indifferent. Not at all. It uttered an extraordinarily significant appeal in order to notify another creature of its race of our human presence next to the little beach, which immediately made it known by means of a few clear modulations that it was keenly interested in that entire affair. An animate being of small dimension, perhaps a hedgehog, stirred under the foliage. A light breeze passed through the air, and caused a few thin eucalyptus leaves to fall. The fig tree affirmed that all was well, and, in front of me, on the sand, little waves with fringes of foam became still, as if to hear better.

They only heard these words, which I repeated in a low voice: "Yes, there's a hint of freshness, all the same."

Then I look a flap of the cape and, pretending to want to protect myself against that hint of freshness, I extended it against Roseline. She did not protest, and even indicated by an imperceptible movement that she was favorable to that protection.

At that precise moment a toad intoned a hymn with a disproportionate voice, as if it deliberately wanted to break the harmony of the landscape and the evening. Roseline started to laugh.

"It has a stentorian voice," she said. And immediately, she added: "By the way, who was Stentor, and why is his voice celebrated?"

I turned my head slightly. The shadow had arrived softly. There was no hint of freshness. I was about to sketch an explanation, but Roseline and I suddenly stopped thinking about Stentor—unless she continued to think about him without letting it show...

POOR PORCASTRE!

In the same way that one can divide the universe into two parts, the sky and the earth, although there is a host of other possible divisions, we can say that there are within us two different beings, one superior and one inferior. I never felt that so strongly as when there was an absolute predominance within me of the inferior being.

That was produced immediately after the evening spent at the little beach. In the midst of that charming landscape, and partly with its aid, my inferior being triumphed. And the result for me was a perfect and tranquil delight in that victory.

I was conscious of that the next morning, in the fashion in which, scarcely awake, I ran to my shutters and opened them so violently that they rebounded. I was more vigorous than usual. Outside, the sun was warmer. The plants were growing with a greater ardor than the day before. I noticed that one of the good God's creatures was marching over my window with an unaccustomed energy.

I then had the surprise of seeing my friend Porcastre surge through the garden gate. He had come to spend a few days. He was staying in the same inn. The proprietor was a very sympathetic fellow. Was I still living an eremitic life? I heard his laughter continue while he was walking back and forth in the garden.

I shouted that I was going to come downstairs. But everything was happening as if in a dream. The arrival of a friend was a very secondary contingency. I was in a state of physical intoxication.

As long as he doesn't talk to me about philosophy, I thought.

Philosophy! And internally, on an invisible blackboard, the inferior being wrote: *Nonsense!*

"If you want to read Plato's *Timaeus*, it's necessary to read it in Victor Cousin's translation. When one comes back to it, you'll see that one comes back Victor Cousin and his translation."

Porcastre was brandishing a tattered book, which I recognized by virtue of often having seen it sticking out of one of his pockets. In order not to waste a minute of the time I had taken to come downstairs, he had taken out Plato's *Timaeus*, on which he had been mediating for five years! I almost laughed in my turn.

Poor Porcastre, thought the inferior man. *He has nothing better to do than reread the* Timaeus. *And how skilled he is! What women he frequents! Oh, the amours of poor Porcastre!*

I knew that, almost every evening, Porcastre went along the Rue Caulaincourt where he lives, took a side street not far from the cemetery and went to spend the evening in a brasserie where he found three or four local hookers.

"I like that feminine atmosphere very much," he had told me. "We all lack femininity."

And one evening, he had made me a long eulogy on the intelligence of a blonde with a thick neck who was known as Loulou.

"Imagine that Loulou had had a little more success. Well, she would have been exactly the type of those courtesans who once discoursed with philosophers in Athens."

The triumph of the inferior man had suddenly rendered me sensitive to elegance. When Porcastre appeared on the threshold of the garden I was in the process of asking myself which of two jackets was the newer. Now I stared at my friend's trousers and observed that they had no trace of a crease and fell back on themselves, rather like the trousers of zouaves.

It is a characteristic of the inferior man to allow his thoughts to show on his faces, to become stupid. I sensed that stupidity in my features, but it did not embarrass me and was rather agreeable.

"Oh, I'm not like you," said Porcastre. "I don't have that impeccable elegance. But it seems to me that it doesn't sit well with your eremitic tastes."

The idea of elegance must have tormented him. With a rapid gesture he pulled up his trousers devoid of braces, exactly as Madame Tournadieu did with her girdle.

What similitude of nature does that similitude of gesture imply? I wondered.

And while my mind was focused on that problem, Porcastre indulged in various pleasantries regarding my pretended solitude and my pretended search for perfection.

"But too bad! It's too late. You remember that we made a bet. It still stands. I've fixed a delay of three days. They only start today, because you only introduced me to Mademoiselle de Lusignan an hour before my departure. Of course! You weren't confident. But now, you have only to stand by."

Porcastre started to laugh, with the heaviest laughter that he had in his laughter collection, and he gave me a great slap on the back.

An irresistible desire took hold of the inferior man, the desire to tell Porcastre about the scene on the little beach. It was a miracle that the one I call the superior man, and who is only less inferior, was able to recover a little authority, in order to stop the words pressing on my lips.

The inferior man made up for it by being internally scornful of the costume, language and manners of his friend, and being particularly scornful of his admiration for Loulou and his conception of women and amour. Puffed up with pride, he gazed ironically at the copy of the *Timaeus* that Porcastre had put back in his pocket, and he went so far as to shrug his shoulders while murmuring: "Plato's *Timaeus*"—not addressed to the poor quality of the copy but to Plato himself.

And the superior being did not have the courage to protest. There was above him the nascent moon, the perfume of eucalypti, the wisdom of the fig tree, and the romantic mystery hidden by the folds of Roseline's cape.

Nature makes use of beauty as an artifice in order to make us descend again after we have permitted ourselves to rise. Who will ever be able to explain why nature, instead of extending a hand to us like a benevolent mother, sets traps for us and toys with our desire?

"Will you permit me to write a letter?" Porcastre asked. His face was filled with a childish ingenuousness. "I promised Loulou to give her my news as soon as I arrived."

Poor Porcastre! I thought. But I was not sure whether Porcastre was to be pitied, and whether it might not be necessary to say: "Fortunate Porcastre!"

GRIMALDI'S VISIT

It was with a sharp surprise that I saw the silhouette of young Grimaldi in my garden.

"Say that it's the Comte de Grimaldi," he said to Antoinette, with a certain emphasis.

I went out immediately and invited him to sit down in the shade of the pine tree, because the spring sun was becoming a little more ardent every day.

He was naturally antipathetic to me. But I professed that sympathy is gained by reciprocity and that it is for the man who has a general sympathy for an ideal to make the first move, so I put an expression of cordial satisfaction on my face.

He made the bracelet he was wearing on his left wrist glint, and his gray-striped suit had a hint of ridicule because of the excess of its stripes. He put affectation into lifting up his trousers to show his silk socks. The force of his jaw filled me with astonishment.

"I don't have the appearance," he told me, "but I'm very sensitive. Yes, I'm sensitive. I have scruples. That's why I've come. I've me to ask you for some advice. I've come to ask the advice of a man of experience."

I told him that I was at his disposal, but that I was subject to error like everyone, perhaps more so."

"To whom can one address oneself, though? Here, we're so far from everything. The most learned man, it appears, is the pharmacist, and I don't know him. Then, I thought that someone who reads so many books, someone of your age, might be able..."

"Yes..."

"Roseline has respectful sentiments for you, which I share..."

"Evidently..."

"What I have to ask you is so special...I'm hesitant."

"Don't be..."

"It isn't to the pharmacist, naturally, that I could...there are things that only elite minds..."

"Speak."

"I ought to tell you first that I belong to a very ancient family."

"I'm not unaware of that."

"Long ago, in a very distant epoch, the Grimaldis already played a role, and a great role."

"We talked about that the other day."

"It's very important to explain the case that I'm going to submit to you. The Grimaldis were the kings of Monaco. I belong to a royal family. Oh, I don't say that to glorify myself. The kings of our day are no longer in the same situation. But you'll see that it renders my case particularly curious. Have you studied psychoanalysis?"

"Not especially, but I know what it is."

"I've studied it myself. I've read a book by Freud. It's very interesting. I'd read others if life wasn't so absorbing. Well, from the viewpoint of psychoanalysis, my case is very particular. It's a subject of study. If I had time, I'd study it as a scientist might do."

"But what...?"

"I'll explain everything to you. But it's difficult to explain! And it's delicate. It's extremely delicate. I couldn't tell it to anyone. Especially not women. I couldn't tell it to Roseline, for example, even if she weren't the cause of it. I'm telling you in confidence."

"Of course."

"Or rather, I'll try to tell you, for it's very difficult. There it is! How can I explain to you that a Grimaldi, belonging to a royal family, has within him a liking for treason?"

Grimaldi looked at me fixedly, advancing his jaw immeasurably. He was wondering what effect what he had just said had had on me. But I didn't understand very well.

"What?"

"I have a natural inclination to treason. I bear it within me. As soon as I have an amity for a man, I search involuntarily for an opportunity to betray him. And if I have a liaison with a woman, I betray her immediately. And that given me a keen satisfaction, but I'm a little ashamed of it, all the same. How can that be explained?"

"I don't know."

"It's very special, very curious. But I can't do otherwise. And I'll tell you something even more curious. I've conducted research into the history of the Grimaldis. Yes, just like a historian. I've gone to libraries. I've sought information from librarians, because I've never had the habit of books. Well, I've seen that all the Grimaldis have an inclination to treason. And the further one goes back the more pronounced that inclination is. Thus, it's the ancient Grimaldis who are the most unworthy. It's necessary to read local history, Local history is very interesting. Grimoald, who was mayor of the palace under Childebert II, betrayed the King. You'll tell me that that happened a long time ago. That's nothing. A Grimaldi committed treason at Cry. Another became famous at the battle of Lepanto, but for treason. And when one reads the history of Lérins Abbey, one sees that it was a Grimaldi who led the Saracen ships, who was the cause of the pillage of the abbey, and the death of Saint Porcarius and more than five hundred monks."

"Five hundred and three. I know the story of the monk Eleutherius."

"Do you know it entirely? The monk Eleutherius had seen Grimaldi leaving with the Saracens. He was miraculously transported to Fréjus by sea and the inhabitants proclaimed him bishop. There was a great influx of the nobility of the land to receive the Seigneur de Lusignan, King of Cyprus, who was about to disembark. Among the nobles, Lorenzo Grimaldi, Seigneur d'Antibes, stood out. Bishop Eleutherius thought he recognized the Christian he had seen at the head of the Saracens. It was indeed him. You see the audacity of the men of my race! I have an old miniature representing the disembarkation of the King of Cyprus, holding the hand of Melusine de Lusignan. In the foreground, near the Bishop, was Lorenzo Grimaldi.

"Well, behold the mystery of heredity! The ancient miniaturist represents him with my slightly prominent jaw. He resembles me—or rather, I resemble him. And behold the mystery of things! My ancestor attempted to seduce the Dame de Lusignan, and might perhaps have succeeded—for the women of old were similar to those of today—but for the intervention of Bishop Eleutherius. And after so many years, there is a Grimaldi and a Lusignan once again, or more precisely, two Lusignans, who find themselves in the same place. I say two Lusignans, because that's where the whole drama is."

"What is that drama?"

"It's about that subject that I've come to see you. You know that Roseline has a sister—an older sister. Well, it's because of the innate taste for treason that is in me that I've tried to please Roseline's sister. I know that there are things that one should never say. There's a secret that must never be violated. You'll understand me. But the case is particular. It's very probable that she and I are going to leave together. I'm talking about Roseline's sister. So, I wanted to ask you...only you can explain it Roseline. I don't like to cause pain. Explain the cause of everything...a hereditary force that is in the race...a force about which one cannot do anything. One is then the victim of fatality. Fatality! Everyone is obliged to incline..."

I replied to the descendant of the kings of Monaco that I would do my best. In any case, my response was of no great importance to him. The essential thing was that he had explained the matter.

"I'd like to know whether, for example, you..."

"What?"

"Excuse my curiosity...I'd be interested to know whether you also, like me, have an inclination to betrayal?"

"No, I don't believe so,"

"It's annoying to be alone. I would have liked...anyway!"

He got up to leave. I saw that he was considering my house with an inexplicable sentiment of smugness."

"You're not badly accommodated here," he said, agitating his bracelet. "I know your house well. I came here five or six years ago with a charming young woman who had rented it. She's dead now. It's extraordinary how one forgets people who die! One even forgets the living."[19]

---

[19] It is not clear why this remark should be included in the text unless the young woman in question is the female ghost of whom mention has been made previously by both the earwig

Having arrived at the wooden gate he wanted to say something that he had difficulty formulating.

"I hope that you don't bear a grudge against me."

"For what?"

"That's true. But I've done well to tell you all that. It's so curious. A Grimaldi who wasn't able to have a Lusignan, centuries ago! And another Grimaldi, with the same square jaw, who has two Lusignans at the same time. There's something astonishing—I'll say more, mysterious—about that."

---

and Porcastre. It is possible that the mystery is abandoned hereafter because the author abbreviated the planned story in order to finish the book before he died, but whether or not that is true, the interpretation of the ghostly presence can only invite speculation, depending on the interpretation of the novel's allegory. It might not be irrelevant that the author appears to have made contact with his ex-wife again before writing the novel.

THE AMOROUS RENDEZVOUS

There is a manner of arranging a rendezvous with someone that has a much more extensive range than its apparent significance of time and place. If a young woman says to you, while squeezing your hand for a long time and looking deep into your eyes: "I'll come to dinner with you this evening..." those words go much further than the promise of sharing the evening nourishment, especially if there has been mention of that dinner beforehand as an entry into matters, and if it has been given, by allusions and reticences, the character of a sentimental gala with an amorous conclusion.

I observed in the afternoon a curious phenomenon caused by that dinner. My books had disappeared. They were no longer there at my disposal. I no longer had the faculty of picking one up, reading it and immediately obtaining an intellectual pleasure. Or rather, they were effaced and veiled; they had retreated into an inaccessible distance, and the incapacity to take one and read it came primarily from myself and a preliminary incapacity of comprehension. At any rate, I no longer had books, and the inferior being was so dominant in me that I rejoiced in it, that I regretted the time wasted, the time devoted to philosophical nonsense, and I proposed ridding my house of all those useless bindings. Yes, I called my books "bindings," in the same way that the vulgar call paintings "frames."

My first concern had been to retain my housekeeper, Antoinette, for the evening. She was usually only there in the morning, and prepared a cold meal for me for the evening, which I requested to be as ascetic as possible. That meal was always too abundant at my age.

"Oh! My poor Monsieur, you're already rather thin!" said Antoinette.

She was quite right! Why had I condemned myself to a miserable evening mal? What had I gained by that? Epictetus, of course, had not even had a table to eat infinitely frugal things, of which I had no idea. But I wasn't a former slave. The Hindu sages, of course, contented themselves with boiled rice that pious people brought them in a ladle, but no ladle was brought by pious individuals and there are differences of climate, and above all, differences in sagacity.

The word "sagacity" formulated in thought nearly made me burst out laughing. Was it sage not to eat when one is hungry in the evening, and to deprive oneself of a small glass of liqueur under the pretext that it is necessary not to obscure one's consciousness?

"Antoinette!" I shouted. "Bring me a bottle of Chartreuse and a bottle of Cognac, the best you can find."

"The best!" Antoinette exclaimed, with admiration.

She viewed the prospect of a splendid repast, which would produce abundant leftovers, favorably. She was moreover, a disinterested soul who only envisaged leftovers in the light of the tastes and appetites of her husband.

"I'll tell my husband I won't be there this evening," she said, knotting her headscarf.

"Aren't you going to miss him at dinner?"

I did not attach any importance, of course, to the solitude of that husband, and only said that in order to throw up the dust of vain words.

"When it's a matter of one's profession!" said Antoinette, suddenly as great as duty.

And she left. A thousand small tasks were imposed on me. I went to pick flowers in Mathieu Lapeyre's garden

"I have people to dinner," I said negligently.

"Oho!" he said. And he cut hyacinths and irises, which he enveloped in large mimosa branches.

He cut large quantities. I sensed that I had been imprudent I employing the words "people to dinner" He was vaguely glimpsing men in suits, women in evening dress and luxurious automobiles parked in the little sunken road on to which my garden gate opened.

"Would you like me to make little bouquets for each person?"

"No thank you, Mathieu."

"And if you need someone to open the gate..."

"No, thank you."

I distributed the flowers all over. I saw to the organization of the cushions.

Antoinette reappeared triumphantly, laden with provisions. It was unnecessary to say any more to her. She was like the pilot of a ship; everything was her responsibility.

"Until now, you haven't let me go. You'll see what I can do."

Suddenly, I was seized by an idea. I had forgotten the champagne. It was just in time. Could one invite a young woman to dinner and not offer her champagne? I went to buy it myself. A grocery large enough to stock champagne was some distance away. I was incompetent to make the choice. Was the most expensive the best? I asked for two bottles, and then changed my mind. It was three bottles that I needed—no, four. Could they be delivered? The errand boy was ill. I loaded myself with the four bottles.

I was obliged to make a long detour in order not to go past Madame Tournadieu. In spite of my instructions the packaging was imperfect and the gold foil of one or two bottle-tops was visible. What would Madame Tournadieu have thought?

The evening promised to be very warm. As I was walking under the pines I was gripped by an anxiety. What if Roseline arrived early? Why not? I started to run, in spite of my burden. Evidently, she would wait. But she might leave again. Would Antoinette understand that she was the guest? Finally, I saw the squat silhouette of my house next to the old pine. I was sweating.

"Has anyone arrived, Antoinette?"

"No one—but it's only six o'clock." And Antoinette added, as she unwrapped the package: "The lady isn't running any risk of being thirsty."

I smiled with pity. Four bottles! What's that? Once...

I was deceiving myself. Alcohol had always made me feel ill. But the inferior being needed to convince himself that he was familiar with heavy drinking.

I had a little time before me. I started pacing back and forth in the garden. Read? There was no question of that. The possibility of books—my books at least—had disappeared for me. Oh, I had better things to do. Life! I was a man who was alive. How fortunate the circumstances were that had brought me to life. I had emotions, I was waiting, I was anxious. That was life. And to think that I had wanted to shut myself voluntarily in a prison of books! I would never read the *Enneads*. I would no longer occupy myself with the afterlife. I would no longer search for the key to any mystery. For a start, there was no mystery. Everything was clear. Monsieur Spéluque was a lunatic who would have ended up turning my head upside down. Only one thing counted, and that was the pleasure of living. I had never experienced it so intensely.

Then I noticed something that filled me with satisfaction. I had run for a long time with those four bottles, which represented a rather heavy load. Well, I was not experiencing any fatigue. On the contrary, my blood was circulating freely. I could, without inconvenience, run the same distance again with eight bottles. And I wondered whether I could have done that before, when I was…in any case, when I was a few years younger. No, I could not have done. My strength was therefore increasing.

"Is it at half past seven that I ought to serve?" shouted Antoinette, from the threshold.

"Half past seven precisely," I replied, confidently.

I looked at my watch and I remembered that Roseline had said, lowering her voice: "I'll be at your house at seven o'clock."

Seven o'clock had passed a few minutes before. She was slightly late. But wasn't lateness customary? Yes, it's a custom as old as the world to be late. And the more the rendezvous has a sentimental character, the longer the delay ought to be. Ordinarily, Roseline was never late. It was a good sign that she was this evening.

I had circled the old pine many times. What was it thinking. Was it conscious of the rendezvous arranged with Roseline? It certainly had some consciousness of it, but different from any that I could imagine. I went back inside to see whether the table was properly set.

Finally, the bell rang. I ran forward, but on the threshold I got a grip on myself. It was necessary not to show too much ardor.

I looked out. There was no one there. The cracked bell rang again, however.

"It must be the milk for the cream dessert," shouted Antoinette.

The child who had brought it was shorter than the gate and I had not seen him. I took the milk.

"Don't hurry too much, Antoinette."

Waiting is always annoying. I made another circuit of the pine, but a little more rapidly. I heard Antoinette drawing a bucket from the well with difficulty.

"I forgot to put the wine to cool, but the bucket is cold." She panted as she added: "It's bad for the asthma."

I went into the little road to see whether Roseline's silhouette might not suddenly appear. The little road was deserted. There was a delightful glow under the yews, the laurels and the mimosas.

"I'll be at your house at seven o'clock," she had said to me...

But time passed. Darkness descended by insensible degrees.

Roseline will certainly come, I said to myself. But was there not an unformulated tradition that dictated that one should be warned when something was changed in an amorous rendezvous? Such a rendezvous escaped the habitual laws of life. Directed by a secret fantasy, it could not conform to normal rites.

"Half past seven passed some time ago," said Antoinette. "Everything will be cold or dried out."

At that moment I heard the cry of an owl that ordinary resounded when night fell. That cry was like a signal. Discouragement took possession of me. Through the open window I saw the flowers that were visibly fading and shedding their petals around the vases in which I had placed them. I felt an immense fatigue in my limbs, to the point that I let myself fall into a wicker armchair. I would not have been able to run with a single bottle of champagne. And I saw the head of Mathieu Lapeyre over the bushes, his eyes wide, wondering where the luxury automobiles of my guests could be.

But no; it wasn't possible. Something must have happened, perhaps a serious accident, and in any case, something very important. Roseline had broken a leg slipping on the steps of the perron of her house. I had noticed how dangerous they were. Or her father had been bitten by one of his snakes, which he had the habit of handling imprudently, and he had died suddenly.

But why hadn't she warned me? The most elementary politeness ordered that. But did politeness enter into it? The mysterious actions of sympathy and desire were above customs. Their movements were not occupied with the preparations for a dinner. If Monsieur de Lusignan had not been bitten and Roseline had not slipped, it was because she had changed her mind. But that hypothesis seemed impossible to me. She had said exactly: "I'll be at your house at seven o'clock." And in the tone of the voice, the gaze and the pressure of the hand there was an irrevocable decision.

And yet...

I was interrupted by Antoinette. She had come out into the garden. She was considering me.

"Oh, the youth of today! This couldn't have happened in the old days. To a young man, perhaps, but to someone of your age...! In the old days, no one would have dared."

She had the gravity of someone offering condolences to a mourner.

"You'd better eat alone. We can't let the dinner go to waste."

And I sensed that she felt sincerely sorry for me. I felt sorry for myself too. I got up from my armchair, though, made a simulacrum of whistling, and said: "All this isn't very serious."

But I wasn't hungry. I retained a hope, but I sensed that it was diminishing as time passed. How inexorable time was in its regularity. Fundamentally, it conditioned everything. When a little more time had passed, all hope would be lost. And I sensed that it was the cause of everything, in a more profound fashion. I was enveloped by time. I was carrying a burden of time by which my being was penetrated. It had made my hair gray, it had sculpted my features, it had given my features an appearance of gravity, which I disowned but of which I could not rid myself. Time, in that form, is called old age. Yes, that was the cause. Why disguise it?

It seemed to me that I had just lit a lamp and that I was going over the small events whose enchainment had produced that evening. Now, I saw that it was a matter, in sum, of a man laden with time, an aging man, who had invited a young woman to diner, without paying any heed to the time he was carrying. The young woman had accepted, and then she had reflected. She had measured the difference in age. Or perhaps she had not even measured it. She had acted instinctively, driven by the obscure notion of time that everyone bars within them. That notion makes it known that, for everything concerning amour, the contribution of time is synonymous with ennui and disgust.

"You can go, Antoinette."

And I also wanted to shout to Mathieu Lapeyre that it was futile to wait behind the laurels.

Antoinette was far away, it was very late, and I was still listening, leaning on the wooden gate, in case Roseline's footsteps might resound in the distance on the little road. There are such strange combinations of circumstances! Anything can happen! The night was bright enough. I saw the contours of trees outlined against the sky. The indifference of things was prodigious. The hedgehogs were pursuing searches in the grass. A cricket intoned its song, and then hesitated, and stopped.

In the distance, an owl uttered its appeal and another responded to it in another direction, and they did not come together all night. One could believe that they would never come together. Perhaps one of the two was an old owl. It seemed to me that its call had something hoarse about it; it resembled my voice if I tried to articulate "Roseline."

And in the dark, in a low voice, I murmured "Roseline!" in order to discover the relationship between the sounds of my throat and the cry of the owl. There was none. It was an absurd comparison. And I told myself that, unlike the owl, I did not have a distant response.

I thought about the length of the night and insomnia. It was necessary to walk in order to tire myself out, in order to forget. I laughed bitterly. At my age one was no longer capable of great efforts. I had already run with the bottles. Old men are rapidly fatigued. I resolved all the same to go into the pines. I left the gate wide open. Who could tell? If Roseline came, in spite of the implausibility of that arrival, she would think that I was not far away.

Once, I would have enjoyed the romanticism of the disappointment and the solitude. But at present, there was no more romanticism in it. I saw a phantom with white hair in the depths of my sadness. I could walk rapidly, simulating for myself a light step, waving the hat that I was holding in my hand, but I knew that a force of ennui was traveling with me, that from now on I was a creature prey to elements of disaggregation, that I had lost the winged secret of youth, the virtue of laughing in company for no reason, of pure innocence in stupidity and pleasure.

In any case, my shadow in the moonlight projected its head forward. I was already slightly stooped. I thought of certain human faces, of a median age, that I had avoided urgently because of the quality of their breath. I had heard it said that one cannot smell one's own. And the bizarre vegetation that only appears in middle age in the nose and the ears—that was what I suddenly sensed coming to life within me, growing forcefully, like a symbolic sign of age.

Then I ran to escape my thoughts. I reached the road. There was a light ahead of me that was oscillating to the right and left. I caught up with it. It was the lantern of a peasant's cart. I retraced my steps.

How short of breath I am! I thought.

The wooden gate was open, as I had left it. The cricket was a little less hesitant, and its song more regular. The shadow of the pine traced a more solemn circle. In what measure did it comprehend human chagrin and the paltriness of that chagrin? Would I have dared to confess to it with sincerity, of there can be a true sincerity of a man talking to a tree? And by what means would it have replied to me?

The entire house was full of an odor of *pâté de foie gras* and cold chicken. The four bottles of champagne, divided in two buckets, were standing upright, like lugubrious futile soldiers. The flowers spread excessively heavy perfumes that made one think of the presence of a corpse.

I thought that, for me, there was only peace in sleep.

THE MASS BEFORE DAWN

But I could not sleep.

A time impossible to evaluate went by. Then, in the distance, at an infinite distance, a bell chimed an hour. I sat up. Silence fell again, and it seemed to me that I heard it take possession of the sky and the earth again with a quiver. I got up quietly and I went to open the window.

It was at that moment that a nightingale began to sing. Perhaps there are nightingales whose songs, as informed naturalists say, are amorous appeals, signals relative to generation, in order that a host of infantile nightingales might be brought into the world. But there are others that sing for the pure pleasure of singing, which are improvisers of the lunar night, which invent stories of birds and men, which develop themes of joy and sadness. And I have sometimes observed, without being able to explain it, that those themes have a relationship with the state of mind of the person who is listening to them.

That nightingale, I understood immediately, did not belong to the category familial nightingales. It would not have a nest nearby. It was a free nightingale, going from one wood to another, and singing while the others slept. At any rate, if it had had a wife and chicks huddling in a nest between two branches of the old pine, it would not have dared to signal its presence by a song in such a loud tone and risk attracting nocturnal owls. That courageous nightingale was careless of owls and it filled the vast night with the resonance of its voice.

Scarcely had it commenced than another voice replied to it—that of a cricket. And it, too, was an exceptional cricket, firstly because of the extent of the sounds that it emitted, and above all by virtue of the astonishing delight of what it was announcing. That cricket had come from far away, with a determined objective, a particular intention. And there was no doubt that it had been waiting for the song of the nightingale in order to sing with it.

The state of mind in which I found myself was so miserable that my first thought was that I would never be able to go to sleep, and I think I looked round the room in search of an object to throw into the branches of the old pine in order to put the bird to flight. I did not find one, and in any case, I was ashamed.

Once, I had been scornful of a certain Delgrade who had talked about a property in the country that was badly situated because it was surrounded by nightingales that prevented him from sleeping at night. One, in particular, sang very close to his window. "I took my father's hunting rifle into my bedroom and I ended up going downstairs. Who knows? I might perhaps kill several and it might make an excellent spit-roast for breakfast."

So, I was almost similar to that Delgrade, eater of nightingales! I started to laugh bitterly.

That was because the two messenger creatures were in the process of singing with the character of an annunciation. They were announcing the reign of the spirit. They were proclaiming, in that corner of the world, the eternal transformation of creatures in progress toward a more perfect form, toward a better soul, more lucid and more conscious of beauty. That was not translatable into words, but the meaning could not escape me. I perceived, without any possible doubt, its elevated range, and a great frisson ran through me from head to toe.

But why was that message being proclaimed in that particular place at an hour when everyone was asleep, when there was the least chance of it being heard? For, resounding as those voices were, they were only resonating for the pines, the mimosas and the wild laburnums.

Certain ideas are so elevated, I thought, that they have to be enunciated in the immaculate hour that precedes the dawn, and have no need of any listener. And suddenly, I thought of the prayer of Eleutherius, which, by virtue of its power, had perhaps impregnated that earth and had made it a magical place. Then again, there was, in fact, a listener at that window, anguished and full of bitterness, but retaining, like an ember beneath the ashes, his desire to understand the world. At the thought that the song was resounding within me, I knelt down and put my hands together.

The annunciators continued their hymn. They revealed the beauty hidden behind changing forms, the immense labor of creatures enclosed in the prison of terrestrial envelopes and seeking to attain the degree of spirit to which each might aspire, in accordance with its effort.

They proclaimed that life is woven with threads of dolor, that every step forward is a wrench in the flesh, a wound in the soul, but that it is nevertheless necessary to advance, for the law is immutable. But they announced the light. There is a light for everyone, which becomes brighter and more beautiful as one discovers it. And it is in suffering that everyone must find his own.

And then my light appeared to me materially. The trees of the garden emerged from the darkness and were outlined against a mobile blue. An impalpable glow, which gave the impression of being produced by their branches, enveloped them. Thousands of tiny drops of

198

dew, invisible until then, became brilliant, lit up like the lamps of a minuscule fairyland, but expanded to infinity. The garden emerged from the mysterious bath of the night, rejuvenated and purified.

And I too had to purify myself. I had gone back down the road of desire. After an attempt to raise myself up, to attain the realm of the spirit, the ineffable realm where the blissful reside, penetrated by serene wisdom and divine love, I had descended again, intoxicated by physical form and the promise of pleasure. I had exchange pure gold for base matter. I had betrayed the cause of God.

My God, how long the road is! How distant perfection is! How fugitive the spirit is! And what traps are extended for us! There is the very beauty that is in the faces of women, the ineffable color of gazes, and the harmony of attitudes. And that beauty is deceptive. It leads us along the retrograde path, toward the material joy of the senses, the blind pleasure whose terminus is oblivion. How to know? How to recognize the good road?

Meanwhile, the light continued to engender itself. Every blade of grass was impregnated by it, and every leaf emitted a little radiation. Every flower had an aureole as a sign of sanctity.

Then I slapped my forehead and reproached myself for my pride. I had thought that the hymn of the bird and the insect were for my exclusive intention. I understood that it was nothing of the sort, that it was resounding for the entire portion of the earth susceptible of perceiving it. For I had the awareness of an immense attention of arboreal creatures: those that lived in the flower beds and the cracks in bark, the inhabitants of the bushes, the ditches and the dust, the trees themselves, the vegetables, the parasites of the vegetables and the confused personality of the stones.

The annunciation of perfection in progress, the duty of working toward the spirit beneath the hard carapace of successive forms was proclaimed to all the beings animated by a current of life, no matter how rudimentary. And all of them were waiting, all of them were listening to the living speech of the messengers.

The wood of the trees creaked. Droplets of gum trickled over the trunk of the pine, and every drop glittered with a fragment of soul-light extracted from the earth by the roots and mutated into solar matter along the channels of the wood. The flowers extended their pistils like supplicant arms. I heard the delicate sound of calices bursting forth in a surge of amour. I saw the antennae of insects agitating in the grass, and sometimes the circle of a flight attested to the intoxication of a dragonfly, the hopeful impulse of a scarab prey to the dream of scaling the sky. The turtle was running hither and yon. A white cat with phosphorescent eyes had leapt on to a gatepost and was crouching there as if pinned by an invisible arrow.

With what an immeasurable amour were the living beings earth and the air attentive! A purity was floating that I had never felt. It was in the design of the veins of leaves, the crystallization of drops of dew, the fluidity of the air penetrated by the presence of the rising sun. I understood that I was participating in a mystical mass celebrated by two creatures animated by the gift of expressing God, a mass for the usage of trees, insects and flowers—and perhaps also for the kneeling man, because the profound speech of the great sounds made by nature is addressed equally to everything that lives beneath the sky.

THE RETURN OF THE SUBLIME FRIENDS

It was a little later, when the sun had already appeared and the morning was already advanced, that I perceived an unaccustomed activity in the house. I had slept, without being able to remember at what moment I had lain down fully dressed on my bed. The window was still open. There was a great peace within me. But what were those sounds, those whisperings, those presences? I was breathing a different air than the day before.

I shouted "Antoinette!" but there was no response. Antoinette arrived early, prepared the coffee, made a simulacrum of order, and then went to the market. I thought that she had already gone. In that case I could not explain the animation of sorts that had reached me, and as the opposite of the sense of solitude.

I ran down the narrow staircase that connected my bedroom to the spacious room on the ground floor that was simultaneously the library, the dining room and the drawing room.

I saw immediately that the cutlery and bottles of the previous evening's dinner had disappeared. But I stopped, open-mouthed, on the steps, so surprised was I by the spectacle that struck my eyes.

I have scarcely formulated those words that I take account of their inexactitude. There was no spectacle, and in reality, I did not see anything. I was, however, witness to something extraordinary.

The books, which had disappeared without anyone taking them away, which had by means of I know not what inconceivable magic been removed from my sight, were back in place. They were offering themselves; they were splendid; they were displaying their striped spines and their labels, on which golden letters shone. And I saw, filling the room, coming from the garden, heading toward the books and disappearing into them, without my being able to explain the mystery of that union, the authors of the books, the philosophers and sages that I had neglected for long days.

In truth, I cannot say that I saw them. I am certain that, if I had finished descending the stairway, I would not have been able to touch them. No, I would not have seized Socrates' mantle, if I had had the audacity to make the gesture, before he was absorbed into the *Phaedo* bound in dark green. And yet they were there. They had come back. I saw Socrates' maroon wool mantle floating.

And they were slightly different. They were accessible. They no longer had the closed faces that were familiar to me; they were no longer similar to silent enigmas. I cannot explain either their manner of existence or the mystery of that presence, nor the relationship that united them with their books, the symbols of their thought, as they emerged from those books or reentered them, as people emerge from and reenter human dwellings. No, I can't explain it, but they were there.

In any case, what's the point of trying to explain it? Everything in life is a mystery. And the operation that consists of making a large plant emerge from a seed is much more astonishing than the presence in your house of long-dead wise men. Besides which, isn't the true miracle in the fact that thoughts that are vast and ungraspable, which embrace the stars, can be combined and condensed on small areas of paper and can, at will, spring forth, expand and embrace the stars again.

Thanks to those presence, certain things that I had not understood until then became clear. The resemblance of certain teachings given at intervals of thousands of centuries, in different parts of the world, were clarified by the resemblance of their authors. The distant Hindu who had written the Bhagavad Gita on sheets of bark with the tip of a reed, had almost the same features—a kind of family resemblance—with the monastic author of the *Imitation of Christ*. One had his hair in long braids and the other a tonsure, but both had in their features the same modesty, the detachment from all things that they taught as the shortest way to attain the divine world.

Jewish prophets passed as if under a door through the striped green spine of an enormous volume entitled *The Sacred Books of All Religions*. They had long hair. Some were haggard and their eyes were sparkling. They had a family resemblance with the philosopher Nietzsche. In his skeletal thinness, the Tibetan ascetic Milarepa was similar to various Christian ascetics. With similar frock-coats, Goethe and Carlyle had analogous silhouettes.

There were some who were exchanging winks, and at least had a certain malignity in common. They were making signs that they had deliberately employed in an abstract style in order not to be understood, and also to appear greater. Those winks were saying: *It is appropriate to dupe limited men slightly.*

And they were divided up into families. There were the desperate sages, authors of thoughts moving and icy at the same time, like Pascal and Marcus Aurelius. There were those who had enclosed themselves in a cosmogony of stone, like Lao Tsu, and smiling sages ready to accept ministerial posts, like Confucius. Descartes was an exception in carrying a sword and, in any case, perhaps because of that useless weapon, he did not seem much considered.

I was astonished to see them so numerous. But those who had not written were brought by the authors of books in which there was mention of them. Their thoughts were mingled intimately, and yet they retained their personal character.

I heard speech:

"I was only an adolescent," said Proclus, "when Minerva appeared to me to consecrate me to the spirit."

"I had the amity of angels, with whom I was able to converse when I pleased throughout my life," said Swedenborg, "and even now, I only have to call them..."

"The angels, who know better than me who has written the Divine Names and established the differences of the hierarchies," said Dionysius the Areopagite.

"Bah! Angels! Only the work counts," said a monk of short stature with myopic eyes. "Who can boast of having written, like me, forty quarto volumes?"

"I don't see them here," said a voice, ironically.

"It's an oversight. They've just been reprinted by the Carthusians."

"Whereas I can see *The Imitation of the Life of Poverty*."

"*The Response to the Forty Questions of the Soul*,"

"*The Tree of Life*."

"*The Man of Desire*."

"The *Ethics*."

"I'm wondering whether it's necessary to write books. I am the man who has been called the unknown superior, the man who came one night to instruct Tauler of the truth and disappeared without giving his name. It was me who interrupted Jacob Boehme, as a child, while he was nailing soles on shoes in order to announce the grandeur of his mission."[20]

And, saying these various things, they all disappeared. A bee starting flying around in the middle of the room. I felt a great serenity. The books were in their place, each with its spiritual promise. I touched them. I moved a few of them around. What joys they held enclosed! But the *Enneads* only had three volumes...

---

[20] In the chapter of *Magiciens et illuminés* translated in *The Angel of Lust*, Magre suggests that the person in question was Christian Rosenkreutz.

MADAME TOURNADIEU

"Did she at least apologize?" asked Madame Tournadieu. And as she posed that question, a crease furrowed her brow and she took on the appearance of an administrator of justice.

I replied that she had apologized by a note sent the following day, and that it was of no importance.

"To you! To do that to you! In your place...and note that she came to me almost bragging about it."

She made the gesture of cutting of a head with the back of her hand.

"And why? I ask you? To go strolling in the moonlight with your friend, the one who dresses badly. It's better to laugh about it."

Under the pretext of a slight threat of rain, Madame Tournadieu had taken me into a little drawing room full of cushions.

"It's here that I come to sit down to dream. Don't you think that there are certain natures that are a little, or very far, from being understood, like Christ?"

"What do you mean?"

"When I dream here all alone, it seems to me that, like Christ, I take all the sins of human beings upon me. I suffer for them. It depends on the days. When the evening is stormy, like this evening, I feel more keenly the evil that has been done. I'm not talking about bad actions directed against me. I always forgive. Such is my nature. I feel above all the harm done to others. Thus, for example, I find that Roseline's conduct has been unworthy."

Again, Madame Tournadieu made the gesture of cutting off a head.

"And I can see her game very well. Anyway, you can see it yourself. She wants to make that handsome fellow, that Grimaldi with whom she goes out, jealous. He's a handsome fellow but I believe him to be of very vulgar extraction. That's obvious at a glance. The jaw isn't deceptive as to the origin. In any case, what does it matter? Roseline will be punished."

The idea of an imprecise and vast punishment put a smile of triumph on Madame Tornadieu's face.

I was in haste to withdraw,

"I have to work," I had said, on coming in. I repeated it.

"Oh, how you work! I'm sure that you work too hard. Do you know what you need? I know what you need. You need a twin soul beside you. Oh, don't protest! I'm not talking about that vulgar companion that men have to take care of their hearth, washing and meals. I'm thinking about the exceptional creature that you need...a woman who will protect you from evil influences, who will prevent harm from reaching you, who will be a little like Jesus Christ. Well? Isn't that the companion you need?"

Madame Tornadieu's eyes were bright and slightly moist. She was looking at me intently, and I had no difficulty in divining that she believed that she was bringing to bear a magnetic force whose power she attributed to herself. One day, I had seen on her table beside her deck of cards books entitled *The Marvels of the Will, The Miracle of the Gaze* and *Power at a Distance*. I knew that Madame Tournadieu claimed to communicate with her sister in Paris without making use of the obsolete means of correspondence. She attributed a great authority to herself, which was only manifest in the invisible.

I was only thinking about the joy of being outside and walking alone under the pines. My eyelids fluttered and I took on, for a few seconds, the appearance of a weak man who might perhaps need to have a female Christ beside him. However, I reached the threshold in the midst of a bath of fluids.

"Thinkers like you need reflections and meditations to make decisions," said Madame Tournadieu, casting a melancholy glance at the cushions of her divan, like a general gazing at a useless army after a battle that has not been fought. "Yes, they're children, veritable children..."

I did in fact have a desire to start running, like a child.

"That large cloud is threatening. You'd do better to wait until all threat of rain has disappeared."

"That large cloud will certainly burst within five minutes. I'll try to get home before then."

THE AGRIPPA,
ALSO KNOWN AS THE EGROMUS

I had received a note from Monsieur Spéluque asking me to come and see him urgently. It concluded: *I have something admirable to show you.*

I felt remorse in his regard. I left for Fréjus immediately.

As soon as I was in his library, I saw his gaze light up, as it does when in the presence in the presence of someone to whom one is about to surprise with an unexpected revelation.

He got up from the seat he occupied behind his table, and could not prevent himself from gesticulating.

"Well, there it is!" he said, in a triumphant tone. "At least I know the dimension of the mystery that we were seeking the other day. At any rate, I have information on that subject."

I was seized by a fit of frankness. I was weary of playing the game of silence with him and making a semblance of understanding something of which I had no idea. I confessed to him that my decision to install myself in the locality did not come from a particular knowledge of an occult order. It was chance alone that had brought me. But since I had arrived I had been witness to certain inexplicable phenomena. I scarcely dared formulate the assertion that one evening, I had understood the language of animals. There was something abnormal, although I did not know what, connected to the influence of the area. I was incapable of explaining clearly what I meant. I merely sensed that there was a mystery, and I would be very glad to have the key to it.

Monsieur Spéluque looked at me for a long time in silence and I understood that he was wondering whether he was dealing with a wily individual, a stupid one, or a sincere one. Perhaps he concluded that I was all three. But how can one stop when one has composed in one's mind a thesis to which one attributes a character of brilliance?

"By chance! You're telling me that you came here by chance? How do you know? There is no chance. You're a link in a chain. You've promised me to attain the truth. But what's surprising is that we're alone, or almost alone, in seeing and marveling. That's the power of conformism. If Jesus Christ, preceded by an angel, were to walk through the streets of Fréjus, everyone would think it was a joke, and the next morning, those who said timidly that they had seen him would be treated as lunatics. Go tell them, then, that you once understood the language of animals, and that there are gnomides that come out of caves nearby!"

Monsieur Spéluque started to laugh with a sincere pleasure, for it is an agreeable sensation to understand what others cannot.

"No, we're not entirely alone in knowing. I've acquired the proof of it. There are people who have come, some moved by a desire to know, others for unknown motives. Do you recall a certain Guillard, a bad man, who was cross-eyed and whose body, on decomposing, gave of a sweet odor, as the bodies of saints sometimes do?"

Certainly I remembered. His house was not far from mine and I had gone there after his death.

"He was one of those who knew. The few objects that had belonged to him were sold at auction yesterday. I went to the sale room in Boudouris and I was able to acquire for next to nothing the book that you're about to see. But I was lucky. A man with a clean-shaven face, and who was also cross-eyed, appeared immediately afterwards. He had arrived late. He asked me in a low voice whether I was willing to cede the book to him. No matter what price, he told me. I refused, of course. But it's him who acquired the green bottle containing a minuscule dorsal spine. I tried to compete, but I understood that my fortune was insufficient. He tripled the bid every time. The entire audience was stupefied that a bone in a bottle could be valued at such a high price. He got the dorsal spine, which is perhaps that of a gnome, but I got the book, the Agrippa, also known as the Egromus.

Monsieur Spéluque had brought a key out of his waistcoat pocket, and he took out of a writing desk, as one takes a precious object, a book of rather poor appearance, the binding of which was shabby and which I would have been ashamed to have on show in the midst of mine.

"It's only a book of popular magic, an imitation of the Albertus Magnus with certain curious modifications. There's an almost complete dissertation on poisons. The harmful qualities of certain plants are described there, and the means of using them. There's a strange treatise on bird droppings and their properties. It's all annotated, with comments. That Guillard was certainly a bad man. His copy of the Agrippa wouldn't be of any interest if it hadn't had an inscription inside the cover."

Monsieur Spéluque handed me the open book, pointing at the inscription, and I read: *The entire region between a river called the Argens and the big rock over-*

looking Roquebrune, from the area that the sea covers to Mont Vinaigre, the top of Saint-Pilon and the grotto where   came to pray...

"It's a very precise determination!" exclaimed Monsieur Spéluque, joyfully. "The same one at which I had arrived. A few centuries ago, the sea still covered a part of the land outside Fréjus. Note—which is significant—that the author of those lines didn't dare write the name of Saint Honoratus And there's another note at the bottom of the page."

There were, in fact, a few words in half-effaced characters: *Decipher the things written on the carapaces of turtles that emerge from the Argens...*

"You see! Who could write on the carapaces of turtles except certain aquatic spirits?"

I remained perplexed. "But what does this delimitation signify?"

Monsieur Spéluque closed his book again, carefully. He made a resigned gesture.

"Know first that the influence of the earth isn't exercised everywhere in the same fashion There are effluvia—waves or radiations, if you wish, to use contemporary parlance—that act differently. And there are places that have a terrible privilege. The great natural laws are violated there. One can see an amaryllis emerge from the ground and develop in one night. The dead body of a wicked man can be embalmed. Perhaps the frequency of the vibrations is simply more rapid? In such a place, the evocation of the dead is easier, prayers have more chance of rising very high, because communication with the superior hierarchies operates more easily. And the power of evil is harnessed in the same proportion.

"Such places have been sacred throughout the ages: Delphi, Montségur, Lourdes. A force passes through them that humans do not know, and utilize haphazardly, some for good and some for evil. It's reported by the semi-historian Philostratus that Apollonius of Tyana hid talismans on these shores when he left the isles of Lérins, which were to serve for the spiritual development of future men. Apollonius would have belonged to those initiates of early times who had the future of the human race in view. They stored a spiritual force in certain magic stones that was to serve in the Dark Ages, when the spirit would be in danger, and they placed those receptacles of force in the most propitious places.

"What is the crucial point of the place where we are? The grotto of Saint Honoratus and Porcarius, the place where Saint Eleutherius lived with a crow and is presently known as the Parc Santa-Lucia, or the one where the Templars came to raise their headquarters between Saint-Raphael and the Valescure? Who can tell? The turtles that emerge from the Argens have hieroglyphs on their carapaces. Once a year, in December—that corresponds to an anniversary, no one knows of what—the tower of the Templars, which still subsists amid houses, is surrounded during the latter part of the night by a vague luminosity, to the extent that I've been able to perceive it from Fréjus.

"You'll be able to witness yourself, after the first hot day, a phenomenon that is produced very close you your house. Between that little house and the sea, about fifty meters away, alongside a small villa called 'Lacerta,' there's an enormous blossoming of wild plants of all sorts. Larches, laburnums, myrtles, lentisks and rosemary spring forth in such abundance that they form a vivacious thicket, perfumed and inaccessible. It's like a small-scale virgin forest.

"At the first sign of summer, enormous swarms of fireflies emerge therefrom—winged glow-worms that make a bouquet of luminous radiance. Certainly, it's not surprising to see fireflies illuminating the nights of hot countries, but this region is entirely deprived of them, except at that unique point. Everything that is marvelous is welcomed by denial or indifference. No one wants to see the light of the Templar tower or to be astonished by the presence of fireflies at Santa-Lucia."

Monsieur Spéluque stopped in order to meditate momentarily.

"Perhaps it's better thus. If there's a saint or a hero to whom a task has devolved, he will be able to discover the propitious place and, without being importuned by the blind, he'll come to wait where necessary for the descent of the divine force. That force is never lost, and expands so variously! It's sufficient for an ordinary man, well-intentioned but ordinary"—as he said that, Monsieur Spéluque's gaze was fixed on me in a wounding fashion—"to come to install himself where Eleutherius meditated, for him to understand what the animals around him are saying."

"Only for a few seconds."

"The time is irrelevant. The misfortune is that the force can serve any ends. The further we go, the more the number of those who aspire to elevate themselves spiritually decreases, and the wicked are increasingly numerous. Between the banks of the Argens to Saint-Pilon, I'm afraid there are a considerable number of them."

"I confess that I haven't noticed anything thus far."

"Evil doesn't allow itself to be known. It has a face like anyone else. When we talked about Monsieur de Lusignan, didn't you tell me that he seemed at first to be

214

simple and benevolent? But you also told me that he collected butterflies."

"Indeed."

"Believe me, it's necessary to mistrust a man who sticks a pin through a delicate body into which the creative spirit has put his concern for beauty. Even his daughter…but that doesn't concern me. The battle between good and evil takes place all over the world, but here it is exercised with more ardor. Where are the talismans of Apollonius? Will we ever know? The grotto of Saint Honoratus was one such place in the time when the saint lived there, and where his disciples came to listen to the murmur of his prayer in the rocks of the mountain. But every beneficent force has its counterpart. On looking in the direction of Roquebrune one night, I saw that the church formed a more obscure mass, like an accumulation of shadows. I sought the reason for that. I discovered that the church in question contains, in the part that is underground, in its foundations, certain statues of demons that were once an object of adoration for a Ligurian tribe that had consecrated itself to the evil forces. Many men of our day practice that worship in another form, and there are many more of them that people think."

I thought about the monastery above Roquebrune, the monk that had disappeared and the tree trunk that had taken on his resemblance.

Monsieur Spéluque had fallen silent and I got up to leave.

"In sum," I said, "if the laws of nature are overturned, if the waters of the Argens carry mysterious forces, if strange creatures live in our proximity, does the man who inclines to perfection in meditation and the study of the writings of masters have an advantage in pursuing that goal here rather than elsewhere?"

"A great advantage!" exclaimed Monsieur Spéluque, while traversing his garden in order to accompany me. "The man of whom you speak could go backwards, even return to the rank of the animal he once was..."

"Damn!"

"But he could go very high, very rapidly, by virtue of a grace that comes to him from the trees, the earth, the clouds, perhaps simply by virtue of a grace."

"But how to anticipate, to know?"

"There are annunciatory signs. The man who wants to see the signs only has to raise his head frequently, to look at the sky above him, especially at dusk. The nuances are more variable then, the vapors lighter. It's the moment when the gods have the greatest convenience to instruct humans by means of little tableaux, designs made with the clouds and errant luminosities. People don't think of seeking the signs; they can't decipher them. It's necessary to walk while looking at the sky."

THE EVENING OF PENTECOST

I remembered the words: "Something always happens on the evening of Pentecost."

Now, it was the evening of Pentecost. A letter arrived from Roseline. It was a child who brought it, and there was no reply. The letter was more of a note, for it only had a few words:

I shall wait for you this evening at nine o'clock under the large eucalyptus.

The large eucalyptus was a tree whose majesty we had often admired together, which was situated behind the park of Monsieur de Lusignan's property, not far from the little iron gate from which no one ever came out. The day was warm and fine; the evening promised to be admirable. How seductive and romantic that rendezvous was!

I had seen Roseline two or three times since the dinner to which she had not come, and with a common accord we had not mentioned it. She had made allusion two or three times to the intense migraines by which she was sometimes abruptly gripped and which rendered her incapable even of writing a note. I had nodded my head without sympathizing with the special fashion of that affliction. We had resumed our relationship at the point where it was before the evening on the little beach.

It is a great verity that any pleasure that is withdrawn from us becomes infinitely greater by virtue of the mirage of the imagination. Perhaps it is only satisfaction that can reckon with the attraction of an unknown pleasure.

Under the large eucalyptus! That place might have been chosen because of the proximity of the park and the facility of going back if I were not at the rendezvous. But Roseline was quite sure that I would come. It might have been chosen because of the symbolic character that the eucalyptus had acquired in our conversations. We had said several times that the shade of the tree and its situation in the landscape were marvelously suited to an amorous rendezvous. We had accompanied those words with gazes and silly smiles that implied in sentimental symbolism that one would like to be invited to that rendezvous oneself.

Then too, the relationship of two individuals forms a mysterious curve that one might trace as precisely as the trajectory that a river follows. The river makes detours; there are bridges thrown over it; it sometimes turns back and can sometimes have a subterranean course and no longer be visible. Now I sensed that the sea was, in this case, in the shade of the old eucalyptus, and that the river must flow into it there.

I did not draw any vanity from it. I knew that the disappointment caused by young Grimaldi and the appetite for revenge were the principal causes of the rendezvous under the eucalyptus. But there is an entire category of events that are such that one does not want to know the causes, and does not linger over examining them.

The arrival of the child bearing the note had not caused my any joy, and my first thought was not to go to the rendezvous, as was my second. It was with the approach of evening, when the wind caused a few pine-needles to fall and plucked petals from the rose-bushes surrounding the well that the third thought surged forth. I wonder whether it was not mingled with some hypocrisy.

It said: *If I don't go to the rendezvous, I won't know whether Roseline went to it herself. If neither of us is there, we'll be in the same situation tomorrow. Whereas, if I go out at nine o'clock and make sure from distance whether she's there, and then turn back without going any closer, I'll be settled in my own mind. I'll have seen the temptation and I'll have vanquished it.*

For it was necessary to vanquish the temptation. Temptation never dies. One can triumph over it, but not suppress it. It remains crouching in a secret corner of the soul. An abrupt renunciation in the wake of a chagrin does not have the range that one accords it, because of that sort of immortality of desire. Perhaps there is a moment when the love of the spirit ends up triumphing definitively over the attraction of the form, but when does that moment arrive?

The evening was increasingly warm and laden with the effluvia of spring. A precocious cicada had given a warning to the world, announcing that thousands of cicadas would soon be wandering in the pines. Then it had fallen silent, or cicadas need a great deal of sleep, like certain humans, and a rule of their species causes that sleep to begin at dusk. Certain perfumes, which had been jealousy kept in reserve by the flowers, were suddenly delivered, emerging from partly-opened blooms. But there was no absolute agreement. There are flowers, like certain convolvulus, of which I could see the rich colors open from my window, which close again as soon as darkness falls. Fortunately, faithful mirabilis were growing not far from the convolvulus, which reared up and opened as the convolvulus closed.

Is there not an equilibrium in us, I thought, *analogous to the one there is in that garden? As certain pleasures disappear, are they not replaced by others?*

And I darted a reassured glance at my books, which, attained by the final gleam of the setting sun, caused their gilt to shine.

Antoinette had abruptly decreed that morning that it was necessary not to waste four bottles of champagne.

"Monsieur will drink them all himself. That will fortify him."

And she had taken it upon herself to uncork one, in order to incite me to drink.

The mystery of certain wines is that they give birth to joy in the soul of the person who drinks them. But it is necessary that there should be a predisposition to joy, a seed susceptible of development. If there is a seed of sorrow, that is what receives an aliment and develops. There was in me a seed of desire, and I felt its living force growing rapidly.

"This wine is excellent," I said aloud, as if I were taking the invisible guests of my house as witnesses.

And I sensed at the same time that desire is accompanied by a craving for joy.

I got up, made a circuit of the table two or three times, and sat down again.

"Did they drink wine?" I said, again aloud, looking at my books.

Why not? The Greeks entertained the highest intellectual speculations during banquets. Plato did not think of branding Alcibiades as a drunkard. But the sages of India were all ascetics. If the Christian mystics, at least those who were in monasteries, followed the rules of their Orders, they drank wine, for the majority of Orders authorized wine. Goethe, Swedenborg and many others participated in dinners in the houses of kings, and the wine must have been abundant and excellent.

"Yes, they drank wine," I said, once again aloud.

A certain warmth expanded within me, obliging me to go out into the garden, and I said, but in a low voice: "It's necessary to fear everything that diminishes the clarity of the mind."

Time passed. What should I do? The clarity of my mind was slightly diminished. It was simply necessary to go to the rendezvous. One attached too much importance to things. One reasoned too much. It was appropriate to take from day to day the pleasure that life brought you. And then if one believed in Providence, was it not an insult to refuse what it gave you?

I went back inside to get my hat. But ought I to take my hat? No, I would go bare-headed. Did Pierre de Grimaldi wear a hat? Did Porcastre? I put the hat down with my right hand while my left hand felt the thickness of my hair, and I experienced a sentiment of surprise on observing how thin that thickness was. I thought of the ease with which I had caught colds for some years. I put the hat on my head and emptied the final glass of the bottle of champagne.

As I closed the garden gate behind me a problem occurred to me. For how many years, exactly, had I had that facility for catching cold that I had not had before? For colds had once been an unknown malady for me. It was about five or six years that they had been putting in a regular appearance. Perhaps seven. That problem was absurd and futile. Why had it cropped up while I was walking along a road bordered to the right by rosemary and mimosas? But that problem drew others after it. There were holes in my jaw that corresponded to absent teeth. I got out of breath when I ran. Certain heartbeats caused me anxiety. And the vegetation in the nose and ears about which the doctor to whom I had manifested my astonishment had said: "It's simply a sign of age."

He had said "age" in order not to say "old age." But I could pronounce the phrase, especially in the solitude of the road where I could only be overheard by the trees. And I articulated, aloud, uniquely for the trees that were around me: "A sign of old age."

For the road was now bordered by trees of various species. I passed under a cedar, and then there were pines, cork-oaks and other trees whose names I did not know. And they were all old. And on considering them, at that moment, I perceived with certainty that they bore within them a great resignation on the subject of time. Incessantly occupied in extracting life from the earth, they were aware of the ineluctable advent of death, and doubtless they were delivering themselves to a mysterious labor of preparation, of which I knew nothing.

But as for me, who believed myself to be placed on a more elevated degree than those taciturn prisoners of terrestrial matter, what was my preparation for death? What was I even doing for the benefit of the last years of my life? I knew that the last part of a man's life ought to be devoted to reaping what he has sown, transforming his past experiences into wisdom. Thus, having meditated on destiny, the best of humanity had prescribed. There was a time when it was necessary to renounce the pursuit of pleasure, in order in order devote oneself to the amelioration of the soul.

And the order of things, in its omnipotence, gave precise warnings that the time had come. The teeth broke. The hair turned white with an abrupt ardor. One sensed the dolor of unknown organs. It was like a clock chiming. Woe betide the man who made a semblance of not hearing it! Nothing happened to him. He continued to pursue pleasure. There was no visible punishment. No one chastised him. But there were the effects of ignorance and satisfied pleasure that one had allowed to develop in oneself, and those ineluctable effects were exercised on the man after death.

I knew that all those who had scrutinized the problem were in accord. It was necessary to renounce, to purify oneself, to try to understand. It was necessary to prepare to live in a world where forms have another appearance and where souls are naked. I knew that. I had repeated it to myself a hundred times. And yet, I was hastening along the road. I had just looked at my watch feverishly. I was afraid of being late.

I was not late. I had arrived at the place where the road bends and I suddenly saw the large eucalyptus, the wall of the park, and the little iron door. One might have thought that the eucalyptus had moved aside the bushes and smaller trees that evening in order to enjoy a more solitary reverie. And at the same moment, I saw the little iron door open, and I saw Roseline appear.

I had stopped, and at the place where I was, she could not see me. She darted a circular glance around the empty space around the old tree, and began to walk around it slowly.

In the gloom, I could only distinguish an oval face amid the blue silk of a headscarf, a supple white form in which the robe scarcely masked the movement of life. Ws it the charm of the solitary space, the fused light of the vanished day still trailing here and there? She had never seemed so delightful to me. In that romantic landscape she incarnated the heroines of whom I had once dreamed, the attraction of youth and amour. And she attracted it all the more because I could only perceive, alongside the whiteness of the eucalyptus, and uncertain and floating silhouette, like the idea that one has of beauty.

Then a force pulled me backwards. Without my being conscious that the movement had been determined
by my will, I took a few steps silently along the road I
had already traveled. Did that force issue from the
depths of myself, or is it true, as so many souls secretly
believe, that we are protected by certain invisible spirits
that whisper to us, when the time comes, decisions that
we obey without being able to explain their origin?

It was necessary for me to go back. No hesitation
was possible. It was an order that came from I know not
where.

I went back slowly, gripped by a great melancholy.

I am breaking the last link with the past. Now, I will
not recommence again the comedy of pleasure to which
the name of amour is given, with its infantile play-
acting, its hopes, and its deceptive and charming joys.
That pleasure I am losing, and it is suddenly clad in an
almost heart-rending attraction. Perhaps that pleasure
was puerile, and was only based on illusions, but I shall
not find it again, either in this life or another. My hair
will continue to thin, my features will hollow out, my
shoulders will droop. I shall walk with my head slightly
forwards, like all those for whom I once felt sorry, with
a pity mingled with scorn, because I saw the visible appearances of old age in them. Never again will I find the
quality of active delight of the man who wakes up in the
morning with the assurance that he will see during the
day a woman whom he thinks he loves. Never again will
I feel the intoxication of the exchanged gaze, the
squeezed hand of the creature who leans over in a
movement of abandonment.

The road climbed a brief slope and then descended
again. From the top of that slope one could see behind,
through an opening in the trees, the place where the large

eucalyptus was. The tree was imprinted with serenity and it seemed, with its open arms, in the tranquil night, to be invoking the gods appropriate to it.

Beside it, similarly white and leaning lightly against its wood, Roseline was standing. She seemed fluid, devoid of weight. At that distance, she was not distinguishable from another woman. She was a woman of the past, the symbol of all the women I had known, those I remembered and those I had forgotten. How charming her silhouette was, even from afar!

She was youth, my youth, which was no more than a shape, a distant form that was about to disappear into the shadow of the evening, and which no human or divine power could return to me, of which no Orpheus could go in search in the Underworld, which no Christ could resurrect.

Beauty, youth, you were under the eucalyptus, and I had to descend on the other side, along a slope where the pines were denser and the darkness thicker!

O my God, I am offering that which I loved the most to the invisible holocaust that demands from humans, without reason, the sacrifice of what is most dear to them.

The darkness did not appear to me to be thicker as I went down again in the midst of the densely-packed pines, and immediately, I had the sentiment that I was marching toward a new goal. Where I was going, I would not be alone. I was awaited.

There is a law of compensation that tends to return in another form that which has been lost. Beauty! Youth! But the spirit is rejuvenated eternally, if one has the will to do it. And there is no limit to the time to enjoy beauty. I had extracted myself from what is known as an amorous rendezvous, but I had another rendezvous in which there was no feminine face, no kiss, no ardor of the blood, where one could contemplate the radiant beauty of ideas.

I started walking rapidly. How much time I had lost! While walking, I had made a detour in order to follow a path from which the sea was visible. And suddenly, before me, there as a rapid circle of light, and then another. It was a flying spark, a little animate lamp. And I remembered the fireflies that Monsieur Spéluque had mentioned. They were multiplying around me. Some were skimming the ground, others were lost in the sky. All of them were, in fact, emerging from a dense thicket of wild bushes, a bouquet of mingled plants that I was skirting.

Was it the sudden warmth of the evening, the first burning breath of summer that was making the fireflies emerge in such large numbers, or was I seeing an intention of destiny, which was suddenly illuminating that corner of the world for me? Was not the evening of Pentecost the evening of the descent of the Spirit?

The path described a circle and came back toward my house. I perceived it with its tilted hat and its appearance of not standing upright. By virtue of a caprice of the wind, the agile flying insects seemed to be gathered around it. It was surrounded by a circle of living light, luminous droplets that were rising and falling, forming a spray and dispersing. And those flying wings seemed to be tracing signs in the blue of the sky. They were words in the language of the gods, which I did not understand, but which it was my prerogative to discover.

I traversed the shadow of the old pine at a rapid pace. I was in haste to return to the room where the books were.

And I thought that never, even in the most beautiful days of my twentieth year, had any amorous rendezvous procured me such a pure and profound pleasure.

THE DARK SIDE OF SOULS

THE DARK SIDE OF SOULS

A man sitting under his lamp in the evening can draw a great deal of consolation from stories of the lives of superior men. By searching here and there in those stories he can cause to spring forth, as in a faded mirror, certain lost reflections of great souls.

If one has just anxieties about immanent justice and divine bounty, one is marvelously comforted by the sentiment that others have experienced those anxieties. The solutions they found were always insufficient and sometimes puerile, but what does it matter? One feels that one is joined by a community of preoccupations to a long chain of anxious men, and that is sufficient to ease the anxiety, or to give it a color of consolatory nobility, thanks to an indisputable antiquity. One is a little like those vain men who are proud to have ancestors who went to the crusades. One is proud of being part of a lineage that has sought Providence and has not found it, but has made other discoveries relative to the soul and the beauty of the world.

By studying the lives of superior men one finds that it is impossible to encounter in the relations of modern life, whatever effort one makes, examples of true benevolence, sadness for philosophical causes and high aspirations. But one is interested to observe that all great souls have a dark side. At some point they touch evil. One might think each has a black thread that binds him. And perhaps that is true, and it is because of that bond that those great souls are among us instead of being elsewhere. If they had broken it they would have disappeared from the earth and humankind would have had no further knowledge of them.

To be sure, it would be better, by virtue of a profound study of a life, to have a response to all the problems one has posed for oneself; but the most impassioning problems can only be resolved by oneself.

In the weaknesses of great men, in their contradictions, even in their cowardice, one sees a trace of humanity that is more moving than an excessively inaccessible grandeur.

When one has followed a great many of those beings who were believed to be perfect, when one has sat under the portals of philosophers, when one has marched alongside the cypresses with the sages, in the ineluctable dark side by which they are followed, one perceives that intellectual thought, even when it emanates from the highest genius, does not lead to anything much. There is a circle in which some go in one direction and others in the inverse direction: the sterile circle of reason. When one has gone around it several times, one has neither more truth nor more hope.

Only the mystics attain the spiritual reality with the fiery jet of their desire. They alone are instructive. And as one is tempted to imitate those who stimulate your admiration, one cannot help wondering what one can do to become a mystic—and that question is itself a portal to a new path.

Plato wanted to burn the books of Democritus that he had in his possession, in the hope of annihilating that philosopher's work. It was necessary for two Pythagoreans who were present to represent to him that he would gain nothing, those works already being too widespread. He never named Democritus in his writings. Democritus was, however, the philosopher he should have cited most abundantly, in view of the fact that it was from him that he drew most frequently.

Diogenes hid a great bitterness under a philosophical bonhomie. The barrel was only a symbol of his affectation of simplicity. One day, at a dinner at which he was eating and drinking abundantly, he saw that Plato was contenting himself with olives. He almost had a fit of rage.

Aristotle, the substance of the thought of the Middle Ages, sustained philosophy and science through all the centuries that it is permitted to us to recapitulate, with an extraordinary pettiness of the soul. He took advantage of the old age of his master, Plato, to supplant him in the Academy of Athens. Throughout his life he sought important positions and obtained that of Preceptor of Alexandria. He mingled, by virtue of ambition, in all the quarrels of the Greek states. The historian Arrian accuses him of being one of those who poisoned Alexander. He was a pharmacist and had a great knowledge of poisons. His body had an inexplicable affinity with oil. He took baths in oil, which he then sold on to his clients, and even during the day, it was necessary that he had on his stomach a leather purse containing warm oil.

Socrates was too good a citizen. When civic virtues attain a certain exaggeration, they lower a man's grandeur. The Athenians resolved one day, at the instigation of a warrior demagogue named Cleon, to take possession of the city of Amphipolis. There was then a pacifist party in Athens composed of sensate and just men. Socrates was not a member of that party. He was one of those who went to lay siege to Amphipolis. The inhabitants of that city, who were defending their liberty, defeated the Athenians. Socrates showed great courage, fighting hand to hand during the rout, taking no account of the fact that he was defending a bad cause. He showed the virtue of courage that one sees in history shared by millions of bellicose men, but is that what one has the right to demand of such a great sage? And is not courage, practiced thus, an immense diminution of veritable human virtue?

The seven sages of Greece! When those syllables resonate, one has an impression as profound as when one hears mention of the Rishis of India, the first initiators of humankind. There is a vague atmosphere of the marvelous around them. Now, we have a few details of the lives of those seven sages. Chilon, according to an inscription at the base of his statue, was the greatest of them. He was passionate about physical exercise, and also an excellent father. He died of joy on learning that his son had come first in a sporting contest.

Paternity and sport—is that really what one demands of an ideal type of humanity?

THE MEASURE OF SINCERITY

In what measure have those who have preached detachment been detached? Have those who have informed others of the reasons why humans ought to be consoled had an interior consolation themselves? And did that consolation came from a knowledge greater than the one they revealed in their writings for some reason of vanity, but to which they made some chosen disciple party? For there are moments of intimacy in which the noblest souls are invited by ambient influences of temperature and light to a sincerity and an absolute self abandonment.

Fortunate was the man who was able to chat familiarly with the Buddha when, in the evening, in the shade of a fig tree, after having taken the bowl of rice indispensable to the nourishment of the body, he forgot that life is dolor in order to contemplate the beauty of the stars.

Fortunate was the man who was a passenger on the same ship that brought Plato to Sicily and was able, when the rocks of Leucadia and Cephalonia appeared, to hear from his mouth before the calm sea the verities that could only be transmitted in speech!

But it is also possible that superior men flattered themselves with a peace that they did not possess in reality. Did they not hide, sometimes, in order to shed secret tears? How do we know whether the austere faces that we admire and want to take for an example were not masks, engraved every day for the naïve delight of disciples? Those sages, having once put their pride in the tranquility of their soul, were firmly obliged to defend that appearance until death, and against death.

It is the history of the sincerity of the masters of thought that it is necessary to believe. But we possess millions of details about men of action and almost none about philosophers or saints. For example, everything has been said about Napoléon and the Maréchals of the Empire, great killers of men and master horsemen, but we are not documented on the manner of death those who spent their lives meditating the problem of human destiny.

Perhaps it is better thus. The serenity of the final hour must be very difficult to attain and it is not certain that it is the wisest and the best-informed about the afterlife who are the most courageous.

But is it really a question of courage?

I was told recently that the man who was known as the master Philippe de Lyon,[21] had retained after his death a face filled with anguish. Madame D., the author of remarkable works on the powers of the spirit and spiritualization of beings, spent the last fortnight of her life crying "Help!" and struggling against invisible forces by which she thought she was being attacked. It is, however, of her, out of all the people I have known in France, that I would have expected the most serene end.[22]

Have those who are believed to be the wisest, by virtue of a wisdom long practiced, repressed desires that

[21] The healer and seer born Philippe Anthelme Nizier (1849-1905), who ran a school of "magnetism" in Lyon in his later years.
[22] Some readers might have assumed that "Madame D" refers to the famous English medium Elizabeth Hope (1855-1919), who used the pseudonym Madame d'Esperance, and held séances all over Europe, but Magre's earnest interest in spiritualism could not have preceded her death by very long. It is, in any case, unclear why he does not spell out the name in full.

will reappear at the last moment? Or, what is more disquieting to think, are they the most clairvoyant, and have they glimpsed something that frightens them? One might think that they were more apt than others to discover a world that they had so often scrutinized. But it is necessary to remember that many ordinary people have acquired in death a revelatory calm, an expression a thousand times more eloquent than any words, the reflection of a sudden, moving and blissful vision.

THE BRONZE SANDALS OF EMPEDOCLES

Austere, clad in white, slightly annoyed and threatening because of the possible projection of that annoyance, the philosophers of antiquity stand in the background of our intellectual life. One has more respect for them than love, and they are all Greeks, even when they are Romans or Sicilians.

Those philosophers have marched at my side during courses at school, they have accompanied me in life, they have been present in hotel rooms, and on promenades at the seaside. They had in their eyes the particular deadness that the gazes of busts have, and there loose robes contained the promise of an edifying and superior life. I knew that it would be necessary one day to put them in their place in definite centuries and that I would draw comfort from their grandeur of soul.

In fact, it is their weaknesses that are more comforting. When one is weighed down by certain faults and the difficulty that human nature has in modifying itself, one is satisfied and reassured to observe that the truly great men, indisputable models of humanity, have possessed faults to a high degree.

Empedocles of Agrigentum was one of the greatest luminaries of those immense and vague times that are known as antiquity. It is necessary to remark and be astonished by the fact that there was one century of history in which prodigious minds appeared almost at the same time, and that those minds were scattered here and there, from one end of the earth to the other, as if a seed had been thrown with a determined purpose. There were Lao-Tsu and Confucius in China, the Buddha in India,

Pythagoras and then Socrates, Plato and Empedocles in the Mediterranean lands. The idea of a sowing with a determined but unknown purpose, of a vast and spiritual plan, is consoling to the highest degree and it is necessary to rejoice in seeing the traces of it.

Agrigentum was then a great city, the number of whose inhabitants is estimated at a million, although that figure must be very approximate. Empedocles possessed one of the largest fortunes in Sicily and in Agrigentum he was simultaneously a popular tribune, high priest, engineer, physician, healer, poet, scholar, naturalist and philosopher. He made laws favorable to the people and had the wisdom to exercise some oppression on the rich. He had the greater wisdom of refusing royalty when it was offered to him, but he did not refuse a kind of triumphal ceremony in his honor with a procession, a glorification of his person, and divine honors. Having refused to be a king, he accepted to be a god.

It seems from what was written but him and what remains of his poems that he was animated by the highest form of intellectual pride. The higher one rises on one scale, the lower one descends on another.

To that pride was added an immoderate love of the splendor of costumes. All those who have depicted him have mentioned a gold headband, a crimson robe and specially, bronze sandals. That last detail has always astonished me. Marcel Schwob, in a portrait that he made of Empedocles, adds that those sandals came from Lakonia, without my being able to discover where he obtained the detail of that origin.[23] It is true that the writ-

---

[23] The title of the book in which Marcel Schwob included his "biography" of Empedocles, *Vies imaginaires* [Imaginary Lives] (1896) gives a strong clue as to the fanciful origin of

er was very well-informed relative to feet, since, talking about Panthea, who was resuscitated by Empedocles, he says that she wore sandals of which even the soles were perfumed.

That a great mind like Empedocles had such a great exterior vanity is what causes surprise. Thus, at the summit of philosophical superiority, one can still wear a band of gold around one's head! One immediately thinks of the mysterious individual whom occultists place at the summit of the human hierarchy and who was known by the name of the Comte de Saint-Germain.

In what is known of his life he is seen occupied in the handling and transformations of jewels. He is represented going to Louis XIV's feasts in elegant costumes with his hands covered in rings. One clairvoyant perceiving, or claiming to perceive by clairvoyance, a meeting of the Agartha[24] in a solitary place in the Himalaya, saw the Comte de Saint-Germain several times with his rings, clad in multicolored uniforms that were always different.

Human perfection can therefore be obtained while retaining certain great faults, a certain paltry pettiness. Contradictions are in our nature, and we know that the highest artistic or intellectual faculty can be coupled with inferior sentiments. Francis Bacon, whose thought

---

the detail—the comment is ironically disingenuous, as are many others in this set of essays.

[24] Agartha was the name attributed by the French occultist Alexandre Saint-Yves d'Alveydre to a subterranean city of wise men, which he located beneath Tibet. Madame Blavatsky appropriated the idea as a core element of her esoteric doctrine, making Agartha the location of the White Lodge, whose members were the custodians of all esoteric earthly wisdom— hence Magre's use of the definite article.

contributed to the formation of the English intellect as we know it, profited from his position as Lord Chancellor to take bribes, making a commerce of justice, enriching himself by all means, and his vanity was such that at the moment of his death he wrote: *I bequeath my name to the centuries to come and foreign nations*. There would be, at least in the foreign nations, a few people who would refuse that legacy, estimating that, in the balance in which everyone secretly weighs values, a great creative intelligence does not compensate for injustice and cupidity.

What has been transmitted to us regarding the death of Empedocles is eminently consoling. Nothing authorizes us to doubt the testimony of Diogenes Laertius. The more mediocre a historian is, the more reason one has to believe him truthful.

Having woken Panthea, the woman with the perfumed soles, from a sort of catalepsy, Empedocles held a banquet in his own honor, to celebrate his medical success. That, at least, was the pretext, for the banquet was in his mind a farewell feast. The physician Pausanius, who was present, says that about eighty people were there. When the meal was over, the guests dispersed. Some went home, while others went to chat in the nearby woods. Empedocles, Pausanius remarks, remained alone at the table. Was that by virtue of an ultimate regret for what he was about to abandon? Eventually, he went to his room, but the next day, his guests were astonished not to find him. They searched for him in vain; there was no trace of him.

A servant then recalled that during the night he had heard a voice outside the house calling "Empedocles!" He had looked out of the window and had perceived a light, which did not make much impression on him at the time, but which he subsequently qualified as supernatural and celestial. Legend, which could not forget the importance of the philosopher's bronze sandal, subsequently declared that Etna had rejected that metal sandal and deduced that Empedocles had thrown himself into Etna in order to be consumed therein.

It is more plausible to think that Empedocles, who was then sixty-four years old, thought that the time had come to withdraw from life in order to escape his obligations. In order not to be importuned, he had not confided his place of retreat to anyone. Nevertheless, a conductor of horses or the owner of a fishing-boat must have had a rendezvous with him on the night of his flight. It was him who came with his lantern to summon him for the departure and it was that modest light that the servant who was not asleep perceived.

In India it is prescribed that every man should spend the final years of his life in meditation far from society. That is a practical rule, a rule of both wisdom and elementary prudence, which only sages obey. They put down the gold band then, as well as the crimson robe, and even the bronze sandals.

Every time that a man obeys that rule, one knows that he has understood the necessity of detachment and preparation for death, and that he has entered into the chain of those who can be taken as examples. Whatever their faults might have been, one can think that they submitted them to the purgation of the purifying flame that is solitude.

THE EXAGGERATION OF THE BUDDHA

The Buddha exaggerated, either to influence people by mans of an enormous affirmation or because what he affirmed was imposed upon him by a special temperament and the particular conditions of his education.

It is reported that his father, the king—the king of a petty kingdom—having doubtless recognized in him a particularly keen sensitivity, wanted to prevent him receiving the dolorous shock given by the sight of illness and that of death. He succeeded in that, says legendary history, and that is not implausible.

One can picture that patriarchal king of the small city of Kapilavastu, in the foothills of the Nepalese mountains, as a benevolent landowner having within the enclosure of his vast estates his herdsmen, his flocks, his temples with their Brahmins and his workshops with their carpenters and weavers.

Young Siddharta has shown since childhood and immoderate taste for philosophy. He is charming and loved by everyone. His father has spread the word to his friends, his wives and his servants. They must spare his exceedingly sensitive son any dolorous image and any painful emotion. His father's gardens are vast and he scarcely leaves them. If he goes out, it is on horseback, surrounded by a numerous company who defend him from any exterior contact. His exclusive taste for things of the mind, as much as the paternal precautions, have isolated him from the true reality of the world. Even in our modern times, one sometimes sees certain young men whose education has kept them ignorant of life for a long time.

Now, he decides privately one day that that ignorance has lasted long enough. He thinks that he has remained enclosed in pure ideological speculation for too
long. He wants to have direct experience of the world,
and he begins with an excursion incognito in the back
streets of the city, those of which he has heard vague
mention as ill-famed and inhabited by a wretched popu-
lation.

He knows about poverty, but only from a theoreti-
cal viewpoint. He must only have seen stylized beggars
and decorative corpses. Now, abruptly, he has before his
eyes a pestilential beggar and a real dead man, clad in
the ugliness of miserable death. He suffers a shock, and
that shock engenders in his philosophical conceptions
the prodigious exaggeration of despair that will tempt
souls in the course of the centuries-for it is the same with
doctrines as with material facts. They need, in order to
be veridical and seductive, to be magnified enormously,
to the point of being beyond nature, so great is human
puerility.

Life is dolor, the Buddha has said. Now, it is not entirely that. In making up the portion of life that is neither
wellbeing nor dolor, which is neutral, one can say that,
for the most part, it is two-thirds dolor and one third joy.
The joy is in the same proportion as fine weather in the
greater part of the world. The third of joy is considered
by the great majority of people as a sufficient justifica-
tion for the fact of existence. In fact, a smaller proportion would still be sufficient for the majority.

But the Buddha in his negative determination, goes
further. He affirms that all joy is vain because, the word
being in a perpetual transformation, no joy is durable.
He does not take account of the fact that many joys are
joys precisely because of that quality of rapid disappear-

ance. To be sure, one would like to retain and prolong them, but a large number would be changed into bleak ennui by duration and prolongation.

His argument becomes more solid and invites reflection when he considers joy as essentially deplorable because it is an element of attachment to existence. It is evidently to that question that the greatest human deliberation ought to be devoted. Pleasure, even issued from the most legitimate affection, engenders the desire for revivification, in order to recommence. We bind ourselves to matter by our love of forms. That love causes us to rotate in the wheel of new existences. For the miserable portion of joy on which we can count, we deprive ourselves of the blissful state of Nirvana—a blissful state only susceptible of attainment by those who are already spiritualized.

Thus Buddhism, which is the world religion that counts the most adherents, has conquered its faithful by offering them as an ultimate recompense something that is incomprehensible for them.

In fact, a promise equally mysterious for ordinary people was made by Jesus when he offered his father's kingdom as an ideal goal. On that subject I remember a significant remark made to me in my childhood by a comrade older than me: "I wouldn't want to go to Paradise, because one doesn't enjoy anything there except the presence of God."

That presence is the equivalent of Nirvana. The Buddha did not judge it necessary to disguise the divine effusion of the spirit by means of the image of a powerful and paternal individual. That doubtless comes from the fact that he was addressing himself to people more cultivated than Jesus' auditors. But what did the immense mass of his believers think when they knew that it was necessary to renounce the portion of worldly joy for that Nirvana difficult to imagine?

Promises of an incomprehensible order have more attraction than the most desirable of known things, and the greatest influence on people is obtained by mystery.

The Buddha promised the Nirvana of which he knew via the experience of reality. Nirvana is the elevation of consciousness to the highest power. In order not to be afraid of that elevation, and even to grasp its extent, it is necessary to have risen very high already.

THE GARDENS OF EPICURUS

The biographers of Epicurus report with admiration that he freed by his testament the philosopher Mus, who was his slave as well as his disciple. That is more a sign of an immoderate liking for possession, for he need not have waited until his death to free him. He spent his days with him, he was on an equal footing in discussion, but he nevertheless maintained him in slavery for as long as possible! And he made a profession of amity as the most precious thing of all!

What has contributed most to the glory of Epicurus is the idea that he had of teaching philosophy in beautiful gardens near Athens. He had founded a little community of which he was the master, the members of which, especially those who were slaves, labored to maintain the gardens and render life mutually agreeable. Doubtless poor Mus accomplished a heavier labor than the others.

Nothing is made to be more rapidly popular than the fundamental principle of his teaching: It is necessary to spend life as agreeably as possible. There is a narrow relationship between wisdom and happiness. It is appropriate to be happy, by means of a calm and virtuous life, without occupying oneself with what happens after death. He thought, moreover, that nothing happened. According to him, the soul was composed of round and light atoms; it lost on dying its properties of roundness and lightness.

The amicable phalanstery founded by Epicurus included women, some of whom had very free mores, so his enemies did not fail to say that his gardens were witness on certain evenings to scandalous scenes. Everything depends on the idea one has of scandal. He has also been accused of delivering himself to inordinate excesses of nourishment, but a letter survives of his in which he solicits a consignment of cheese in order, he says, to add it to his bread and "finally" have a good meal.

"I am an Epicurean," all those have said throughout the ages who put pleasure above everything else but nevertheless want to give themselves a certain philosophical gloss.

Epicurus was less of an Epicurean than his disciples, because he obtained his principal pleasure in the search for the secret of things. That research caused him to write a large number of books in which he intercalated numerous passages from other philosophers, while neglecting to indicate that they were quotations.

The gardens of Epicurus are more immortal than the philosopher himself. The gardens, with their trees and their amicable benevolence, are extraordinary useful to humans. Unfortunately, the names of the species that grew around the philosopher's house have not been preserved. They must not have included eucalypti. Epicurus would have been penetrated by their influence merely by virtue of the perfume of their bark, and he would have discovered a less limited horizon for human destiny.

THE BEARD OF EPICTETUS

It is surprising, and perhaps consoling, to think that certain men have been able to lead a life exempt from desires and approaching perfection without any hope of future life and happiness after death. It is consoling and disappointing at the same time, but every disappointment bears within it a hidden consolation. It is admirable that human nature has been able to attain such a high degree of disinterest, for one can hope to equal it; but one is afflicted that sages who have scrutinized the problem of the afterlife throughout their lives have not been able to find sufficient certainty to support the legitimate hope of life after death. Is it the case, therefore, that those sages had glimpsed nothing n the course of all their research?

What a great name is that of Epictetus, and how little the average educated man knows about his existence! He was a slave, poor and deformed. Almost as the same time as him, Marcus Aurelius lived, who was sufficiently well-made physically, an emperor who enjoyed almost unlimited material power. Each of them has only left as a valuable trace one small volume of moral thoughts.

Often, sitting beneath one's lamp, thinking about the infinitesimal capacity one possesses of acting upon one's peers, one says to oneself that if, by some miraculous change of fortune, one suddenly enjoyed supreme power, one would transform humankind. Marcus Aurelius, who attained one of the highest summits of human wisdom was an emperor, and he changed nothing materially; his greatest action was exercised unknown to him, by the book in which he expressed his good intention and his resignation to the law.

Why does the poverty of Epictetus please me? It is similarly very agreeable to me to think that Ammonius Saccas, the founder of the Alexandrian school, the master of Plotinus, was socially a simple street-porter, a carrier of bags. Epictetus was poor and wanted to remain so. History does not say whether he had opportunities to make a fortune and rejected them scornfully, but I am pleased to suppose so. Thus, I am quite sure that a man has led a life absolutely exempt from desires and has found compensation in his solitary thoughts.

Epictetus lived in one of the suburbs of Nicopolis in Epirus, in a little house that had no door. That absence of a door entails a disdain for cold. Nor did he have any furniture, except for a straw mattress and a lamp whose nature history has transmitted to us; it was bronze. Perhaps it was a gift and perhaps it had some value, because a thief stole it from him. That was a subject of joy for Epictetus, for that theft made him sense that he had taken pleasure without being aware of it in an unnecessary and excessive luxury. He replaced the bronze lamp with a clay lamp of minimal value.

The existence of that lamp enables one to suppose that Epictetus read before going to sleep, which is a great self-indulgence. An absolute conformity with nature would have prescribed a contentment with the light of the sun or that of the moon.

People came a long way to consult him, for in those days people consulted philosophers as they consult physicians—or, rather, healers—nowadays. Philosophy had become a profession. There was a philosophical uniform, which consisted of a long beard and a torn cloak. One party of popular opinion was opposed to philosophers because they were ridiculous, or because they disdained to exploit their admirers, and Domitian had them imprisoned or exiled.

Unlike many other sages, Epictetus prescribed neatness and practiced it. But he was prejudiced with regard to beards. During a conversation with Arrian he criticized a young man because he was clean-shaven.

He taught virtue: virtue in the most elevated form, perhaps excessively elevated. In climbing the moral summits, virtue dresses itself in a kind of protestant authority inseparable from a certain ennui. He was scornful of pleasure in all its forms and never enabled a glimpse of the slightest prospect of future life.

"I have time," he said one day to a disciple. "Let us see, therefore, what ought to be drawn from the conversion of syllogisms. When all is going well, sailors have the right to light the fire, sing and dance."

I wonder whether it is not better, truly, to sing and dance with the sailors than to occupy oneself with syllogisms. But that great philosopher employed his leisure in "drawing himself from their conversion." How much more admiration I would have felt for Epictetus if he had wept, on observing the theft of his bronze lamp, because he was attached to that object! Nothing is more alive and personal than a lamp productive of light, and I see in Epictetus' indifference in replacing the companion of his evenings with a clay lamp a dryness of heart that diminishes him—all the more so as he gave that petty event as an example frequently enough for it have flown through the ages in histories of philosophy.

Did Epictetus gaze at the sea with emotion from his doorless threshold? No text indicates that. I am afraid that he might have judged that contemplation unworthy of a true sage. When nothing distracted him from his thought, instead of occupying himself with "the negative syllogism," as he assuredly did, how much better he would have done to go and pick up sea-shells on the beaches of the Gulf of Ambracia! The slightest indication of playing with children or familiar pleasantries would have rendered him more admirable in my eyes. Even a glass of wine, drunk with a disciple at sunset, would brighten his face with a warm and benevolent color. No drop of wine trickled into his beard, which must have been strangely stiff.

Many centuries after his death, in the environs if Nicopolis, pious Christians opened a tomb, the tomb of "a pagan of old." All the bones of that pagan had been reduced to a handful of dust. All that subsisted intact was a beard. I am sure that it was the beard of Epictetus.

THE MISSION OF MOHAMMED

Mohammed was anointed with perfumes from head to toe and had an extreme liking for women. As soon as it was well-established that he was the prophet of God, he assembled a harem. The people of Medina thought, in any case, that a prophet of God ought to have more wives than other men. They were passionate to know which one was the favorite and it required special legal dispositions to limit the actions of the curious who came by night to discover the spouse with which Mohammed was sharing his bed.

Murder was not at all repugnant to Mohammed, although he did not commit it himself. There was a Jewish poetess in Medina named Asma, who wrote ironic poems against him. Humor was foreign to the prophet. He instructed one of Asma's relatives to kill her. He did the same for one of the leaders of the Jewish aristocracy named Kaab, whose only crime was not to believe in him

An ancient law of Arabia obliged respect for caravans during one month, the sacred months of Ridchal, in order to permit them to make a pilgrimage to Mecca. Security was then assured to them, even by the worst brigands of the desert. Mohammed did not hesitate to violate that ancient law and he ordered the pillage of caravans, under the pretext that the merchants were unbelievers, but in reality with the aim of possession of the stolen booty.

Reentering Mecca victorious, he forgave many of his old enemies, but he had a woman put to death who had written poems wounding his vanity. That was a crime he could not forgive.

It was at the moment of that reentry to Mecca that he destroyed, in order to proclaim the unity of God, the three hundred idols that populated the Kaaba. A significant fact is that he insisted on ripping out and destroying personally a wooden dove sculpted with great artistry. The dove has always been a symbol of the pure spirit.

Whence came the extraordinary prestige that the man in question had, and what was the secret cause of the immense role he played?

That former conductor of caravans, having become the husband of a rich widow, led in Mecca until his fortieth year the life of a wealthy merchant, with his wife and children. Then he acquired a taste for meditation. He neglected his business and frequently withdrew to certain caves of Mount Hira. There, what are nowadays called phenomena occurred. He heard inexplicable noises, confused voices. He had the sentiment that a supernatural power was seeking to make him comprehend in order to confide a mission to him. His wife Khadidja came to the cave and took account of the phenomena.

Finally, one night when Mohammed, increasingly versed in the science of meditation, was approaching ecstasy, he perceived a light so dazzling that he lost the sentiment of it. When he came to, he saw beside him a being that he subsequently identified as the angel Gabriel and who, by virtue of the bizarrerie and the indirect methods that one always remarks in the manifestations of the beyond, commenced by crying out to him: "Announce!"

"What shall I announce?" he replied, as anyone would have done.

Then the form, instead of speaking, deployed a silken cloth on which were written the words that figure at the head of the Koran, and in which it was said that he had to announce that the Lord was the author of all grace. Then the vision disappeared.

It was renewed some time afterwards, to speak words of great beauty to him—a beauty all the more striking because other words said to him subsequently in the same manner were sometimes mediocre and incoherent.

For twenty-three years Mohammed received advice, moral laws of great elevation and orders of extreme cruelty, emanating from a supraterrestrial world. That force was sometimes personified, and he continued to consider it as the angel Gabriel.

One cannot accuse Mohammed of having believed himself, by virtue of an unreasonable pride, to be the successor of Moses, Jesus and other great prophets. His faith in his mission only came after his visions and because of them. He was chosen.

Was there not in Arabia a more spiritually elevated man who could have fulfilled the mission of proclaiming the unity of God while giving a personal example of greater detachment from the passions and less fury with regard to his enemies? A prophet who would not have counseled believers to exterminate pitilessly those who did not think like them would have been more useful to humanity. At least, we suppose so, in the present state of our conceptions of good and evil.

One might reply that only an individual of that nature, deeply steeped in violence, could direct the violent. But when Mohammed violated the truce of the sacred month, for an unjust pillage, he scandalized all the honest and moderate men of Medina. He went further than his fellow citizens' capacity for evil.

If Mohammed was chosen, by whom was he chosen? By a general consciousness of the Arabs, materializing in light, form and voice, to strike the missionary spirit? By his own superior soul, wanting to enlighten the inferior soul of the merchant? By the powerful directors of human races who labor with persistence and impotence for the perfection of humanity—if they exist?

That choice would then be proportional to the mediocre knowledge that they must have of humans, in view of their solitude, their more elevated preoccupations and the sadness of their failures.

THE SONGS OF NANAK

Nanak was one of the greatest humans of the human race, but the Occident does not even know his name, although his influence is exercised over millions of people. He lived at the beginning of the sixteenth century and he was the prophet of a large part of northern India.[25]

Like many prophets, who did not know at the beginning of their lives the extent of their destiny and the necessity of chastity to bring their mission to a successful conclusion, he committed the error of marrying. Confucius and Ramakrishna fell into the same trap. Nanak even had two children.

He is the most seductive of all the great religious prophets because he was a poet, and he never separated poetry and the lyrical impulse from the research of the divine.

He was the son of the steward of a rich Rajput in the environs of Lahore. In his youth he showed himself incapable of devoting himself to any work. Having obtained the position of director of a warehouse from his brother-in-law, he linked himself with a bohemian musician named Mardana. He spent all his time with him, playing the rebec and searching for the most appropriate music to accompany religious hymns.

He had the custom of going to take a bath in the river at sunrise. One morning, emerging from the river, as he went into a nearby forest, he had a vision of God.

---

[25] Guru Nanak (1469-1539) was the founder of Sikhism; his name still remains relatively little known in the Occident.

He saw a supernatural light and heard a voice that said to him: "I am Brahma and you are the divine Guru."

An analogous vision accompanied by a voice is generally the prelude to the career of great missionaries: the apostle Paul on the road to Damascus, Swedenborg in a London inn. Jacob Boehme knew his mission by virtue of a ray of sunlight with a particular brightness, falling on a pewter tray one day while he was mediating in Goerlitz, and Van Helmont by virtue of a gleam in a crack in a wall.

Nanak knew that his mission was to show Hindus and Muslims that it was the same God that they worshiped under different names, and that he had to preach that unity in the world. As Hindus and Muslims wore different costumes, he adopted a bizarre and slightly ridiculous costume participating in both religions, with the headdress of Muslims and the sign of his Hindu caste on the forehead.

On the point of quitting his family definitively, with his companion Mardana, when his wife begged him to stay he dared not tell her the irrevocable character of his departure; he replied vaguely: "Your sovereignty in my heart will last forever... Perhaps you will come to join me..." And later, when his mother threw herself at his knees in order to make him return to the familial hearth, he seized his kithara and intoned a mystical song by way of his sole response.

Whatever prestige of the truth might have, even in a messenger of God, how reduced one is by that human weakness on the part of someone who, by a rigorous sincerity, ought to have closed the door to all hope!

He did not recognize the authority either of the Vedas or the Koran. He was the enemy of all prejudices, all rites and all habits that petrified the soul, and he attempted to liberate humans from them.

His life reproduced the principal features of the existence of great masters, temptation by the demon or the expulsion of merchants from the temple. However, the gods granted him one favor that very few received, and which became very useful to a saint traveling on foot in hot countries. When he went to sleep under a tree, the shadow of that tree stopped rotating in accordance with the movement of the sun and only recovered its normal place in celestial geometry when he awoke.

He lived to be very old. Sensing death coming, he gathered his relatives and friends and went to lie down under an acacia. He composed a poem, read it aloud and asked the audience to sing it in the tone that he had indicated. While it was being sung, he extended a sheet of cloth gently over his face. When the song ended, he was dead.

THE DANCES OF CAITANYA

Almost at the same time as Nanak sang, Caitanya danced. Caitanya was another great missionary of northern India who possessed an ecstatic love of God. That ecstatic love, as well as his teaching and his admirable wisdom, he manifested by dancing.[26]

Dancing has lost its religious character for us, but in India it has remained a sacred manifestation of divine love. Shiva, the third person of the Hindu trinity, is represented as the great cosmic dancer who leads the eternal round of planets and creatures.

Caitanya had the privilege of being born to pious parents during an eclipse of the moon, which is a sign of the favor of destiny. He was married at sixteen and one cannot know the measure in which the kiss of the beautiful Laksmi counterbalanced in his soul the taste for study and religious controversy. A woman's kiss must have had a certain attraction for him, because, when Laksmi died of a snake-bite, he married the beautiful Visnupriya.

He was twenty-three when he had the revelation of the invisible world and the love of Krishna gripped him so imperiously that his relatives thought him mad and summoned the most reputed physicians in order to treat his loss of reason. The sudden advent of veritable reason is almost always confounded with madness in that fashion.

---

[26] Caitanya Mahapreabhu (1486-1534) was the founder of the religious movement nowadays most familiarly known in the Occident as "Hare Krishna" after its most widespread mantra.

It was then that, having entered a school of Vishnonites, he commenced to dance in a circle every evening in the house of another devotee, chanting poems to Krishna to the sound of cymbals and drums.[27] Then he departed to proclaim in the world that there is no greater truth than love. The exaltation of that love impelled him to frenetic dances in which he found a foretaste of union.

One day when he was walking with his disciples he saw a shepherd playing the flute. That sight caused him to evoke Krishna and threw him into such emotion that he fell to the ground, prey to delirium. A group of Pathan horsemen arrived. Their leader suspected Caitanya's disciples of having made him absorb a drug in order to rob him. A violent argument ensued. In the meantime, Caitanya recovered his senses, but instead of immediately giving a clear explanation of what had happened to him he began a mystical dance around the disciples and the Pathan horsemen. By the effect of the dance and the speech that followed, the Pathans were converted to his doctrine and became his disciples.

Once, traversing the Jumna on a raft, he found the blue of the waters so moving that he dived into them in order to embrace the suavity of the color. It was necessary to watch over him; another time he threw himself in the sea because of its beauty. He died of a wound in the foot that he had caused by striking the ground with excessive rhythm in the intoxication of a dance.

But in a sage as filled with perfect amour, who thinks of nothing but rejoining the divine essence by means of ecstasy, how can his excess of rigor be explained?

---

[27] Author's reference: "See S. Chakravarti, *Caitanya et sa théorie de l'amour divin.*"

He considered chastity to be essential and had made a vow not to look at any woman, including his wife. He demanded a similar austerity of his disciples. When he learned that young Haridas had asked a woman for alms, and, in consequence, must have looked at her, he expelled that scandalous disciple and rejected his presence with such rigor that Haridas, crushed by the weight of his crime and his master's wrath, committed suicide.

It is impossible to know anything about Haridas' past. He must have been a charming young man and I think, like him, that it is always necessary to look women in the face, especially if one is asking them for alms. But a little is known about his future. There was no chastisement for him in the afterlife, where moral men affirm that suicides are severely punished. I even think that the glance that earned him the malediction of his master followed him like a lamp and illuminated his path.

THE VIOLENCE OF LUTHER

The reformer Luther is the only one among inspired men who, instead of a divine archangel, saw the Spirit of Evil in person in the course of his solitary meditations.

He was in the castle of Wartburg, where he had taken refuge, and where he spent nine months. It was there, he recounted, that he had a conversation with the king of Christian demons, who had become visible to his eyes. He identified the Spirit of Evil with human reason, which he found "more abominable than any fornication." He argued bitterly with his vision and doubtless did not have the upper hand in the debate; he threw his inkwell at the figure. The inkwell must have traversed the transparent matter of the vision, for it broke against the wall. The trace was shown off at the castle of Wartburg for a long time with the veneration that the testimony of the anger of such a great man merits.

Luther was sensitive to the fornications that he qualified as abominable. One of the first points of his reform, perhaps the most important in his eyes, was to authorize priests to marry. He took advantage of that permission himself, and married Catherine de Bore, an emancipated nun, and she bore him six children with an extreme rapidity. He said that nature does not permit a man to do without women, any more than nourishment. Once, in the pulpit, he advised the husbands present that, if their wives refused to do their conjugal duty for any reason, they should call upon their maidservant to replace her.

He was unusually violent, and the vulgarity of his language, which attained an extreme never surpassed, provoked the joy and admiration of the vulgar men of his time. His hatred of his enemies was so powerful that he considered it as a real entity susceptible of being bequeathed by testament. "I hate Erasmus," he said to his disciples. "I instruct you in my last will and testament to hate that viper Erasmus."

He had an enormous appetite for eating and drinking. Some time before his death he formulated his essential desire in a conversation on the subject of his illness. "I ask nothing of physicians except to use the gifts of God, to eat and drink what I please."

And in the same conversation he, who had succeeded in everything, said: "Men are nothing but devils. The best one can hope for is a brief moment of happiness and then to disappear."

One can compare that remark with that of the great optimist that Goethe was: "I can truly say that in the entre course of my seventy years I have not had four weeks of true happiness."

THE SOLITUDE OF SPINOZA

One evening as Spinoza was returning to the furnished hotel in which he lived modestly, a madman who
was lying in wait for him threw himself upon him and
tried to stab him with a knife. It transpired subsequently
that the madman had no valid reason for striking the philosopher. The only one was that Spinoza was in contradiction with the ideas of the rabbis of the synagogue of
Amsterdam.

In the same way, the insane often hurl themselves
upon philosophers, as if they were obeying a secret law.
Just as there is a variety of humans who assassinate ty-
rants, there is one of those who aspire to strike thinkers.
How can the motive of such creatures be explained? It
seems that they would have difficulty replying to that
question. The hatred of thought is in certain individuals
profound and primordial. There are beings who, from
form to form since the beginning, perhaps without
knowing it, have been on a path to which thought is contrary, and represents a loathsome element.

Spinoza changed residence after the attack by the
enemy of thought and realized a miracle of solitary life.
He loved poverty sincerely, refusing offers of a pension
several times. Doubtless he was one of the rare men who
knew that one goes further in the research of the infinite
if one is detached from material goods, the minimum of
which is represented by a few items of furniture and a
family carpet.

As life had taken him for a symbol, his sisters, the
only beings with whom he might have been united,
showed on the occasion of a petty heritage a savage cu-

pidity. They fought, although there was not even a bed included in the division.

An important man, having gone to see him, was afflicted by his worn, holed and dirty dressing-gown. He offered him a new one. Spinoza refused it. He liked his old dressing-gown, Solitary men are affectionately fond of certain familiar objects.

Apart from that of hermits, there was no solitude greater than Spinoza's, face to face with his thoughts. He exercised a métier in order to live, polishing long-range telescope lenses. Permitting others to see further than ordinary sight in the physical world, he succeeded in distinguishing another life himself, behind the veil of the one that was before him and which he scrutinized so intensely.

In his perfect solitude, he had no hope of an afterlife—nothing but that of dissolving into the universal order. "The greatest good is the knowledge of the union that the soul realizes with nature entire." Can that knowledge suffice to fill life when one is confronted by a poor rented room with telescope lenses, the faces of landladies and sometimes another philosopher who comes to talk about lofty problems?

Who can ever say what the thoughts of that solitary man were on the Sunday afternoon when he died? The family with whom he was lodging left him in order to go to Vespers. When they came back, he was dead. There must have been the sound of bells. It was the twentieth of February, and perhaps afternoon sunlight, already oblique, traversed the window panes of his bedroom. Can having written the *Ethics* suffice to fill a soul, even one as vast as Spinoza's?

Did he remember the young woman about whom he had thought at the beginning of his life and from whom he remained separated by timidity? My God, what if it appeared to him that the *Ethics* and all human philosophy were of no importance? What if the columns of his temple, made of the substance of his books, had silently crumbled around his death-bed?

He had sacrificed his entire life to informing humans that God and nature are only one. I say an ardent prayer that he did not abruptly glimpse the vanity of that notion. For there are such traps. Some things are of formidable importance to us and then, one evening, for no reason, they appear to have the weight and extent of a soap bubble. One can tell oneself that one only has to blow more bubbles in order to enjoy a new mirage, but it is necessary that it is not at that precise moment that one loses one's breath.

THE REVELATION OF INVISIBLE WORLDS

THE PRESENCE OF DESPAIR

There is a despair of the morning and a despair of the evening, and those two sisters willingly clasp hands during the day.

One sometimes wakes up with a desire precipitately to reenter the empire of darkness from which one has just emerged so imprudently. There are shutters clicking and milk bottles colliding on a stairway somewhere. An automobile horn evokes a traveler who is cold, in a taxi, with his trunk alongside the driver, heading for some desolate railway station. One is afraid of being cold, of rediscovering objects and beings...

One closes one's eyes again...

The despair of the evening is like an aging queen with inflexible features. She has a black stick and she hits you with it. Every blow evokes a memory, but not good ones—never the good ones.

Forgotten bad deeds revive abruptly and bite your soul without letting go, rather like certain insects that hold on to you with their jaws even when they have been cut in two with scissors. And the black stick also causes regrets to revive that one had thought completely dead, but regrets of a special, inferior, miserable nature, especially those related to missed opportunities. At some moment in life one might have been able to satisfy some desire, and one did not, out of stupidity—especially those relating to women. One believed oneself to be sheltered from that quality of bitterness, but no. It is like the odors that penetrate so thoroughly the jar that contained them that no disinfectant or corrosive can succeed in extracting it from the pores into which it has penetrated.

And then, no book, no known wisdom can serve. They cannot bring anything more. There is a savant conspiracy between the external world and oneself. One cannot receive anything and nothing is sent. One is imprisoned in walls of ash with no possible deliverance. One can fill the room with blinding light by switching on all the lamps or remain in darkness, huddled like a hunted beast; it is the same thing. One is tracked by nonexistent forces, by a presence of annihilation.

How can the enemy be vanquished? How can one be surrounded by luminous perspectives at all hours? Is there a secret of eternal joy?

THE MOUNTAIN OF SERENITY

Perhaps awake, perhaps asleep, I followed a road that had just presented itself to my sight. It descended with an extreme rapidity between melancholy trees. On raising my head I perceived that there was no sky above me and that the road was subterranean.

No signposts! No lanterns hanging on poles! I went down, pushed by a force of descent, wondering where the light might be coming from that permitted me to distinguish, to the right and the left, images, faces and scenes of life.

Nothing but things already seen! Sometimes, it was an individual that I recognized as a long dead friend who was fixed in an attitude of eternity. He made me a sign to go further, and I continued to descend.

The landscape was increasingly desolate. The vegetation was sparse and singular, as if struck by petrifaction. I distinguished the silhouettes of women. They made me signs from afar: signs that gave the impression of saying: *The opportunity was missed! What's the point? That which has been will be no longer.*

And I was still descending, endowed with a strange speed, and I thought about that astonishing hero named Arne Saknussemm who, perhaps by the same road, had reached the center of the Earth. But I knew that I, personally, was marching toward the center of dolor, and I wondered what relationship could unite those two astonishing centers.

I traversed with a light celerity carboniferous terrains in which there were imprints of dead ichthyosaurs and antediluvian cicadas, the design of whose wings was visible. I glimpsed the tombs of giants, phantom dol-mens. I saw to my right masses of coal and schist that plutonian forces had disturbed, and to my left volcanic corridors between frozen lava and basalts covered with crystals, like tears wept by mountains saddened by being buried far from the light.

And I finally reached, or thought I reached—which is the same thing—a lake with metallic waters, the flu-idity of which must have been less than that of terrestrial waters. It was a viscous lake, and yet confusedly reflec-tive. It was surrounded by a beach composed of an infin-ity of tiny gray seashells, and on leaning over I saw that they were fossil and mortuary seashells representing the deformed heads of animals or humans who were all sad—a sadness all the greater because it must go back thousands of centuries.

I was tempted to sit down and wait, immobile, until the moment of my death—but no; next to that lake of despair there is neither peace nor repose and one cannot say: "Finally!" It is necessary to get up and go on, to walk around its interminable waters on the beach of dead seashells, where footfalls make no sound, in a light com-ing from below, the mere perception of which is painful.

I saw several roads and discerned certain indica-tions that made me think that there was perhaps a differ-ent advertisement for every man. On one of those roads there was the trace of a foot, the nails of whose shoe were in the form of a cross. Above another rose a white bird from which a feather was detached. I saw it fall with a spiral motion because of its lightness. On the third road there was no perceptible manifestation. I recalled how many times symbols had lied, how many signs had turned out to be empty of meaning, and I took the third road, which, according to my weary mind, had every chance of leading toward oblivion.

It was a perfectly sinister road where one lost the notion of space, with the result that I no longer knew whether it was rising or descending. And I followed it for a time variable between one second and eternity.

Suddenly, it turned, and an extraordinarily fresh and aromatized wind blew toward me. Was it by virtue of a mysterious game of nature, a bizarre illusion of subterranean worlds that, in the region of the solitary lake, caused one to lose the sentiment of proportions? But I took three or four steps and I found myself on the summit of a high mountain bathed by celestial air.

I saw horizons unrolling harmoniously and valleys succeeded by mountains with a regularity that I had never remarked before, the observation of which was an unexpected blessing for me. The clouds were rising and falling. In the distance, a sea was in its immemorial place and making the movements appropriate to seas, which have been commanded by a general order. At the moment foreseen by my destiny, I appeared on that mountain in order to enjoy relationships with the earth, the light and the expanse.

I was penetrated silently. I occupied the exact point of the world that was necessary. I felt tranquil and joyful, with a certain perfection coming from the experience of my journey. I knew henceforth that the lake of despair is not far from the mountain of serenity.

THE ROOT OF DESPAIR

The root of despair plunges into egotism. Anyone who loves all beings will be bathed in an inexhaustible mildness. But the most difficult thing of all is to love one's neighbor. One can easily love a dog, a cricket or a woman, but all beings! And if one succeeds in loving all beings, how can one avoid being torn by the sight of their suffering? The ugliness of faces is an obstacle to love, the permanence of evil in souls is a more powerful obstacle, and divine silence causes an anguishing uncertainty to float overhead.

And why has the law, to which it is necessary to conform no matter what, wanted the annihilation of egotism, since it has made the gift of oneself accompanied by an unalloyed bliss. Every time that nature tries to attain her goals, she offers the creatures who are her instruments an intense pleasure as compensation. Physical creation by means of a sexual act is recompensed by a brief joy. That joy is not devoid of analogy with pain. Mental creation is followed by a more durable joy, but which is accompanied by torment. Whereas any manifestation of affection produces naturally a delight whose purity becomes greater as the disinterest becomes greater and the gift of oneself more complete.

The world manifests a prodigious design of unity, and whoever collaborates with that design is recompensed by a blissful delight. But the world manifests in parallel an equally prodigious appetite for division. And from that is born the temptation to go against the law, because in division there is an illusion of joy in which human pride takes pleasure.

It is necessary to obey the law. We are prevented from doing so by certain vertigos that blow over us like tempests. Those tempests are unpredictable. There is no meteorology of the soul. From the depths of the horizon blasts of nothingness suddenly hasten. Then, all the best-established certainties are overturned, like the tents of a camp of travelers by a tornado. One finds oneself naked on sterile sand. One says to oneself: *What if everything is a lie? What if there is no perfection, no afterlife, no state of nirvana? Has not the tempest that has destroyed everything, in sum, an origin as divine as the faculty of construction that had permitted me to establish solid shelters, or what I believed to be such?*

It is necessary to tear out the root of despair. For that, it is necessary to have the certainty that a more beautiful life is hidden behind the miserable life that unfurls before us. Now everyone can find by means of his own perspicacity, his own attention, by listening to the silence and examining the shadow, the proofs that ignorance demands, the proofs of the reality of an invisible world.

Nature seems not to want that discovery. She has organized a schema very skillfully, in order that it should not be possible to pierce the enigma. She has arranged matters so that every proof of the afterlife has a counterpart in reality that makes the proof turn back against itself. But all the layouts of nature present a slight fissure through which one can pass one's head in order to see further.

Methods have been prescribed which require more or less time to follow, and more or less vigorous purifications of the body and soul. But even without practicing any method, by presenting oneself with one's natural impurity and hope at the edge of the invisible world, one can hear a word or see a face, a grotesque or terrible image, which gives the certainty that there is a marvelous life to discover.

THE ADVENT OF THE SIGN

Ramakrishna has said that living faith can be given and received in a more positive and more tangible fashion than any other material thing.

Thus, someone can come into your house one day and hand you faith, like a precious object! Or it can be the consequence of an encounter. And that encounter might occur at any moment.

But what is the faith in question? Ramakrishna speaks of the living faith. For here is also the dead faith. Now, the difference is essential. The word faith means ordinary faith in God, the God of a religion, and a series of complex and almost invariably absurd dogmas, for they come from verities so deformed that they are unrecognizable. That harsh and forbidding faith cannot be given like an object, in passing or in the course of a conversation, and received with ease. One cannot slip a skeleton into a hand.

The living faith of which Ramakrishna speaks is faith in the pure Spirit, in the Absolute. It is joyful, winged, deprived of punishments and recompenses. It is a communication with the original force, from which one can receive an unalloyed felicity if one can find the secret of one's accord with it.

All saints and all visionaries, and even simply those who have meditated intensely on human destiny, have had at one moment of their life a sign or a revelation of the invisible world and of the accord that they might have with that world. How many destinies have been orientated by small supernatural events! Even Descartes had three symbolic dreams.

The moment of their life at which the sign is manifest is ordinarily marked by a violent dolor, the loss of a cherished individual or the sharp sentiment that one is not living in accordance with the law whose orientation one has secretly glimpsed. The sign is most frequently the appearance of a flame or a luminous face, sometimes a voice giving an imperative order. Some have seen a transparent individual beside them. Others have been visited by Jesus Christ or the Buddha. The revelations have sometimes come after an appeal, after an anxious wait. But at other times, they have presented themselves abruptly without any apparent reason, because the person's hour had sounded on the invisible clock of his soul.

It has been possible to indentify that revelation with Christian grace. In that case, the person who receives it is the object of a favor originating from a capricious God who chooses certain beings and not others. But religion has nothing to do with the veritable revelation. The spiritual vase of the soul receives one more drop of spirit, a drop ordinarily mingled with a tear, and it overflows toward its source.

It is not necessary to believe in a personal God to receive the grace of the spirit. It comes from a more immense source.

Revelation can be manifest in a different manner, but the result is similar. The individual experiences a delightful joy that words have difficulty expressing. His forces of love are infinitely multiplied. He understands the insignificance of his life. His heart beats with that of all creatures. He senses passing through him the torrent of the suave delight that is the intimate essence of everything that exists, and which death must give to those who die detached.

One discovers in almost all mystical experiences the same mechanism of revelation. It is at the moment when the soul abandons itself, and recognizes internally its submission to the law, that a mysterious door opens, that the sign is made.

But the person who sees nothing arrive, the person who appeals in vain, ought not to cease to believe in the magic of his appeal. There is no appeal without response; the response is only more or less belated. It is necessary never to forget the words of Swedenborg:

"A divine law appears to exist, in accordance with which our will awakens the will of God."

THE UTILITY OF ILLNESS

I have been forced to observe by personal experience that the state of illness, of slight illness, is more favorable to the discovery of and the access to another world near to ours, another world more beautiful, which is like an ideal counterpart.

It would be preferable, more moral and more exemplary exclusively to glorify the health of the body as the source of all marvels. In a healthy body one has clearer and nobler thoughts. Not always, in fact. All people charged with instruction have unanimously taught that it is first necessary to have a healthy body; even in the mystical domain, it is said that there is no possibility of self-improvement if one does not have lungs, muscles and a circulatory system capable of certain exercises that guide the spirit along the way.

That is an obvious verity and I adhere to it fully. The state of health is superior to the state of illness and it is necessary to seek the health of the body and that of the soul with love.

Personal experience, however, informs me that a slight state of illness pushes you gently, without your being aware of it, toward a sort of frontier, an intermediate zone in which one has the faculty of perceiving in the distance a double of our universe, of which ours might only be a physical refraction and not the true reality.

In the same way, a little moral disequilibrium, an abnormal excitement, favors intuitions. It creates resonances of new and profound emotions. What is called inspiration is nothing other than a disturbance, a temporary disorganization of the mental faculties. Ideas vibrate differently, associating with more rapidity, and of the new groups they form, one of the more audacious sometimes reached a point that the others have never attained.

Complete health is a benefit that no one would ever think of refusing, but if nature has inscribed in its formidable book certain troubles for your organism, it is necessary not to be overly afflicted by that, but to seek to obtain an advantage therefrom for the knowledge of invisible worlds.

There are in illness points of contact with those words that one cannot have in a state of health. The dreams of fever are not incoherent inventions but deformed images of the reality that is beyond our senses. It is sometimes by virtue of fever that an indication is given to the mind, because it is the state of disturbance that permits its reception. How many apparitions have been perceived, how many admirable words heard, of which one did not take account because they were perceived in a fever?

For those who attach an inestimable value to the certainty of the afterlife, illness merits rehabilitation.

THE APPARITION OF THE LAMP

Perhaps personal experience ought to remain secret and there are things that ought not to be revealed. Perhaps there is a mystery that one abolishes by describing it. But is not silence the equivalent of annihilation, and is not the duty of speech as imperious as the duty of silence?

The example I can give is very minimal. I am not giving it to serve as an example to someone who wants to follow the same research as me. I am obeying an internal invitation to recount.

That evening I had not sensed the courage to make any appeal, any invocation to powers living or dead. The apartment was deserted, I sensed that the street was deserted behind the walls, and my soul was deserted, like the immense world in which I sensed that I was lost.

I do not know why a terrible word came back to my memory and appeared to me as if it were written in letters of fire in an invisible book:

There are men for whom life is a torture...

Certainly, I was not one of those men. Life had never been a torture for me, and I had even extracted numerous, varied and delectable joys from it. The source of those joys had dried up, that was all. Or rather, it had been replaced by another, more abundant and purer source devoid of all bitterness but from which I drew in solitude. No, I had no grounds for complaint, and, face to face with the past, I owed it an action of grace.

"Praise be to life and its multiform beauty, to the pleasure of human love, to the richness of thoughts that one finds in books, to everything that is charming and perishable!" I formulated with my lips. But in the depths of myself was written: *There are men for whom life is a torture...*

I had known some of them. They had lived and they had died. I saw them again. Their characteristic was an apparent enthusiasm for life: a desperate enthusiasm; an enthusiasm that went as far as desiring death in the hope of a higher life. I had lived intimately with two or three of them, but there were others that I had only glimpsed, in gatherings or in cafés, especially in cafés. I remembered the shining eyes, the particles of genius scattered in speeches at marble tables, sometimes flashes of hatred. And they had left neither works, nor sketches of works. Their actions had only been essays and usually stillborn essays. They had been useless to their fellows, perhaps harmful. And I cherished them without any valid reason, perhaps solely because life had been a torture for them.

I listened for a long time to the sounds of the city and the night, to know whether anything particularly extraordinary was happening: the fall of the Eiffel Tower, or the seven blasts of the trumpet of the Apocalypse, the signal for the end of time. I assured myself with a secret regret that there was nothing but the moan of taxis moving through the endless sadness of the streets, and, here and there, a lamentable gramophone tune hanging on to a window like a poisoned bird. Then I thought that when there is no end of the world in prospect, and one cannot rid one's mind of those for whom life is a torture, there remains an ultimate, profound refuge full of forgiveness and forgetfulness, and that refuge is slumber.

Toward that refuge, which has always been accorded to me a little before midnight, I precipitated myself with ardor. That ardor was a flight. I fled what was around me, the books and the benevolent photographs; I fled the people of memory, always ready to appear at the slightest sign; I fled my own thoughts, my own insignificant life; above all, I fled those for whom life is a torture, whose faces I saw again, dolorous and grave, their cheeks marked by alcoholism and a certain laughter more atrocious than any sorrow.

And I wondered whether, of those companions that I had known and who had disappeared, I was not the survivor. Was I not a member of that desperate family, who had resisted life because he had been more favored by fate, who had been able to create chimeras, depict them, whisper them in the form of idols and worship them, in order to have a reason for living? But sometimes the balloon of ideas burst; there was no longer anything there, and I found myself similar to my brothers the alcoholics, the desperate, those for whom life was a torture.

Oh, to pass quickly under the portico of sleep! To enter into the world of nocturnal things, perhaps dreams, almost certainly silence and repose.

And for that, in order to forget everything, it was only necessary to flick the switch of an electric lamp, stretch out the arms in a cross, as if dead, and wait.

In reality, that is not what I do every evening. When the light is switched off, I take advantage of the peace of darkness to collect myself, to attempt to communicate, by the surge of thought, with the superior forces of the spirit, which I imagine as personal entities susceptible of hearing me. And sometimes it happens that I have, if not a response to my request, at least a little sign permitting me to believe that my aspiration was known, and that my silent words were not lost.

But that evening, the virtue of request was not in me. My soul was like a stone, like a sealed tomb. I only sensed a profound and sincere desire for oblivion.

And it was then that the beyond manifested itself to me for the first time.

What creature of the beyond, what supremely attentive intelligence gave me, in exchange for despair, the gift of living light?

The obscurity of my bedroom was compact and I was lying motionless with my eyes open. In front of me and a little to the right, with a gripping rapidity, a light sprang forth, of a bright, pure and dazzling gold. And in the middle of that light, with the color and relief of life, was a lamp: a lamp of an obsolete model, a lamp of old, with an ordinary tapering foot and a beak for turning the wick.

Now, I recognized that lamp perfectly. It was the lamp of which I had made use in my youth, which had cast its mediocre but faithful light in my student room. To that lamp, once, I had given the form of amity that one gives to certain familiar objects when the number of possessions is restricted and the objects render you the precious services that matter renders to mind. When more modern rooms had permitted me electric lighting, I had kept the lamp as a souvenir of certain evenings of cold, solitude and hope, with which it was linked and of which it had been the soul. Then the years had passed, changes of residence had succeeded one another and the lamp had disappeared. There had never been a precise moment of disappearance. I had regretted that loss. But I could not believe that it been thrown in the rubbish. It had dematerialized and, by virtue of a mysterious ascension, had returned to the abode of eternal flames.

Now, it had descended again. Not for long—I estimate at five seconds the time for which it was presented to my eyes; but that time appeared infinitely long to me. It was long enough for me to be conscious that an event of a marvelous order had occurred, and that the event in question was produced by a golden glow, and that the lamp of my youth was at the heart of that glow.

And immediately, the lamp disappeared and was replaced by the image of a Buddha, a standing Buddha placed in such a fashion that the light that had surrounded the lamp aureoled it in a perfectly harmonious fashion and resembled the painted gold leaf that is placed around certain statues of Buddha in order to represent the luminous aura that envelops them.

The Buddha did not remain before my eyes any longer than the consciousness I experienced of the reality of its image. It reentered into the fluid gold that surrounded it and that gold itself was attenuated, dissolved, and disappeared, giving way to the normal darkness that, logically, must not have ceased to fill the room.

An impression of rapture remained within me. The word rapture is the only one that I can employ in order to designate a state very different from the intellectual delight that I might have obtained from the satisfaction of having been the witness of an extraordinary manifestation violating the rules of nature and indubitably external to me. That impression of rapture must have overlapped slumber and I rediscovered it the next day when I awoke—after which it was effaced, as beauty is effaced when it is expressed, and amour when it has cast its breath of enchantment.

Whence came that messenger apparition that preserved me from the fall? From the unconscious, to which people now confides the role of explaining everything:

the unconscious, parent of dreams, creator of better and worse? A testimony coming from the utmost depths of myself, and in consequence from my unconscious, imperiously asserts the negation.

Are there, as I believe, hierarchies of beings superior to humans, and do those beings, in certain cases, and for reasons that escape us, intervene?

Or is it necessary to believe that I received the message of a living being—a very powerful living being who could send his thought over a great distance? Once, I had the favor of approaching one of the men who have arrived at the highest degree of spiritualization, the only man who, to my knowledge, has attained the spiritual plane, manipulating forces at will and able to distribute them. Had I not remained, unknown to myself, in rapport with him? Space would not have been an obstacle to the transmission of his thought, and more than it is for a modern apparatus for transmitting radio waves. Had he not made use of his power to preserve me from a danger?

It was to that hypothesis that I rallied. For the greatest danger of all is perhaps despair, and the aspiration of the soul toward annihilation. Certainly, the days succeed one another, each bringing its particular tonality, its color of good fortune or misfortune. I would probably have found better thoughts the next day. But it is possible that, in the general economy of the spiritual life, the plunge into slumber with a surge of despair has a great importance, and that a superior and protective intelligence thought it good to preserve me from it.

Whatever its origin might have been, I understood the language of the symbol. It said:

The lamp of your youth is still burning. Here it is, still close to you. Once, unknown to yourself, you made a pact with the light; remain faithful to that pact. Here, to remind you, is the image of the man who, on the earth, has approached the truth most closely.

It was only the next day, I confess, that I saw again, but more veiled and more distant in my memory, the faces of men for whom life is a torture.

It was only then that I realized how favored I was among all those who are inscribed for torment. For those vanished brothers there had been no sign, no consolatory apparition. They had not even had within them the faith in such signs. They had been reabsorbed by the great destructive force without the slightest indication of the divine. They had departed without a lamp.

Where were they now? Through what avatars of transformations had they passed? And at what moment of time would they finally be given the sweet rapture that the golden light procures?

THE EVENING OF JUDGMENT

I had appealed and they had come, one by one, all my past bad deeds, for there cannot be for a man the serenity of the evening if he has not summoned them to appear before him and has not absolved himself of them.

For a long time they had remained in the background of my soul, but I knew that there had to be a day of final judgment for them and that I had to be the judge.

But in all those bad deeds I only heard the ordinary evil caused to other creatures. For me that evil had been like a ball that I had sent back with an automatic movement, after having received it in the intoxication of the game. Of good and evil, I had only been a bit-part player charged with receiving and launching. Those bad deeds did not have to be judged. If they were to have consequences, they would be as insignificant as their own substance.

It was a matter of a more subtle evil, and bad deeds that had touched the profound domain of the soul.

One day, when I was walking in the summer sunlight through the countryside near the Mediterranean coast I had perceived a black cat in front of a very poor solitary house. It was a kitten, particularly thin, threadbare and melancholy. It seemed imprinted with the desolation that only beings deprived of all affection have. There must also have been a drama of nourishment there. The cat did not reflect the joy in living that young animals have. It seemed to possess a precocious consciousness of its solitude and the evil fate that had caused it to fall into the hands of harsh and indifferent masters.

I stopped and I took it in my arms in spite of its protestations and its fear, and I stroked it gently with my
hand. The protestations ceased and the cat seemed suddenly to abandon itself. It raised its head toward me and
I saw in its round bright eyes something akin to a distracted stupor. At the same time it emitted a bizarre
murmur that was not the purr of satisfied cats, but expressed the bliss of an admirable novelty.

I put it back in the place from which I had had taken
it and I continued my route. It was a little road that
snaked between pines. After a minute, on turning round,
I saw that the cat was walking behind me, with an un-
steady gait. I made a gesture to order it to stay and has-
tened my step. But the cat had made a rapid decision. It
had abandoned its birthplace and it was giving itself to
me.

In vain I gave it a further order to go back. It strove
to run. I wondered what I ought to do. Could I steal it
from its masters, whom I did not know and who must be
bad masters? But it was not that scruple that retained me.
I imagined the embarrassment that a cat would cause me
in the hotel where I was staying, the sight that I would
present in traversing the hall of the hotel carrying that
pitiful creature, and my ignorance of the care that needed
to be given to a sick cat.

I started to run along the road. Then I heard a desperate voice behind me, without analogy with any animal voice, and I saw that black, bristling, caricature of a
being, trying with all its might to catch up with me. I had
the cowardice of increasing my speed, and it was only
after a long distance, and when the road had turned several times, that I ceased to hear the appeal of the creature
to which I had revealed what love is.

In the darkness of its absolute misery, it had not known that there was anything else in the world than the fear of the strong, hunger and solitude. And I had made it know goodness and had immediately snatched away what I had just given it.

And that bad deed I had accomplished—exactly the same one—with human creatures. Was that, then, a greater evil deed? Is there a hierarchy in the scale of the evil that one does, according to the degree of development of the beings to which one does it? I am not sure about that.

It was in the time of my youth in Toulouse, when I still distinguished poorly the differences established by the social order. One day, I passed a young woman in the street who seemed charming to me. Perhaps she was. I followed her, I returned to the vicinity of her house and I perceived that she had the custom of looking out of a ground-floor window. I did not make any connection between the particular quarter where the house was situated and the presence of the charming young woman at a window from which communications with passers-by are quickly established. It was summer, in any case, and it was normal to be sitting behind open Venetian blinds. I went back to the street frequently and, as a first move, I sent a bouquet of flowers, via the intermediary of a child, to the young woman that I dared not approach directly.

It is not customary in our day to send flowers to a professional hooker. That gift was so abnormal that it produced an immense effect, for the bouquet arrived at dusk, at the hour when everyone in standing in doorways and in the frames of windows.

A strange amity resulted from it, in which my timidity was able to retain the character of amity.

"Since you read a lot," the young woman at the window said to me once—for she had seen me with books under my arm—"lend me a book. I'll read it, even if there are verses."

Now, at that time, I had just bought—and it had been a serious material effort for me—the latest book by Henri de Régnier, entitled *Episodes, sites et sonnets*.[28] It was, so far as I remember, of a rather mysterious symbolism. I feared that it might be incomprehensible. On the contrary, it was read and reread, learned by heart. It became a sort of Bible of an incomprehensible cult, perhaps that of the elevation of the soul: a cult that is celebrated at every degree of the human scale.

I do not know what happened in me. It was not because I discovered what modest career my friend had been called to follow. It was only later, with a little more experience, that I understood that. Something happened within me that might be called a sudden indifference, a taste for change, or to which one can give any name one wishes. I interrupted the intellectual rapport that I had maintained faithfully and which had taken on a sentimental coloration of its own accord. I abandoned the volume of Henri de Régnier and the person who had made a breviary of it. I did not go back to the room

---

[28] The book in question was published in 1891, when Magre would have been fourteen. It does not feature in the account of a suspiciously similar brief relationship with a prostitute rendered in Magre's *Confessions*; as to whether either anecdote is true, one can only speculate, but it is worth noting that this particular anecdote can be seen a contraction of the theme of his early novella *La Tendre camarade* (1918; tr. as "The Tender Comrade"), which must have been based in similar feelings of remorse based in personal experience—sentiments that were obviously long-lasting.

where my desiccated bouquet had been conserved as the testimony of I know not what ideal, which is forever forbidden to certain creatures. That inexplicable thing I had enabled her to glimpse; I had brought it, and my absence annihilated it.

It took years for me to realize that my departure, which must have been interpreted as a kind of scorn, was a cruelty colder than any insult. From the person who had believed that the best thing in the world, amity, could exist, I have taken away that faith. I had permitted her to rise by a degree in the scale of emotions and I had allowed her to slip back by abandoning her. Was that not the sin against the spirit, the only one that is unforgivable?

But are there sins that are not forgiven? Especially if one has brought them into the light of consciousness, if one has seen their causes and one has created contrary causes that will give rise to good deeds when their hour of realization has sounded?

And I summoned other bad deeds into the light. They all had a family resemblance. They resembled one another by virtue of the egotism with which they were imprinted, by the self-love that they had manifested.

What is known as the Guardian of the Threshold is not a redoubtable monster, the sight of which cannot be borne because of the hideousness of its face.[29] It is one-

---

[29] I have translated *le Gardien du seuil* straightforwardly, because it became a common motif of the literature of the French occult revival, detached from its usually-unacknowledged source. However, the English original of Edward Bulwer-Lytton's novel *Zanoni* (1842)—one of Madame Blavatsky's favorite sources of inspiration—the entity in question is called the Dweller on the Threshold.

self; it is one's own soul. It is necessary to look it in the face in order to take account of its pitiless pride and its faculty of annihilating everything that happens to encounter it in one's life—a faculty that is developed in the image of divine nature.

For nature wants the expansion of beings and never ceases to give to the strongest, who are also the most pitiless, recompenses of beauty and power. But only up to a certain limit! There is a point at which it is necessary to stop, to render what one has received, to abdicate one's former royalty. One drop more and the vase overflows! There is a solemn evening of the recapitulation of acts and thoughts. It is necessary to take up oneself the trumpet of God, make it resound and awaken one's own dead.

Emerge from the shadow in which you repose, base deeds, secret thoughts of evil, unexpressed jealousies and impure intentions! Appear with your double attached to you, the remorse that you must some day bring into the daylight! Push before you the brother with the poisoned body, the tenebrous larva, in order that it can be dissolved by the virtue of the light. Come, all of you, from the depths of the past in order that I judge you!

It is sufficient for me to see you, to reduce you to nothing with the cortege, which I have been told is infinite, of your effects. This evening I am closing the immense book in which the effects and the causes are inscribed, the former born from the latter, with the fidelity of a mathematical law. The long series is concluded. I am stopping the birth of evil by my redemptive will. I am turning the last page and I am tracing at the bottom a cross, the most ancient sign employed on the planet by humans, the cross of the spirit.

THE EXPLANATION OF PAIN

The presence on earth of evil and pain remains inexplicable. Those who have made the most profound researches in order to provide an explanation of it have been obliged to declare, as a last resort, that it is a problem surpassing the comprehension of the human mind.

Now, there is in William James' book *The Varieties of Religious Experience* an astonishingly suggestive page in which an explanation, and even a legitimation, of pain might perhaps be found, resulting not from a hypothesis but from direct experience.

William James reproduces the story of a woman who recounts what she has sensed under the influence of ether taken before a surgical operation.

"I wondered if I was in a prison being tortured... I became unconscious again... A great Being or Power was traveling through the sky, his foot was on a kind of lightning as a wheel is on a rail, it was his pathway... He moved in a straight line, and each part of the streak or flash came into its short consciousness only that he might travel. I seemed to be directly under the foot of God, and I thought he was grinding his own life up out of my pain. Then I saw that what he had been trying with all his might to do was change his course, to bend the line of lightning to which he was tied... He bended me, turning his corner by means of my hurt, hurting me more than I had ever been hurt in my life, and at the acutest point of this, as he passed, I saw... The angle was an obtuse angle and I remember thinking as I woke that had he made it a right or an acute angle, I should have both suffered and 'seen' more...

"He went on and I came to... I did not see God's purpose. I only saw his intentness and his entire relentlessness towards his means. He thought no more of me than a man thinks of hurting a cork when he is opening wine... And yet, on waking, my first feeling was…that in that half hour under ether I had served God more distinctly and purely than I had ever done in my life before... I was the means of his achieving and revealing something, I know not what not to whom, and that, to the extent of my capacity for suffering."[30]

It is known that ether has an inexplicable property of evocation and metaphysical lucidity. Under its influence, great problems are clarified; everything appears luminous, easy and veridical. But that extraordinary effect disappears after a very short time and one cannot recover the verity that one had seized, and which has fled.

William James' experimenter has remembered. Her story is gripping and it becomes atrocious because it is plausible. In the general economy of the world, in which we know that nothing is wasted, it seems that only pain is wasted. According to this, it is not. On the other plane it takes a geometrical form; it is transformed in order to serve for unknown operations, the secret of which escapes us.

That a being of a divine character, terrible by virtue of its indifference, considers our pain as an angle to be

---

[30] William James, *The Varieties of Religious Experience*, Lecture XVI. I have reproduced the original English text that is equivalent to Magre's French version, which is somewhat paraphrased, perhaps by the translator of the French edition he is citing—although he gives no reference, and might be translating from the English himself, a trifle freely.

flexed, over which it slides with ease, even if that image is only a symbol, nevertheless has an appearance of verity. And a proof of that verity is given by a reaction of spiritual elevation that pain procures for the person who experiences it, if not always, at least in certain cases, in accordance with personal capacities.

For it happens that pain debases without compensations of any sort. But perhaps there are pains that serve the gods, and bad pains that have no profit whatsoever. How, then, can they be recognized? What is the touchstone of human pain?

And if we recognize that our pain is of the kind that is useful to the gods, there remains the matter of knowing in what measure it is just that we suffer in order to permit them to run over angles that are more or less acute or obtuse. The protestations that we might raise, although futile in appearance, are perhaps registered as mysteriously as the service rendered by our pain. They might serve as a counterweight in an unknown balance. Perhaps our non-acceptance diminishes the sum total of pain.

Consciousness is the great purifying spring. If we can measure our suffering and imagine its unknown utility, perhaps we can even succeed in transforming it into enjoyment. The person who suffers for nothing has a right to despair and to curse the unknown cause of his pain. But if he knew that he was participating in a sublime endeavor, he would doubtless accept it and request to suffer more.

Pain remains the greatest secret of the earth.

PRAYER TO THE SUN

O paradigm of luminous essences, source of subtle emanations, you who change into light the compact darkness of infinity. O Sun, you are surely the only God to whom it is necessary to return, after having toured the circumference of possible gods! Perhaps you are only a spark in a vaster and higher spray, but for us you are the ultimate end and the supreme beginning. And before the mystery that envelops all Powers, it is you to whom I address myself, as the sole visible Power, generous and eternal.

I know full well that you cannot respond directly to human pleas, but you respond indirectly by making wheat grow for the person who is hungry, vines for the person who aspires to intoxication, appearing in the morning for the person who is afraid, and descending behind the horizon for the person who aspires to nocturnal repose. For you give the appearance of rising and descending, and there is no better wisdom for humans than that image of decline and rebirth.

O Sun, I am one of those who has need of the continual presence of your radiance. I sense life drawing away from me in the lands where our fiery silver circle is not seen. Moreover, I cannot explain why the Earth has that strange inclination on its axis, and why, in certain unfortunate regions, so many opaque larvae called mists and so many liquid humors of the air called rain intercept you in our eyes. The tissues of my body perish from not having your warmth in their substance, and far from you my soul is sick, no longer having the energy to launch forth.

I please myself believing that there are solar spirits that live in you, creatures with bodies with a marrow of fire, which move in your oceans of incandescence and enjoy delightedly the continuity of flame. By the same token, there must be an unimaginable opacity of darkness elsewhere that must absorb beings that are voluntarily blind and infatuated with their own ignorance.

O Sun, remove me from the formidable celestial current that, according to the ancient philosophers of India, bears humans toward their ancestors. Deliver me from the lunar attraction that summons the dead, by the law of their gravity, toward that planet of frozen volcanoes and valleys of extinct metal, in order to mineralize them in the hardness of new forms.

O Sun, summon me to you, enable me to rise toward your light, stripped and purified. Let nothing remain of the stone of my bones and the moist matter of my flesh but a light gas, a vapor so transparent that even the wing of a butterfly could not trace a design thereon. Bring back to an imponderable essence everything within me that is terrestrial. Dissolve, volatilize, and annihilate all the elements to which I have attributed the virtues of a separate being, in order that I will be nothing but a drop of the element of fire in the bosom of your radiant intelligence.

IN PRAISE OF THE SPIRITUAL FORCES

I thank the spiritual forces that came to settle upon me when I appeared in the terrestrial light in a modest house in the Rue du Taur in Toulouse, not far from Saint Sernin. It was shortly before noon in the month of March, and, as the astrologers put it, under the sign of Pisces.[31]

I thank the spiritual forces for having recognized in my mother's face a similitude that pleased them and directed them to the narrow Rue de Taur, far from sunlit spaces since the morning that had been floating and playing, passing under the shadow of the steeple of Saint Sernin.

Once they were called fays or godmothers. Sometimes they were distinguished around cradles. There were large ones and small ones. People had difficulty understanding that it was the gift of themselves that the godmothers gave to their godson. In any case, people ceased to perceive them, and even to believe in them.

The house in the Rue du Taur was old and dark, the soul of the child they came to inhabit was rebellious, vivacious, avid for enjoyment. A harsh law, the one of that descent! Harsher still is the one of the slow transformation through the blood of an unstable body! There was one of them whose name I knew from the very beginning, and which I have never forgotten; she was called Obstinate Hope, and I have always sensed her presence.

---

[31] Magre was born on 2 March 1877. under the astrological sign of Pisces.

I thank them for their patience. They are neighbors of evil creatures, almost faceless larvae, hideous inhabitants of interior sewers. They have witnessed struggles; they have seen me stumble and fall. I thank them for having permitted me to get up again. I am only thanking them now because, at the time, I was ingrate and could only incline before myself.

I can render testimony that twice, I sensed that my hour had come, and that my forehead had been touched by the secret golden wand that marks the term of lives. I can render testimony that twice, that term was postponed by the intervention of spiritual forces that I had within me, the ones that had once come to the Rue du Taur, after having played in the midday air around the steeple of Saint Sernin.

Why did they exercise that protection, if it was one, and not a punishment? Doubtless they were anticipating some unspecifiable task on my part. There was a role to be played, a battle to be won, I do not know on what field and in what order of facts and ideas. Perhaps I have not understood what it was necessary to do or, in the darkness, have mistaken the road. I know today that signs are never lacking, that there is no darkness so thick that glimmers do not mark out the path for the person who knows how to look within him for the correspondence of those glimmers, but I was a poor ignoramus, I betrayed myself, I lost the battle every day and I marched without counting the dead.

And now the evening has come and I see the glory of God!—of that which people have called God, and which can bear other names: life in motion; the terrible and resplendent transformation; order and chaos; innumerable evil and invincible bounty; the mystery in the golden mask; and the beauty that envelops all things in her solar crimson robe.

I have attained the true knowledge of the invisible world, that which comes from nature. Whoever has penetrated the secret of things has penetrated the secret of gods. For the spirit moves over the waters and in the forms of the earth. It is sufficient, in order to glimpse it, to have seized an Ariadne's thread, which is perhaps a drifting thread of spider-silk, or to have understood a password, perhaps transmitted by a bird.

Have I seized the thread of spider-silk that is necessary or have I stumbled, one evening when the moon was beginning to rise, over an enchanted scarab that touched me with its antenna? In the depths of the pond I have seen beyond the gaze of the frog and I have understood the relationship that unites the spider with the root of the aquatic reed. In the damp silt I have contemplated the birth of protozoa.

On the hill, walking among the old men that the vine stocks are, I have sensed the future intoxications of the wine rising through the ligneous channels of the wood and expanding in the grapes. I have contemplated the virginity of the rose on which the moth with the death's-head has just settled. I have understood the message of the cypress and the prophecy of the eucalyptus.

I have seen the glory of God and I am stirred thereby in the marrow of my being. I do not know why it has been given to me to have access to that splendor, since the battles have been lost, and I have not realized that which I had a right to expect of myself, which the spiritual forces had designated to me. I would have liked to sing hymns, to struggle in competition with savage animals, to be rolled in the clouds by the wind, driven by strange cries like marine birds over the masts of ships.

Perhaps the least deserving are those that are recompensed. Perhaps it is sufficient to have once understood a mother's gaze to have seen the spirit is its serene glory. But why is there something to comprehend? Is it not sufficient to allow oneself to be borne along by the water of the river, with one's face turned toward the sky?

Praise be to the spiritual forces that give wings to humans! Praise be to what is known as Obstinate Hope, which enables triumph over discouragement; to what is known as the Love of Visible Nature, and which enables the invisible world to be understood; to what is known as the Delight of Detachment, which is the smallest, the most fragile and the only one that sometimes abandons me. They are what permits one to live, and put benevolence on the face of death.

INVISIBLE BEAUTY

Whoever has seen dolor has seen beauty. It exists behind the features of the poorest people, and in the depths of the most distraught eyes. Let the wretched be consoled by the idea that they carry within them a veiled light that brightens down below and is perceptible at a great distance.

The most perfect beauty inhabits hovels and haunts prisons and labor camps. It is in the icy alignment of hospital beds, it is exhaled in the blood and sweat of slaves, those who are enchained to labor, to alcoholism, to remorse for the evil they have done. But it is necessary to be able to recognize that beauty; it is necessary to have interior eyes to perceive it, for it is invisible.

Those who sacrifice their days to care for the sick, those who climb sordid stairways to diminish poverty, are those in search of beauty. They know where it is hidden, without being sure of enabling it to spring forth. The missionaries who go to the accursed islands to which lepers are exiled, are lovers of beauty. They sense that the deformities, the stupor of gazes beneath swollen and dead eyelids conceal a divine mystery. For whoever has seen dolor has seen beauty—but they do not always understand what they have seen.

None of the rites of life have the importance that is accorded to them. Duties are almost all masks that have been painted by the most skillful, and behind their deceptive austerity hides pitiless egotism. Some give the pretext of social duties, others proclaim loudly that they have founded a family, and others say that they have found God. They are deceiving themselves, either by design or unconsciously, in order to enjoy pleasure with more avidity. But there is no other real objective on earth than to discover the beauty of the world. Beauty is stronger than laws, than morals, than virtues. It is the secret law of nature, the virtue of God.

One does not discover it in serenity. Torment is the privilege of elevated souls, and woe betide those who have yielded themselves to the profit of a facile peace. The person who, by means of his meditations, his disinterest and his quotidian wisdom, has finally merited drinking the unintoxicating wine of the tranquility of the evening, must mingle a drop of poison with that wine himself: the poison of the torment and the eternal dolor of human beings, of which he must demand his share.

For it is an unfathomable mystery that nature has created a resplendent beauty with landscapes with tranquil lines, serene statues and ideal virgins reflecting the ardor of pure hearts, but has wanted that the highest sentiment of perfection to spring from the utmost degree of dolor and participation in that dolor. Dante spoiled his paradise for having made too many angelic wings palpitate there; a little sickening stupidity remains attached to innocence.

Beauty is not picked like a flower on the side of a road. It is necessary to wrench it harshly from a muddy matrix. It is like the mandrakes engendered by the tragic semen of hanged men, for which it is necessary to go in search under the gibbet by night, which moan when one extracts them from the earth, but which become an amorous little creature whose suavity is made of its former misery.

All those who have burned with the fire of true beauty are those who have descended into the infernos of the soul and have known the anguish of pathos. They have embraced dolor with the same desperate joy that one would have in embracing the phantom of one's mother on the day after her death. They have felt pity. They have measured the cruel indifference of the gods. They have revolted and blasphemed.

Sublime artists, saints or accursed, they have approached the key to the enigma, they have touched the profound secret of nature that is in the intimate liaison of beauty and dolor, and which creates one with the other by means of a sacred chemistry. They have found their salvation in the tempest. For all the wisdom accumulated by the centuries informs us that it is necessary to be shipwrecked in order finally to be cast up by the sea on the isles of silver springs and golden lemon trees.